ABINGTON 11/14/2013 C:1
50687011263384
Gramont, Nina de.
Meet me at the river /

W9-AMT-375

meet me at the river

also by nina de gramont

every little thing in the world

meet me at the river

nina de gramont

Atheneum Books for Young Readers
atheneum   NEW YORK LONDON TORONTO SYDNEY NEW DELHI

atheneum

ATHENEUM BOOKS FOR YOUNG READERS
An imprint of Simon & Schuster Children's Publishing Division
1230 Avenue of the Americas, New York, New York 10020

ATHENEUM BOOKS FOR YOUNG READERS
is a registered trademark of Simon & Schuster, Inc.
Atheneum logo is a trademark of Simon & Schuster, Inc.
For information about special discounts for bulk purchases,
please contact Simon & Schuster Special Sales at 1-866-506-1949
or business@simonandschuster.com.
The Simon & Schuster Speakers Bureau can bring authors
to your live event. For more information or to book an event,
contact the Simon & Schuster Speakers Bureau at 1-866-248-3049
or visit our website at www.simonspeakers.com.
The text for this book is set in Palatino LT.
Manufactured in the United States of America
First Edition
2 4 6 8 10 9 7 5 3 1
Library of Congress Cataloging-in-Publication Data
Gramont, Nina de.
Meet me at the river / Nina de Gramont. — 1st ed.
p.   cm.
Summary: Stepsiblings Tressa and Luke, close as children, fell in love as
teens, and neither the disapproval of those around them nor even Luke's
death can keep them apart as long as Tressa needs him.
ISBN 978-1-4169-8014-8 (hardcover)
ISBN 978-1-4169-8281-4 (eBook)
[1. Love—Fiction. 2. Death—Fiction. 3. Stepsiblings—Fiction.
4. Family problems—Fiction. 5. Family life—Colorado—Fiction.
6. Colorado—Fiction.] I. Title.
PZ7.G76564Mee 2013
[Fic]—dc23   2012030307

for cassie wright

october 25, 1966–november 26, 1998

in dazzled memory

prelude one

TRESSA

My mother doesn't know that Luke comes through my bedroom window. How could she? He never makes a sound.

My room is on the third floor. There's no trellis, no neighboring oak tree for him to scale. It's not logical to think he would appear, his hands on my windowsill, followed by an ankle, and then his whole entire self. He leaps through the window as clear as morning, exactly the way I remember him. He lands on my carpet and glides across the floor to sit on the edge of my bed. If there's moonlight (and when he comes there's always moonlight) it shines cleanly, without ever casting shadows across his face.

Carlo lifts his sleek head and thumps his tail on the wood floor in greeting. My poor pup used to sleep beside me, on the bed, but these days he's too old and creaky to haul himself up. So there's plenty of room for Luke.

In the early days, when Luke first reappeared, we would try to touch each other. I could see my hand pushing his hair behind his ear—it's always too long—but I couldn't feel the impossible smoothness except for in my memory. I could see his hand, the uneven knuckles wide across my knee, but there was no warmth, no sense of skin on skin, only the painfully lovely sight of it.

So we've stopped trying to touch. It's just too sad, seeing without feeling. And it's the opposite of sad, the two of us together again, cross-legged on my bed, facing each other. Our own hands on our own knees, talking through the night.

There's never any noise from downstairs—no stirring footsteps, no water rumbling through the pipes. When Luke appears, every anxiety disappears. There's only me. There's only him. There's only us. I never recall that exact moment when he exits and sleep enters. I just open my eyes minutes before the alarm sounds, and I know everything else—his presence, his words, his promise of return. I don't feel tired, though I can't have slept more than a few hours.

I feel, in fact, wide-awake, far more alert than after nights when he hasn't been here. I can still see Luke's fingers, hovering tactfully above the paper-thin skin on the inside of my wrist, and I know that he'll be back. I know exactly what's brought him here, and I don't feel afraid or ashamed. What I feel is alive, and in love, and I am almost ready to start remembering.

prelude two

LUKE

It may feel like I'm back, and I am, sort of. I can tell you anything you want to know about the past. But when it comes to now, or the time just after? I don't get it, not at all.

Tressa and I try to talk about it but that never works. There's no problem when she talks about the past. I can understand her fine. Then all of a sudden she must be talking about now, what I've taken to calling the after-Luke, because everything gets muffled.

"Tressa," I have to say. "I can't hear you."

When Tressa talks about the after-Luke it's the same as trying to touch her. I see her lips move but I don't get the words. She might as well be speaking French. Tressa actually *can* speak French, and back in the day I used to like that. Sometimes I'd even ask her to speak

French, and I would sit there listening without knowing what she said. But now everything's different, and if I'm honest it drives me crazy. I want to know what she's saying but I can't, just like I can't feel her cheek or her hair or any other part of her body. It's funny, because when I reach down to touch the dog I can feel him lick me, and I can feel his fur. Maybe if Carlo told me about now I'd understand what he was saying.

I know it must bug her, too, but she never acts like it. Probably she doesn't want to hurt my feelings. When we were little kids, her grandmother was always saying, "Tressa, gentle!" Not that Tressa *wasn't* gentle. It was just the kind of thing you say when a kid tries to touch something breakable. But her grandmother said it so much, I thought that was her name.

"When will I see Tressa Gentle?" I was always asking my parents. At some point I figured out it wasn't really her name, and I stopped calling her that for a long time. But then when we got older, and things got different, I started again. I called her Tressa Gentle when we walked by the river. Back when I could feel her skin and hair.

These days when I come through her window, I want things to be the way they used to. So I smile and say, "Tressa Gentle," and she smiles back. I can see the old maps she drew, tacked on the wall. I try not to think about the blank spots, where new ones must be. If I don't worry about what I don't have, maybe I can just be glad to see her, and be here in her room, talking about the past.

I can't visit anyone else, not my dad, or my sisters or my mom. I want to visit them but I don't know how. I can only get to Tressa.

When I'm not with her I must be somewhere else, but I can't tell you about that, either. I can tell you about my life, and I can tell you about Tressa's life, because she pretty much told me everything. I know what happened to both of us from the second I was born right up until those last seconds in the river.

I wish I could tell my mom that those last seconds weren't so bad. But I can't tell Mom anything. Not anymore. All I have left is me and Tressa, so I come back to her every chance I get.

part one

piecing it together

(1)

TRESSA

I, of course, can tell you about now. It's everything else I don't like thinking about. Not that now is so terrific. It just happens to be my only option—a concept that concerned doctors, therapists, teachers, and most of all my mother have worked very hard to impress upon me. So for their sake I am here, in a bizarre limbo, living with Mom and her husband in the southwestern part of Colorado.

Rabbitbrush is a tiny little Christmas card of a town nestled in the San Juan Mountains. My mother grew up here and then spent most of her life—and most of my life—trying to escape it. The town is very pretty, but it has a bit of an inferiority complex. Although we're not far from Telluride, we're not quite close enough to share its tourists. Local developers and the town council are always trying to dream up new ways to entertain visitors, especially in the summer, since building our own ski area isn't realistic.

Paul, my mother's husband, wants to build a drive-in movie theater on the parcel of land near town that my grandfather deeded to my mom, years ago, so that one day she could build a house there. Now of course she has Paul's house, but Grandpa says Paul will use that land commercially over his dead body, and then he looks over at me apologetically. I shrug to tell him it's okay. Nobody likes to say the word "dead" around me anymore, as if avoiding the word will help me forget the concept. I never realized how often some version of "dead" appears in everyday expressions until people tried to stop saying it. Last week my mother used the word "mortified," then clapped her hand over her mouth, as if that Latin root might send me running for the medicine cabinet, or the graveyard, or wherever they think I'm going.

Certainly not to the graveyard, where Paul had half of Luke's ashes buried. The other half belongs to Francine, Luke's mother. It used to bother me, this weird division of something that used to be whole. Used to be *Luke.* But now that I know those ashes aren't Luke, not at all, I think: let them do whatever they need. My sister Jill told me that Francine plans to scatter her share from the top of the Jud Wiebe Trail in Telluride on the anniversary of his death. This sounds much more like Luke than the quaint but lonely graveyard, which I haven't visited since Luke—the real, whole Luke—started coming back. If anybody notices I've stopped going, I hope they find it comforting.

But truthfully, nothing could be comforting enough to stop my mother from worrying about me. This afternoon she stands waiting for my school bus at the end of Paul's driveway. Ordinarily it's Carlo who waits there, and with a sinking feeling of dread, I wonder where he is. The past few days he's seemed more sluggish, not at all his usual self.

I can see my mother from where I sit in the very back row. It's late November, the week after Thanksgiving, and I know I should probably feel embarrassed. I'm eighteen years old and riding the school bus for my second shot at senior year, which I am repeating, not— thank you very much—because I didn't finish that last month but because the school officials, like Mom and Paul, are determined to keep a close eye on me. Even though I took all my exams and passed them, nobody could stand to let me graduate and go to CU the way I was supposed to. And even though I've had my driver's license for more than a year, nobody wants to let me touch a car. Nobody ever *says* I'm not allowed to drive; they just come up with some very good reason why I can't have the car when I ask. So I've stopped asking, and they all seem relieved.

All this means that what was supposed to be my first

year of freedom has turned into a thinly veiled version of house arrest, which actually is fine with me. "This isn't meant to be a punishment," my mother said back in the summer, when I was still at the hospital and she told me that I couldn't graduate. I nodded, not because I didn't want to be punished but because if I were to be—and if I could choose my own punishment—it would be a whole lot graver than an extra year of high school.

"Hi, Mom," I say as I step off the bus. She smiles and presses a steamy mug of hot cocoa into my hands. I look down into the mug and see a fat marshmallow bobbing and floating. That marshmallow looks so hopeful, refusing to be dragged under or melted by the thick, hot liquid surrounding it. Mom must have timed it out very carefully for the cocoa to still be hot and this marshmallow un-melted. This kind of domesticity is new to her, and it always makes my heart hurt a little, especially when it's directed toward me.

I glance at my mom, who wears maternity jeans and a baggy, wheat-colored Henley shirt that probably belongs to Paul. She's got one hand resting on her huge, blooming belly. Her hair is long and tousled and bleached almost the color of her youth. Mom has always been a wiry, athletic woman; her collarbones still protrude and her arms are corded and toned from prenatal yoga. She has a good face, my mother, with wide blue eyes and high cheekbones, a face that moves without creasing. If I squint, I can block out the weariness she still carries from last year, and the loss of elasticity along her jaw. I can almost believe the illusion of young mother-to-be.

In reality my mother is forty-five years old with three grown children. Almost as soon as she and Paul remarried, they decided they wanted another baby. This meant a long stretch of fertility drugs and in vitro, followed by two miscarriages, followed by an egg donor and this about-to-be sibling who shares exactly zero of my DNA. My sister Jill says she finds it ironic: our mother, at this late date, having a child she actually intends to parent, and it's not even related to her. Mr. Tynan, my English teacher, says that "irony" is the most persistently misused word in the English language, but I know that in this case Jill's using it correctly. Every time my mother turns down a cup of coffee, I picture her pregnant with me—a joint in one hand and a shot of tequila in the other. With Jill and Katie, Paul's daughters, she was more conventional—probably a cigarette and a glass of wine.

Still. When I see my mother trying so hard—putting so much heart into this latest transformation—I can't help wishing her well. I know what it feels like to long for last chances, even when you know you might not deserve them.

The bus pulls away, and my mother still stands there, looking hopeful and expectant. I want to ask about Carlo, but I'm afraid of her answer. So I bring the cocoa to my lips and sip. To my surprise, it tastes amazing: rich and chocolaty and exactly the right temperature.

"Thanks, Mom," I say. "This is delicious."

"Do you like it?" she asks. "I made it from scratch. I got the recipe off this great food blog."

I stare at her. There are times, lately, when my mother seems completely foreign, as if some alien being has entered her body and turned her into the exact kind of mother I used to think I wanted. In these moments I perversely want the old one back, and luckily, she has a way of obliging. For example, right now she sees the expression on my face and realizes she's gone too far, so she laughs—like the old transient Mom making fun of this new Happy Homemaker.

I want to laugh, too, but worry about Carlo prevents it. Mom must suspect this, but she doesn't say anything, just hooks her arm though mine. We start walking up the hill to Paul's house. It's a big place, not too over-the-top but still impressive. Paul made a lot of money buying land in Telluride before its big boom in the late eighties, right after my mom left him the first time.

"Where's Carlo?" I finally ask. For a second the words hang in the air, and despite everything I learned last year about worst-case scenarios, I can't stop hoping for a happy answer. *Carlo's sleeping upstairs in that sunny spot by the window.* Or, *Look, there he is, waiting on the porch.*

But Mom says, "Carlo's at the vet."

I stop. She stops too, and I try to read her expression.

"Why? What happened?" I force my voice to stay calm, then ask the hardest question. "Is he going to be all right?"

"Well," she says carefully, "he looked very bloated this morning, and he wouldn't eat, so I brought him in. Dr. Hill said he had a lot of fluid in his belly. He drained it, and now he's running some tests."

"Why would he have fluid in his stomach?"

My mother looks at the ground for a minute. She does not love facing reality. For example, she's had an amnio and a million ultrasounds but will not find out the sex of her baby. She says she wants to be surprised, but I know the real reason. She is hoping against hope to have a boy for Paul and can't bear being disappointed a moment too soon. When you have three girls, you probably think your body's not capable of producing anything else. So I know it's a feat of strength on my behalf when Mom looks me in the eye and tells me the truth. "Dr. Hill thinks it's congestive heart failure."

"Congestive heart failure," I echo. I have no idea what that means, but it sounds so ominous. We start walking again. Mom puts her arm around my shoulders, and we go through the front door in silence. Inside, my eyes travel past the foyer into the dining room, with the long table and its multitude of chairs at the ready for a big holiday gathering, and the sideboard crowded with family pictures. It's exactly the sort of room I thought I'd never have in a house where I lived with my mom.

Most of the pictures are of Jill and Katie, my older sisters, but crowded in there somewhere are one or two of me. There are no pictures of Luke. I wonder if Paul would like to retrieve old ones from wherever they were stashed, years ago. Probably he does want to but doesn't do it, because of me. If he thought about it for even a second, he would realize that upstairs my computer files are crowded with hundreds of pictures of Luke. I wish I could bear to open them. I could print one out and sneak it into a frame. Place it here with the rest of us.

Even though Mom just told me that Carlo's at the vet, I realize my ears are waiting for the *click clack* of his nails across the wood floors. Mom sees the look on my face and says, "Tressa. Dr. Hill didn't say anything. He didn't offer any prognosis. But Carlo is old, he's very old, especially for such a big dog."

My heart constricts in a panicky way. Carlo is twelve years old, half-Newfoundland and half-collie. I know my mom is right. I also know, standing there in the foyer with the infantile school bag over my shoulder, that I don't care how old Carlo is, or how long a dog his size is supposed to live. I just want him with me. I want everyone I love with me, well and safe, right where I can touch them. In my head I make a quick and terrible calculation. If Carlo dies now, it will be just about exactly six months between them.

I put down the mug and twist my ring—the pearl ring Luke gave me—around my finger. "Remember," I say to Mom, my voice verging on wobbly, "when I was a little kid, how whenever I drew a picture of myself, I'd also draw a picture of Carlo standing right next to me? I couldn't draw me without drawing him."

My mother hesitates for a fraction of a second, and I can tell she doesn't remember this at all. My grandmother would remember. Her sewing room is decorated with pictures and maps I've drawn; the oldest ones are going yellow and crinkling around their thumbtacks. But Mom just nods, her face completely blank.

"Hey," she says, steering me toward the kitchen, toward the consolation of food. "Let's not be all doom and gloom. Maybe he'll be okay."

I think—I don't *want* to think, but can't stop myself— how Paul will feel, how he'll look at me if Carlo dies so soon after Luke. But my mom is staring. She has arranged her face so carefully. She wants so badly to be optimistic, and young. I know exactly how many cracks in that illusion are my own doing. I know this, and I understand that I am far from blameless, and that the least I can do—apart from staying alive—is pretend to believe in her version of our life together.

We go to Dr. Hill's before closing and pick up Carlo. I don't want him spending even one night in a cage on cold linoleum. While Mom talks to the girl at the front desk, I go in back where the dogs are kept, half expecting someone to stop me. But nobody does, not the techs or the assistants. It's a very small town, and everybody knows my story. I imagine they want to sneak peeks at my wrists, which are covered, as always, by long sleeves pulled up to the middle of my palms, but when I accidentally meet a tech's eyes, she's not looking at my arms but at my face, and her eyes are full of sympathy. And it has nothing to do with my wrists. I look away, not meaning to be unfriendly, just not wanting to cry. Not here, in public.

Carlo lies splayed out in a large wire cage. As I approach, he thumps his tail and then lifts his head. He knows the sound of my footsteps. He has always been a pretty dog, with the shiny black fur of a Newfoundland and the same breed's floppy ears, but slender and sleek like a collie, with a long narrow nose. When I open the door to his cage, he pulls himself out and crawls into my lap. He's too big for this—his limbs spill over mine awkwardly. I can feel his bony ribs and hips pressing into my legs, and I stroke his glossy head.

My grandfather gave me Carlo one summer when I stayed with them. I was six years old, Carlo was six weeks old. Grandpa said we were both puppies. He put Carlo into my lap and the dog flopped down in the circle of my legs. At the time, Grandpa still taught English at Rabbitbrush High, and he chose the dog's name. He said that Emily Dickinson's father gave her a Newfoundland named Carlo to protect her on long walks in the hills. I remember nodding as Grandpa told me this. I had no idea who Emily Dickinson was, and I didn't care what we named the puppy. I only felt so glad to have company—someone who might come with me wherever I went.

"That's the point," Grandpa said, "to have someone with you wherever you go."

"What if Mom won't let me keep him?" I asked Grandpa, keeping my eyes on the tiny black puppy, the sleek silk of his head.

"Oh, she'll let you," Grandpa said, his voice a firm and insistent growl. "She'll let you, all right." And I knew that it was settled.

When we get back from the vet, I tell Mom I'm not hungry for dinner and go upstairs with Carlo. Last summer, during my stay at the private hospital in Durango, I received talk therapy in addition to medication. I felt too awkward questioning the psychiatrist, but Dr. Reisner, the therapist, promised me that Prozac was a weight-neutral medication. I have no idea why I packed on so many pounds in the five months I took Prozac; maybe because I just stopped caring. But with Luke coming back, it feels important to look as much like my old self as possible, so now I'm medication-free, and I try to skip meals when I can. Yeah, I know, not the healthiest way to go. So on school days, instead of eating the lunch my mother packs for me, I pick tansy asters behind the baseball field and leave them on the front porch of Luke's house. Francine, his mother, used to complain that those flowers grew everywhere in Rabbitbrush except her front yard. Midday, when I'm supposed to be in the cafeteria, Francine is safely at work. I like to picture her, later in the afternoon, coming home to the bouquets. I imagine her bending down to scoop them up and arranging them in the lopsided ceramic vase Luke made for her at summer camp. Sometimes I hope she knows it's me who leaves the flowers; other times I hope she thinks it's someone else.

Now Carlo and I sit upstairs in my room, the room where—I suddenly realize—I have never been alone, because this dog has always been with me. There's a bandage across his belly, but I can see already that the bloat is coming back. I kneel and curve my arms around his body to lift him onto the bed. I expect him to be heavy, cumbersome. It surprises me how easily I can manage.

I crawl into bed next to him. I have been curling up beside this dog forever, since he was barely bigger than my head, and since he was nearly twice my size. This dog has lived with me summers at my grandparents' house. In winters he has lived with me and my mother in tepees and yurts and tents. He has lived with me in what seems like hundreds of apartments, shacks, houses, and trailers that my mother moved in and out of. He even came with us the four years we lived in the Marquesas on a fifty-foot sailboat.

I don't remember ever facing the world without this dog. "Sometimes I think you love Carlo more than you love me," my mother used to accuse, and I would duck my face in apology because I didn't want her to know that she was partly right. I could count on him to always put me first. Now I am terrified to tell Luke about Carlo, even though he won't be able to grasp it, and I am heartbroken to face Paul. I lie on my bed, curled around my dog, tracing the extra dark lines surrounding his brown and watchful eyes.

My stomach growls, mournful and deprived. Familiar dog breath envelops my face. Carlo's nose feels cracked and dry, and I recognize the expression on his face, grim but loving. And I know that tonight—for however many nights—he works hard to stay alive, for one reason, for me. I know I don't deserve his devotion, any more than I deserve Luke—coming back to me, through my window. But come back he does, which must mean something. Right? Maybe it means I have the right to small hopes, like my dog getting well.

Last year at this time I was a girl with things to do. I took pictures and drew maps. I played guitar. I babysat three afternoons a week for Genevieve Cummings. I found ways to sneak out and meet the boy nobody wanted me to see. Now it's all I can do to move through the day, waiting and hoping that same boy will make the unlikeliest and most welcome appearance. It's been more than a week since I last saw him, and tonight the moon is on the wax. My window stands open, and the air carries in the first thin strands of wood smoke, and the barest hint of snow. I run my hand over Carlo's rib cage, treasuring its rise and fall, willing that movement to continue. I know what it feels like to stick around because you don't want to cause someone else pain, and I almost want to tell him that he can go. But then comes a flood of sadness. And I see Luke, running alongside that rushing river.

Downstairs someone turns on a faucet, and from the way the water gushes—not turned off at intervals— I can tell it's Paul. I tighten my grip on Carlo, and even though I have sworn to give up everything that brings me happiness, I can't tell Carlo what he needs to hear.

(2)

LUKE

The first time I saw Tressa, a hundred butterflies landed on her head. We were four years old, lurking in my backyard next to the bush with big purple flowers. Usually the butterflies hung out on the flowers, but I guess they liked Tressa's white-blond hair.

Land on my head too! I thought. But they didn't. It made me jealous, so it was hard to like the way Tressa looked under all those butterflies. But I did. She looked like a girl from a Disney movie. I half expected bluebirds to start flying around her head too. Or maybe a fawn would come out of the woods so she could pet it. Our moms were there talking, but I didn't listen to them until my mom said that Jill and Katie were Tressa's sisters too. "But Tressa's not your sister," she said.

Looking back it seems like complicated information

for a little kid. I remember that Tressa and I looked at each other and frowned. We felt exactly the same thing, which was weirded out but also kind of fascinated.

The butterflies started flying back to their bush. Our mothers kept on talking. It turned out Tressa and I were born on the very same day. This is the kind of thing a kid thinks is amazing. Right? *We have the same birthday.* Tressa was much smaller than me, barely up to my nose. She had blue eyes. I looked like my mom, which is to say I looked like an Indian. Black eyes, black hair. But me and this little blond girl, we had the same sisters. We had the same birthday.

Before I met Tressa I wished I had a twin like Jill and Katie. Then Tressa showed up and I felt like I'd gotten my own, different kind of twin. I just wished her mom wouldn't keep taking her away. It bugged me to think of Tressa out there in the world. For some reason I always felt like she needed me, even when we were little.

She needed me when we got older, too, just like she needs me now, which I'm pretty sure is why I'm still here. I know I didn't go straight from the river to Tressa's room but that's the first thing I remember. Time had passed, but I still don't know how much. Maybe I climbed up the wall of the house. But I don't remember that, so I could've just shown up at her window.

Once I got inside her room, I could see her sleeping. It felt like I hadn't seen her in a long time. She had her brow scrunched up like she was concentrating. She looked like she was worrying instead of resting. I wanted to tell her I was there, but I didn't want to wake her up. So I backed away toward the wall. Carlo must have heard me because he wagged his tail. His tags jingled and startled Tressa. She sat up.

It's hard to explain the weirdness of that moment. I can't really think of a word for it. Me knowing I shouldn't be there and at the same time thinking, where else *would* I be? I thought she'd maybe be scared of me, but she just jumped out of bed and ran across the room. It almost felt like the old days, when she'd come back to Rabbitbrush after being away for a long time.

"I knew it," Tressa said. She hugged me, and for a minute we thought everything was like it used to be, until after a couple minutes we realized that we couldn't feel each other at all.

"It doesn't matter," Tressa said. She grabbed the collar of my shirt. "I don't care. You're here. That's all that matters. You're here."

And so that's when this other life began. Like the old one, what I mostly think about is Tressa. What I want is to get into her room. And when I can't do that, I concentrate on what I remember about our lives, which is pretty much everything.

Here in the after-Luke I can watch the whole thing like a movie whenever I want. Look. There's Tressa's mother.

She's sixteen. Her parents, the Earnshaws, have lived on their cattle ranch for three generations. I'm surprised that Hannah looks pretty perfect, not rebellious at all. What I see is a pretty girl, a good athlete, a straight-A student. Captain of her softball team.

Nobody knows better than me about growing up in Rabbitbrush. Your whole life happens outside. They strap skis and skates to your feet as soon as you can walk. When I think of being a kid, I think of hiking, rafting, skating, skiing, rock climbing. Hannah's life looks pretty much like mine. She does every wholesome thing you'd expect from a kid growing up in a small mountain town. Not like me, she doesn't do anything you'd worry about.

Hannah graduated from Rabbitbrush High. It still had a prom back then, and her date was my dad. Afterward they both went to CU, and then they moved to Telluride, and Hannah got pregnant. They had the twins but didn't get married for more than a year. "About time," Mr. Earnshaw said when he made his wedding toast. Jill and Katie were there somewhere, toddling around on the hill.

Tressa's grandfather looks really young, making that toast. It kind of blows me away. I don't see a single gray hair on his head. Pretty soon he's going to sell his cattle and almost all his horses, plus a bunch of land. But for now he's got more than four hundred acres, and cows grazing on the hill.

I can't stop watching that wedding. I stare at Hannah, trying to figure out if she looks anything like Tressa. By

the time Tressa was a teenager her hair'd turned brown.
But Hannah always stayed blond. Also she's taller than
Tressa. I think Hannah's beautiful but not as beautiful
as Tressa. If Tressa heard me say that, she'd laugh and
call me a liar. Not many girls will admit to being pretty.
Once I had a girlfriend named Kelly who admitted it.
Hannah would have. But not Tressa.

After the wedding my dad and Hannah came back to
Rabbitbrush. Hannah lasted six months. Then one morning she just took off. After my dad went to work she sat
down at the kitchen table and wrote him a letter. She left
it lying flat on the table and then drove the twins over
to her parents'. Hannah told her mother she'd be gone
awhile but she didn't say how long. She didn't say, *Mom,
I need to disappear for eight years.* She just said, "I need
a little time to myself," then drove down the driveway
and kept on driving.

I'm sorry, she wrote in the letter to my dad. *I do love
you. I just can't do this right now.*

Before the river I'd heard about that letter but I'd
never seen it. Now I can look over Hannah's shoulder
while she's writing it, and I can look over Dad's shoulder while he's reading it. There's nothing in there about
the twins so he figures she took them with her. I watch
him drop his face into his hands. To me he looks like a
kid, even though he's older than I'll ever get to be.

Dad looks too young to be anyone's father. He

looks too young to pour himself that glass of whiskey. After the first glass he starts drinking from the bottle. By the time Hannah's mother calls to ask when they'll pick up the girls he's too drunk to go and get them. I can tell from the look on his face that he's scared. Probably he thinks he's way too young to be a father all by himself to two little girls who're still in diapers.

And that's where my mother comes in.

(3)

TRESSA

I have an appointment to speak with Mr. Zack, the college adviser, which presents a problem. Luke's mother is the guidance counselor, and her office sits in the same little block of offices by the principal, just a few doors down. Part of me wants to see Francine more than anything else in the world. She was always such a good listener. If I didn't have to avoid her but could walk straight into her office, I would tell her about Carlo being sick and how worried I feel. But I know how much she hates seeing me, how the sight of my face is like a billy club at the back of her knees. By far the worst thing about school is the risk of inflicting myself on Francine, and that's saying something. So much about school is awful.

For one thing, I don't really know anyone. My class has graduated. And even if they hadn't, I barely spent two years at Rabbitbrush High before Luke died, and I never got close to anyone else. All of Luke's friends were also friends with his ex-girlfriend Kelly, so even if it hadn't been for my social lameness, it would have been hard to break in.

"I don't understand that," Dr. Reisner said last summer in therapy. "Why couldn't you make friends on your own?"

I tried to explain that I'd shown up at enough strange schools not knowing how to do the right things, and wearing the wrong clothes, and saying the wrong things. In a way it hurt most of all in Rabbitbrush, which was the one place in the world I should have belonged. But by the time I came back here to stay, I had never even owned a pair of mittens. I didn't know how to ski, or snowboard, or ice-skate. I could try my best to learn but could never catch up to the kids who'd been doing those things since the age of three. I would always be clearly *not* a native. This is truer now than it has ever been, because everybody knows the whole story about Luke and me, and how everything that happened was all my fault.

It's one thing to resign yourself to life, another thing to actually have to live it. With Carlo so sick, all I want to do is hold my breath until I can escape school at three thirty. I don't want to have to sneak down the corridor to Mr. Zack's office. Francine's office door is propped open, and I wish I could make myself invisible for the millisecond it will take me to pass by it. Luckily, within a few feet of her door, I get the feeling her office is empty. I don't glance sideways to confirm this. I just scoot past as quickly as possible, and land in the chair across from Mr. Zack with a sigh of relief. A too-loud sigh of relief, because Mr. Zack looks at me with an extra dose of concern, and I realize then that I should have knocked.

He doesn't say anything about that, though, any more than he lets himself stare at my wrists, which are covered by the long sleeves of my cotton turtleneck sweater. Instead he goes right into talking about my academic situation. Last year I took three AP classes, and this year I am taking three more. Even though the school didn't let me graduate, they are giving me credit for all the classes I took last year, so that when I finally get to college, I'll be that much closer to my sophomore year.

"You can stick with your deference at CU," Mr. Zack tells me, "but why not also do a couple more applications and see what happens? You might end up at a better school."

"CU's a good school," I say, slumping in my chair across from him. I pull my turtleneck up over my chin. If I could, I'd wear it up to just below my eyes, my hair spilling down and covering the rest of my face. Hidden.

"It's good enough," he says. "But maybe you'd be happier at a small liberal arts school. Your grades and

SATs are very strong. You won that photo competition last year. That's something new for your application."

I don't say anything. Last year, when Luke and I were applying, it seemed so stupid that I had a stronger shot at more prestigious schools. Luke was better than me at almost everything. He was better at guitar, and sports, and making friends. Better at just generally living in the world, which is probably why he never bothered too much with schoolwork.

"That photography contest is coming up again," Mr. Zack says. "Have you thought about entering?"

Last year I won that contest with a close-up of a mule deer munching on the blue mist spirea behind Paul's house. I'd been going through a phase of just carrying the camera with me, and got a lot of great wildlife shots. Now the camera sits in my bedroom closet, on the top shelf, high enough so that I can't see it when I open the door. Its battery has likely been dead for months. There's nothing I want to record. But since saying all this would just alarm Mr. Zack, I tell him, "Sure, maybe I will."

He goes on listing colleges. "Stanford is a long shot, but it wouldn't hurt to try. Or Colorado College, if you want to stay in state."

"Aren't those superexpensive?" I ask. My inflection rejects the suggestion, even though just yesterday I got an e-mail from Isabelle Delisle—the only friend I managed to collect during all my mother's years of wandering—who, coincidentally, told me that she planned on applying to these very schools.

Mr. Zack shifts his shoulders. In addition to his duties as college adviser, he coaches the ski and lacrosse teams—both of which Luke competed on. As I watch Mr. Zack gracefully tilt back in his chair, I think how he must miss Luke too, and I wonder if it's hard for him to sit here talking to me. If it is, he does a good job covering it up—looking straight at me, his brows kind and quizzical, challenging my financial worries. In a town of modest incomes, my stepfather is known for his wealth. I consider pointing out that Paul is not my *father*. But of course Mr. Zack knows that, as well as he knows that my grandparents have kept themselves afloat for years on the money they made selling pieces of their land to the Nature Conservancy. They would gladly empty out their bank accounts and sell more acres to send me wherever I want to go.

"You could apply for a scholarship," Mr. Zack says instead of pointing out those other options. "All I'm saying, Tressa, is that your grades are strong enough to get you into a competitive school. And you'll have this whole extra year under your belt. Boulder is very big. You might find it more daunting than you realize. A person can get lost in a sea of faces."

Without meaning to I close my eyes. It's not that I want to go to Boulder. It's that I really want to stay upstairs in my bedroom waiting for Luke. I can't think about the future any more than the past. I don't want either of them to exist.

"Tressa," Mr. Zack says gently.

"I'm sorry, Mr. Zack," I say, opening my eyes. "I'll think about it; I will."

He places his chair back on the floor and leans toward me. I can tell he doesn't quite believe me, and I don't know how to convince him of what's not true. Sometimes I think the only thing that would make the adults in my life happy would be X-ray goggles. They could stare directly into my mind and see whatever thoughts would indicate progression, recovery, a rosy path ahead.

"Look, kiddo," he says. "I know applications are a pain, but I also know it'll be worth it. You let me know if you need any help. With anything."

I stand up. Mr. Zack's office has two doors, one that leads back out into the hallway. The other door goes through the faculty lounge, where students are not allowed. From there I could sneak into the hall-way between the library and the gymnasium, avoiding Luke's mother's office.

"Mr. Zack," I say. "Do you think it would be okay if I used this door?" I point to the one to the faculty lounge.

He pauses for a moment, and then glances at the other door, as if Francine might walk by and see him grant me permission to escape her. Then he nods, and tilts his head in the direction I requested.

"Thanks," I say, and duck into the small, bright room. My sneakers squeak over the linoleum, and the smell of hours-old coffee hangs thickly in the air. Only one faculty member sits at one of the four large round tables—H. J. Burdick, the new English teacher. He started teaching here last year. H. J. is one of those natives I'm surrounded by. He graduated from Rabbitbrush High the same year as Jill and Katie. He lives next door to my grandparents, and his sister, Evie, and I played together once or twice when we were little.

He looks up from his book, *Lord of the Flies*. "Hey," he says, blinking behind wire-rimmed glasses. I can't tell if he recognizes me, not only because we've had so little contact but because he seems so distracted. His hair is shaggy, and there are stains from dry-erase markers all over his Polartec vest. As it happens, the Burdicks are the only family in town to boast a history more tragic and bizarre than my own, but you'd never know it from looking at H. J. His long legs, crossed under the cramped table, are way too casual and relaxed for a teacher.

By the time I say "Hi," wondering if I'm supposed to call him Mr. Burdick, he has turned back to his book.

"I have to teach this fifth period," he says, not looking up. "And I've never read it. Can you believe that?"

What I can't believe is that he'd tell me. I stand there, blinking at him, and then say inanely, "Mr. Zack said I could use this exit."

H. J. doesn't blink or shrug, just keeps his eyes on the pages of his book and says, "Feel free."

I hustle out of the lounge. The door closes behind me with a suctioned whoosh, and I have barely let out my breath in relief when I hear a passing student's voice, light as trickling water, announcing that I've walked directly into what I meant to avoid: "Hi, Mrs. Kingsbury."

My heart sinks. Francine still uses Paul's last name, so to my own mother's annoyance, there will always be this additional confusion between them—the two Mrs. Kingsburys. And of course it's not *my* mother coming down the hall but Luke's, and it's too late to pretend I haven't seen her. To make matters worse, the girl walking beside her is Kelly Boynton, who used to go out with Luke. Kelly and I seldom run into each other; someone must have planned our schedules very carefully, one of the benefits of this small-town school, everyone knowing our histories.

Kelly Boynton has short blond hair and wears long sleeves pulled down to her palms, like mine. Her eyes are red-rimmed, and she has her arm hooked through Francine's, who listens intently as she speaks. I can't make out Kelly's words, but I can hear that her voice is laced with tears. The truth is, even before Luke died, I felt guilty around Kelly. Now that I know what it feels like to lose him—lose him for good—that guilt is magnified about a hundred times.

Francine listens to Kelly so gently, exactly the way I

imagined her listening about Carlo. They haven't seen me yet. For a moment I wish myself invisible; better yet, gone. Like the guy in that old Christmas movie who gets to see what his hometown would be like if he'd never been born at all. Only in my case, when I came back to see what became of Rabbitbrush without me, everything would be set right. Kelly would be walking down the hall with Luke's arm around her, not crying but smiling. And Luke would be not a ghost at all, but equally happy beside her—*alive*.

All my life I thought of Luke as belonging to me. I always thought I was special because I'd known him so long. But now that I have the chance to think about it, I realize that Luke belonged to Rabbitbrush much more than he ever belonged to me. He went to preschool with these kids, and elementary school. They learned to ski together before Luke ever set eyes on me, when they were chubby little toddlers, bundled up and not using poles. While I was off with my mother, Luke was here. He belonged to everyone. More specifically than that, he belonged to Francine, and to Kelly, at least for a little while, before I showed up. Luke pretty much even stopped going to parties because I hated them, and I wanted him to myself. And now, beware of what you wish for. Nobody in the world can ever see him again, not even his mother, except for me.

Dr. Reisner used to tell me that guilt is a function of grief. "You'd feel guilty no matter how Luke died," he said. "If he'd died in a plane crash, or from an illness, you would feel guilty. It's one of the things we feel when someone we love, someone close to us, dies."

But Luke didn't die in a plane crash, or from an illness. As Kelly and Francine make their way toward me, I remember a conversation Francine and I had the first spring I came back for good, after one of my mother's miscarriages. "You have to be very gentle with her," Francine said, which surprised me, because I knew that she loathed my mother. "There's not a worse loss. It doesn't matter at what stage the loss occurs. Children are the only people who can't be replaced. You can replace a spouse, or a lover, or a friend. You can even replace a mother if you do it early enough. But a child," Francine said. "There's no replacing a child. There's no hope of recovery from that."

Now here she comes, with no hope of recovery, walking down the hall from the library beside Luke's old girlfriend. Francine is not a native of Rabbitbrush. She grew up on the Northern Cheyenne Indian Reservation in Birney, Montana, and came to Colorado when she won a scholarship to Fort Lewis College in Durango. Francine's hair is thick and black like Luke's, and today she wears it loose. It hangs straight, nearly to her waist. Since last spring the strands of gray have multiplied.

Francine sees me. I can tell by the way her neck stiffens. Should I speak? Smile? Certainly I shouldn't smile; she needs to see that I'm miserable. It's only fair that she gets to think of me as incapable of experiencing any kind of happiness or peace ever again.

Kelly's eyes flitter and land on me. She looks stricken. Francine tightens her grip on Kelly and positions herself more firmly between us, not looking my way even for a second. I can read the avoidance in every muscle of her body. Her eyes don't move or even blink, they stay so intent on looking at Kelly instead of me. Francine's eyes are Luke's in their shape and their dark, dark color. If I hadn't seen him so recently, if I didn't feel sure I would see him again soon, those eyes alone would have struck me to the floor.

I lift up my hand and waggle my fingers in the barest, lamest wave. Francine must see it from the corner of her eye; I see her flinch at the shoulders, as if I have prodded her with something electric. I want to whisper, *I'm sorry*. I always want to whisper, *I'm sorry*. I wish I could do something for her, and the only thing I can think of is to not say anything, and obey the distance she imposes.

The air between her shoulder and mine is full and terrible as our bodies pass. Francine's hand twitches, like she's resisting the reflex to wave back to me, and somehow in that moment I realize she must know it's me who's been leaving the tansy asters. The picture in my mind changes. I see her arrive home every day to find those flowers and to her they're like a bitter practical joke, asking for something she can't possibly be expected to give.

*   *   *

When school lets out, the sun is shining, and I decide to walk to my grandparents' house instead of taking the bus to Paul's. It's a long walk, but I have my hiking boots on. It's been more depressing than ever, riding the bus, now that Carlo is too sick to wait for me at the bottom of the hill. Yesterday my mother and I took him to the vet to have the excess fluid drained again. Dr. Hill talked me into letting him stay the night. I hope that Grandma or Grandpa can drive me over there to get him—Mom and Paul are going for an ultrasound in Durango and won't be home till late.

I head off down the side of the road, picking up my step as I cross the turnoff to Luke's old house. Before long I'm walking past the Cummingses', where I used to babysit their daughter, Genevieve. Through the kitchen window I can see a teenage girl—the new babysitter—at the sink. I picture Genevieve sitting at the table eating a snack, and I wonder if she remembers me. Three days a week I used to pick her up at preschool and bring her home. Probably these days nobody would trust me with their kid.

I turn onto Arapahoe, the steep, winding road that leads to my grandparents' house. Above my head the sky looks blue the way it only ever does in Colorado. Crayola should make a crayon called Colorado Blue. The color is so vivid and deep but at the same time very pale; on some of these clearest days, it hovers on the brink of periwinkle.

In front of the Burdick house, which signals the approach of my grandparents' driveway, I see the daughter—Evie—sitting alone on the front porch, a fat paperback open on her knee. Without thinking, I feel my footsteps slow. Evie waves politely. She's a year or so younger than I am, and we don't know each other very well.

I stop by their roadside mailbox, the name Burdick printed across it in faded blue letters. The year before I came back to Rabbitbrush, Evie's mother died of breast cancer and her father—out of his mind with grief—committed suicide. Before everything happened with Luke, I was horrified by that suicide—leaving behind a fourteen-year-old girl who had already lost her mother.

When both the Burdicks were alive, this house was pretty. The mother used to plant window boxes in the spring, and Mr. Burdick used to paint the house a new color every few years. In fact, it was one of the measures I used to gauge my absences—if the Burdick house was the same color when I returned, then I hadn't been gone too long. Now the house is not unpretty so much as wanting repairs. The window boxes are still there, just full of untended dirt and empty of flowers. Mr. Burdick's last color choice—a bright, pale yellow—is peeling, and the gutters are full. A couple shutters hang off their hinges, a few months or one strong wind away from clattering to the ground. The place has the look of one of those formally grand Victorian houses in Boulder or Durango that's been taken over by students. My grandmother says that H. J. has enough on his hands taking care of Evie without worrying about upkeep. Sometimes in the spring and summer my grandfather sneaks over while they're at school and mows the grass. Probably next week he'll clean out their gutters. I don't think H. J. and Evie even notice.

Evie surprises me by getting off the front stoop and trotting across the lawn. "Hi, Tressa," she says. Her voice sounds airy and musical. She has darker hair than I remember—so dark that it's probably not her natural color. Backing up this assumption is her face looking back at me—fair, translucent skin and very, very dark eyeliner. She has pale brown eyes flecked with green. Despite the makeup and dyed hair she looks about thirteen.

"Hi, Evie," I say.

"I haven't seen you much at school," Evie says, as if this is unusual.

"I'm sticking mostly to class and the library," I say.

"Bummer they made you do over the year," she says. I can't remember speaking to her during these last, terrible months, but her voice implies this is the continuation of an abandoned conversation. And it probably is, just not a conversation she had with me.

"It's not so bad," I say.

"Oh, good," she says. "Where's your dog?"

I pause, then flicker my eyes toward the hill. Maybe

she'll think he ran up ahead of me. But no. If she knows enough to expect him, she'll also know that he never ventured very far from my side.

"He's sick," I say. "He stayed at the vet last night."

Evie does a little double take. She looks too upset by this news, too troubled. I find myself frowning. "It's no big deal," I say quickly, uneasy because the words feel like a lie. "Just old-dog stuff. He'll be fine."

"Oh," Evie says, obviously not convinced. "That's good."

The front door of her house opens, and H. J. walks out wearing an apron and carrying a long wooden spoon that he waves in our general direction, squinting as if he can't tell exactly who we are without his glasses. I can't tell if he's calling Evie inside or saying hello.

"H. J.'s making corn chowder for dinner," Evie says. "He makes his own bread. You want to stay and eat with us?"

"Oh, no," I say, too quickly. "I need to go pick up my dog. But thanks."

"Sure," Evie says. "Maybe you can come over another time."

"Thanks." I stand there for a moment while Evie jogs back across the yard. She and H. J. go inside and close the door behind them, and I think for a minute about everything the two Burdicks have been through, and everything they've recovered from. It's impressive and sad at the same time, how life has gone on—nothing but peeling paint and too-full rain gutters to reveal all that sorrow, and all that loss.

My grandmother stands on her farmer's porch, holding up one hand to shade her eyes. I wave as I walk toward her.

"Tressa," she says. "I knew you were on your way here. I could feel it in my bones. Should we go rescue Carlo?"

"Yes, please," I say.

"But first come in and have a snack." This has always been my grandmother's greeting: "Come in and have a snack." When I was little, the words sounded exactly like, *Welcome! I love you!* My mother tended to ration and then run out of food. I remember once, during a summer we spent camping at the San Francisco Hot Springs in New Mexico, I got in trouble for eating the last two granola bars from the cooler in her tent. She made me sit in time-out on a rock overlooking the springs. Vacationing college students soaked nearby, and I recited the food I would eat if I were at my grandparents'. "My grandma gives me peanut butter and jelly," I said, "and she makes me eggs and gives me strawberry milk. I can always eat more if I want to, because my grandma loves me. She has Oreos. She makes chicken pot pie."

In fact, I still have a hard time, whenever I cross my grandmother's threshold, not devouring everything in sight—as if I can't be sure my mother won't appear and steal me away, back into her on-the-run world of limited food. But of course now I need to lose weight, I need to look like myself for Luke, so I follow my grandmother into the house and say, "I just want a glass of water."

Grandma frowns, as if I have rejected love itself. She compromises by pouring a glass of orange juice and pressing it into my hands. We sit together at the Formica kitchen table. She wears a loose forest-green cardigan and blue jeans. Her gray hair is cut short and is un-styled; it falls choppily just over her ears. Grandpa may have cut it for her. She has pale blue eyes like my mom, with lovely, intricate crinkles all around them. I don't suppose she has ever had any interest in appearing younger than her chronological age.

"I saw Evie and H. J. Burdick on the way over here," I tell her.

Grandma clucks her tongue, sympathetic. "The poor Burdicks," she says. That's what everyone has called them these past few years, and Grandma and I realize at the same time that's probably how everyone refers to us now. The poor Kingsburys. The poor Earnshaws.

Grandma reaches out her hands and closes them around mine. I can't feel the cool dryness of her palms through my sleeves, pulled up almost to my fingers, but Grandma squeezes insistently. "Would you like to bring Carlo back here, honey?" she asks. "You can both spend the night."

I would like to stay here tonight and every night. But

Luke has never come to me at my grandparents' house, so I shake my head.

"Where's Grandpa?" I ask.

"Fishing. He might bring home some trout for dinner." Grandma pauses and says, "Shall we walk down and ask if he wants to come with us?" The tone of her voice is hopeful and apologetic, and my heart shrinks up into a tiny little pebble.

Though Grandpa has sold a parcel of land here, given another away there, my grandparents still own more than a hundred acres. The Earnshaw property spills down from the tip of this mountain peak almost into town, abutting the land not far from the high school and the supermarket, where Paul wants to build the drive-in movie theater that would only be open in the summer, the one that Grandpa swears he will never allow.

I love this place, my grandparents' land. When I was little, and far away, all I ever wanted was to come back here to stay. On the first map I ever drew of Rabbitbrush, a red-crayoned heart represents the house. It's still the place I want to escape to whenever I feel down or lost or blue. The only animals still on the property are a pair of old draft horses, Sturm and Drang. They graze all day on the surrounding hills. It's been a long time since they had any work to do, and apparently they miss the activity. If I were to take the time to run and get Grandpa, Sturm and Drang would follow me like a pair of dogs, their huge furry hooves plodding patiently behind me.

The three of us would find my grandfather standing by the river, patiently casting with his own homemade flies and the rod his father gave him when he was twelve. It would make everyone so happy—the sight of me walking these hills like nothing had ever happened, those two huge, crazy horses lumbering behind me.

Grandma sits across the table waiting for my reply, her face full of hope. I know that she worries about me, and that she loves me, and I want to act, for her sake, like everything's okay.

"Tressa," Grandma says, and I can tell she's going to say something I'm not ready to hear. I slide my hand out from under hers and hold out my palm like a crossing guard, hoping the halting gesture seems firm but not rude: Stop. No. Don't say another word.

I don't want to talk about the river.

(4)

LUKE

Tressa told me all about that day in New Mexico when she got in trouble for eating granola bars. Now I can see where her mother put her in time-out. Tressa just sits there by the water. I know that look, Tressa's mad look. I guess she's like five or six because she doesn't have Carlo yet. She said this happened in summer but I can tell that's wrong. The air feels kind of chilly. Soaking in hot water seems like a good idea. So maybe it's March or April.

She and her mom and her mom's latest boyfriend have been camping on the other side of the river. Tressa's scared to death of that river and I don't blame her. Every morning the boyfriend piggybacks her across. When the water hits her legs she grabs on to that guy so tight that sometimes he pretends he's going to shrug her off. He's kidding, but I still want to push him over, and if it weren't for Tressa on his back I'd go ahead and do it.

I never met Tressa's real father, never even saw a picture of him. She only met him herself a couple times. Generally it seemed like he didn't really exist. Tressa says she thinks of all her mother's boyfriends like one father that she never got to know. So it's interesting to see this guy, one father in a long string of them, ending, I guess, with my dad.

At the hot springs Tressa sits on the rocks wearing a ratty bathing suit. Her white hair is crazy tangled. She looks like a little Tarzan girl, all bony and wild. Her eyes are kind of sunken in her face. I would hate seeing any kid this scrawny, and I get mad at Hannah. So does everyone else at the hot springs. Tressa rattles off the list of what her grandma would feed her. At this point she's already lived in Ireland and Baja, plus a bunch of different states. She has this special kind of accent, likes she's not from anywhere except everywhere. She sounds way too grown-up for a little kid.

I can tell the college girls are pissed that Tressa's hungry. One of them shoots dirty looks at Hannah. The other one gets out of the hot springs and digs out a pear from her backpack. She hands it to Tressa. I can see Hannah's watching but I can't tell if she feels guilty because of her sunglasses and floppy straw hat.

Here's how it goes. I stand there on the rocks a few

feet from Tressa. It's like watching a movie, but at the same time I'm part of the movie. I'm inside the picture. Then all of a sudden Tressa looks up from her sticky hands. She ate the whole pear, core and all. We look at each other. She smiles. Then she stands up and steps into the water. Hannah doesn't say anything. Time-out must be over, or else she doesn't care. Tressa floats on her back with her eyes closed. I realize I've been crouching, and I get up so I can soak in the hot springs too. The next thing I know, I'm climbing through Tressa's window. I land in her room at my dad's house. She sits up in bed, all grown-up and waiting for me.

"Tressa Gentle," I say, and she smiles.

She's not scrawny anymore. Her hair's dark and not tangled. But something's wrong. Something's missing and I can tell she's been crying. Not only that, something's changed in a way that makes it hard to stay. The room goes blurry like it wants to disappear. *This is the after-Luke*. I'm not supposed to be here.

But Tressa says, "Don't go." It takes all my strength to walk over to the bed. We sit there looking at each other. I see her mouth move but I can't understand the words.

Tressa takes a deep breath. I know that look on her face. I know it so well that maybe I can stay. From the way she raises her eyebrows I know she's asking a question. She wants me to do something for her. I can hardly stand it, how much I want to understand.

"Never mind," she says after a while, and this time the words come through. "I'm just glad you're here."

I can't speak just yet. If I could, I'd say, *Where else would I be?* The only place I can ever be anymore is with her. Tressa does something she hasn't done in a long time. She puts her hand on top of mine. I want to feel her skin but all I feel is air.

"It's so frustrating sometimes," she says. "I want to *feel* you."

I move my hand like I'm pushing her hair off her forehead, but I don't actually touch skin. She smiles then does the same with me.

"Remember that day," she says, "at your mother's house the summer before last? You were supposed to go with her to the bluegrass festival in Telluride, but you told her you were sick."

"She didn't believe me."

"But she went anyway. Even though she probably knew exactly what we would do."

Back in the day, Dad didn't want Tressa and me to be together. But Mom didn't really care. She thought he went about the whole thing wrong. "He's turning them into Romeo and Juliet," I heard her tell a friend. Mom didn't want us sleeping together, obviously, but she didn't mind if we hung out. On that particular day Tressa and I knew she would be in Telluride for hours, so we could do more than hang out, we could do anything we wanted. And what we wanted, surprise, surprise, was to lie naked on top of my bed. Which, as I recall, was pretty painful in its own way.

"But I stopped you," Tressa says, reading my mind as usual. "I always stopped you."

"Doesn't matter," I tell her. Even though it did kind of drive me crazy, I'm being totally honest. It doesn't matter. Kelly never stopped me. And even though I liked her, maybe even loved her a little, I'm not showing up in Kelly's room. I don't want to be with anyone except Tressa.

I remember that day when my mom went to Telluride. I may have pushed a little too far, and Tressa got mad at me. So we put our clothes back on, and while I worked on calming down, Tressa drew a map of the trees outside my window. I closed my eyes and listened to her pencil scraping on the paper. It sounded confident, like she knew exactly what she was doing.

"You can look now," she said, and when I opened my eyes, there was this whole gray and white world, these crazy shapes I saw every day of my life but never noticed before. I wanted her to color them in but she liked the picture the way it was. I taped it on the wall next to the window. I wonder if it's still there.

Now Tressa leans back on her pillows. Out of nowhere she grabs her nightgown and pulls it over her head. She pulls her legs out from under the covers and stretches them next to me. So she's lying there naked. There's just enough light for me to see her clearly. It's almost worse, seeing all that skin and knowing I can't feel it. I want to take my clothes off too, but I know I can't. In a weird way it's so much like it used to be, and at the same time it's so different that I want to laugh. Or cry.

"You can try," she whispers. I know she doesn't mean my clothes but her skin. To touch it, feel it.

I shake my head. "I can't. I know I can't. It hurts too much to try."

She leans back against her pillows again. I lie down next to her. Face-to-face we stare at each other. Obviously, Tressa being naked distracts me. But I can't shake the feeling that something important has gone missing. Something should be sitting on the floor next to the bed. I can see Tressa's lips moving, but the sound of her voice won't turn into words.

But then for a second, even though I can't hear what she's saying, I get it. Like a flash going off on a camera. I see what's supposed to be here, I see what's gone, and I understand exactly what she wants me to do.

When Hannah and my dad got married again, Hannah wanted to turn into my mom. That's what Tressa said, anyway. She said her mother was sick of being a hippy and wanted to be a normal, carpooling mom. The sad thing is that my mom always wished she were a free spirit, which is what people used to call Hannah, which seriously irritated my sisters. According to Jill, "free spirit" is a nicer way of saying "deadbeat."

Of course it messed with Jill's and Katie's heads, the way Hannah left them behind but took Tressa along with her. It didn't make any sense. Tressa's father wasn't in the picture, but Hannah could have left her with the Earnshaws. In fact, a couple of times she did. But then, after a month or so, she'd come back for her. She never took the twins with her, not one single time, but she took Tressa over and over again. She had three kids living in Rabbitbrush and she only ever left with one of them. Tressa says it's because she was the only one who never complained, and it's true that she never did. Not until they told her that she couldn't see me.

When Hannah left the first time, her letter said she was gone for good, but nobody really believed her, at least not at first. My dad and her parents figured she'd get in touch.

She never did. She didn't write or call, she didn't even send a postcard. Obviously she didn't e-mail. I'm not sure there even was e-mail back then. The point is, nobody knew if she was alive except my father. He knew she was alive and that one day she'd come back. He used to tell my mother this before they got together, when she was just the twins' babysitter. Mom had just gotten her graduate degree in Social Work but she didn't have a real job yet. Dad paid her at first. "And then he married me," Mom used to say.

You can see for yourself how everything lined up.

My mom fell in love with my dad and then she married him. My dad married her, he maybe even loved her, but at the same time he still thought about Hannah. He still wanted Hannah to come back.

I feel bad for him. But I'm not sorry Hannah ran away. Otherwise I wouldn't've been born. Neither would Tressa. Everyone knew about me from the beginning, but no one knew about Tressa until four years later, when the thing everybody more or less gave up on happened, and Hannah came back to Rabbitbrush.

(5)

TRESSA

I want to tell Luke so badly that Carlo died. When I see
him come through the window, I feel too sad to smile
back. I try my best to tell him the whole terrible story—
how I refused to let the vet put my dog to sleep.

"He's in a lot of pain," Dr. Hill said. I knew this was
true. I *knew* it. Carlo lay on the metal table, the small
room smelling of ammonia from both urine and cleaners,
along with that very particular scent that frightened animals emit. I ran my hands over and over his still-glossy
fur, hating the ragged rise and fall of his chest, and the
glaze over his eyes. I also hated the way Dr. Hill already
brandished his syringe full of death, confident of changing my mind. Grandma stood behind him, watching
me, her eyes full of tears. I wished *she* would make the
decision, and at the same time I understood it was my

responsibility. He was my dog. And how could I say, *Yes, go ahead, plunge that needle into Carlo—who is a person to me, a beloved person.* How could I be an accomplice to killing my dog?

By the time we headed home, I already knew the decision was entirely wrong and selfish. Carlo lay on a red Indian blanket in the back of Grandma's car. She had folded the seats down so I could lie next to him, my faced pressed into his neck. At Paul's house we each had to take an end of the blanket and carry him out to the grass. I wanted him to feel the sunlight.

That's how we sat for the longest time. Poor Carlo, not caring at all about the sunlight, just finished, just wanting to be gone. I sat next to him, my hand on his head, watching his breath get shallower and shallower. Watching him fight for those last moments—going the hard way instead of the peaceful one Dr. Hill had offered. Stupid, selfish girl.

"I'm sorry," I whispered to Carlo. I leaned over him, listening to his last breaths. "I'm so sorry."

Carlo closed his eyes—lovely white, furless lids. I guess I expected to feel relief when his breathing finally stopped and his pain ended along with the ordeal of watching him die. By now I should have figured out that death never brings any kind of relief. It just brings sorrow, and guilt, and the insane, maddening, screaming wish that you could redo the one single moment in time that might possibly change everything.

* * *

In the morning I run downstairs, expecting Carlo to still be in the grass where I left him. To anyone else it might seem morbid, but I want to stroke his fur one last time.

"I'm so sorry," Mom tells me. "Paul already took him back to Dr. Hill's." I don't ask what for. Probably to be cremated.

I walk outside and sit down next to the spot where Carlo should still be. The blanket's gone too; the grass underneath is bent sideways in his shape, and I run my hand over the blades again and again, deepening the indentation.

Mom walks outside and stands over me. I don't have to look up to see the worry on her face. "You can stay home today if you want," she says. "We can go for a drive or something. Go for a hike. Or just hang out. Anything you want."

I think about going for a drive with my mother. I think about the two of us, getting into a car and driving for a thousand miles and never coming back. Knowing this isn't a possibility, I say, "No. Thanks. I want to stay busy."

Her fear—that I won't be able to handle this—makes me even sadder. But then so does everything else—the memory of Carlo's painful last breaths, the inability to tell Luke about it, the worry I constantly cause, and the image of Luke's last moments, which I've been able to push aside since he started coming back. I give the grass one last, smoothing pat, then go inside and get ready for school. When I walk out the kitchen door, my mother is close behind me, holding it open. I know she'll stand there until she sees me get on the bus. I know what she really wants is to walk two steps behind me, all day every day, so she can see for herself that I haven't done anything to hurt myself.

At the top of the driveway, my grandfather's truck putters up right at the same moment as the school bus. "Oh, look," I hear Mom call. "It's Dad."

Grandpa rolls down his window and waves the bus driver away. Then he pulls into the driveway and gets out carrying a small guitar-shaped case. "Tressa," he says, striding toward me on long legs. From a distance he hasn't changed much since he first gave Carlo to me. But as he gets closer, I see all the years that have passed. He holds his arms out to hug me, but instead of walking into them I sit down on the stoop. Grandpa seems to understand that if I let him hold me, I'll fall apart. He sits down next to me, and my mother closes the door as if to give us privacy. I hear her step lightly, back into the kitchen, but I know she's hovering close enough to hear our conversation through the open window.

Grandpa puts his broad hand on my knee. I know it's meant to be a reassuring gesture, but even though he is solid and strong, that hand looks old to me. It looks craggy and liver-spotted, and I find myself looking ahead to another loss that I simply won't be able to bear.

I suck in my breath, which sounds wet and shaky with tears. The thing about deciding to live, even if you're determined not to be happy—your body goes ahead and battles sorrow without you.

"You know," Grandpa says, "one thing I've been thinking about Hannah is that it took almost losing you to turn her into a real mother."

Grandpa says this kind of loudly, like he wants Mom to hear. Inside, something bangs a little too hard into the sink. Her parents will never forgive her for all those years she went away. But while Mom hasn't exactly been Francine, she has had her moments—her own peculiar strengths—and I don't like to hear these digs.

"She's always been a real mother," I say, hoping she'll hear that, too. Then, to apologize for disagreeing with him, I put my hand on top of the little guitar case.

"What's this?" I ask.

"It's a ukulele," Grandpa says. "For you."

"A ukulele?" The word coming out of my mouth sounds so ridiculous that I laugh.

"You never play your guitar anymore. I thought maybe you'd like to try something new."

He slides it into my lap, and I unlatch the case. Inside is a yellow ukulele. It looks much too cheerful. "It's yellow," I say.

"Isn't that your favorite color?"

"Sure." *When I was ten*, I don't say.

Grandpa moves his hand from my knee to the top of

my head. "I miss hearing you play guitar," he says. He's the one who gave me the guitar, for my eighth birthday. An old Martin, much too nice for a little kid. My mother hated having to drag it around with us. But she did it, for me. I feel like pointing this out to Grandpa but don't want him to answer by putting her down.

So I just say, "I don't know why you'd miss hearing me play. I was never much good at it." If Grandpa contradicts this universal truth, I will know I am a lost cause. The only time I ever sounded halfway decent on guitar was when Luke or Grandpa played with me, drowning out my clumsy strumming.

Grandpa, who plays every string instrument there is, says, "So, now you can be not much good at ukulele. I'll teach you. We'll have fun." He's the one who taught me to play the guitar, and I loved taking lessons with him even though I never managed to learn more than five or six chords. Now I pluck a string of the ukulele, still in its case. The sound vibrates, startlingly cheerful and out of place—as if a palm tree just sprouted on the lawn next to the aspens and pines.

"You need a ride to school?" Grandpa asks.

"I guess I do. Since you sent the bus away."

Grandpa reaches over and snaps the ukulele case shut. We stand up and walk to his truck. Grandpa doesn't say good-bye to Mom. Lately his general annoyance with her is heightened by her giving that land to Paul.

As we pull away, I see her, watching us through the kitchen window. She waves to me, and I can tell she's trying to look like she's not crying. Carlo lived with her, too, all these years. I wave back, suddenly sorry I turned down her offer to stay home.

The day passes in a lonely fog until lunch, when Evie Burdick finds me in the cafeteria. Outside, a drizzling rain has started spitting against the windows. It might very well ease into the first real snowfall of the season. Here in Rabbitbrush it almost always snows by October, and this year is no exception. But there hasn't yet been a real *dumping*, the sort to make everyone pile onto skis and snowshoes.

Evie slides her tray onto the table across from me. She wears faded jeans and a skimpy Johnny Cash T-shirt. I'm huddled in a thick wool sweater. I remember how cold I always got when I had zero body fat, and think that Evie must be freezing.

"Hi," she says.

"Hi," I say back. "Aren't you freezing?"

She laughs. "Everybody always asks me that. I never get cold."

"Never?"

"Never."

I usually make my own lunch, but this morning Mom made me a turkey sandwich and packed it into an insulated lunch box along with an ice pack. She also gave me a stick of string cheese, an apple, and a thermos of pomegranate-grape juice. I sip the juice and bite into the apple but try to avoid the rest of my lunch. My fingers have gotten so fat that the pearl ring Luke gave me digs into my skin, creating a cracked and itchy indentation. If I don't start losing weight soon, they'll have to cut the ring off me with metal pliers.

Evie's tray is piled with food from the cafeteria: chicken nuggets, a slice of pizza, SunChips, a Diet Coke, and a package of little chocolate doughnuts. She slides her book onto the table. I try to peek at the title for a possible conversation opener, but she turns it over and dives into the pizza. Ordinarily I would make some excuse and clear away. Maybe I would bundle into my coat and sit under the awning outside, or just toss my lunch and hide out in the library until my next class.

But I remember the other day, when Evie asked about Carlo. Weird, but I find myself hoping that she'll ask again. All day I have felt so sad. It seems, I don't know, disrespectful, not to talk about him.

Evie doesn't say anything; she just eats her food. I want to ask her how she managed, in those weeks after her parents died. Last spring I couldn't stand living in this world anymore. I just couldn't, I wasn't capable. The impossibility of Luke being *gone* because of that one stupid moment. The very second that moment passed, it was too far away to ever make right. And the further away I got from it, the *more* impossible it would be to ever go back and fix it. The guilt and the loss were too huge. I couldn't continue living, not even for Carlo or my mother. Not even for my grandparents. I understood that I ought to, but I just couldn't.

Sitting across from one of the few people who might understand that feeling, I want to say something meaningful, or tell her about Carlo. Instead I find myself saying, "How was the corn chowder?"

She glances down at her tray, confused for a minute, and then remembers. "Oh, it was pretty good. H. J.'s a decent cook. He's very into it these days. He stops at the grocery store on the way home from school, and as soon as he walks through the door, he just starts cooking. He even said something about culinary school, after I leave for college."

She says this so nonchalantly, as if it hardly matters— the two orphans, living together. I glance at the back cover of her book and see the title, *Lover of Unreason*.

"Is that for school?" I ask.

She looks at me, then slides the book into her lap without glancing down at it. "No," she says. "Just something I'm reading on my own." I wait for further explanation, but she doesn't offer any. Instead she says, "Hey. H. J. and I are going to ski in Telluride on Saturday. Do you want to come?"

Telluride is only fifty miles north of us, so the weather is pretty much the same, but for opening day the snow cannons will be working overtime. I almost say no to

Evie's invitation. Then I remember my mother peering out the window this morning, how I should have stayed with her, and in a flash I see a way to make up for it. She would be over the moon about me accepting this invitation, a normal social activity. Still, I can't quite bring myself to say yes. "You guys probably won't want to ski with me," I say instead. "I just learned a couple years ago, when I came back."

"I don't mind," Evie says. "And H. J. loves to ski with beginners."

I have a hard time believing this. Even with Luke, who taught me how to ski and couldn't have been more patient, I could feel him longing to abandon me for the black diamond slopes.

But Evie shrugs. "He says it's more interesting skiing with someone who has something to learn. He gets tired of the whole shredding culture. He says all anyone talks about in this town is ski equipment and snow conditions."

I nod, knowing exactly how H. J. feels.

"He'll probably move away at some point," Evie goes on. "But he says it's sunny here three hundred days a year, and he already knows everyone's name. And he has his job. And, you know, he has to wait till I'm done with high school."

Evie looks back down at her plate, and I wonder if this is my moment to tell her that I'm sorry about her parents. I try to remember the details of her father's suicide, how he did it, and I realize suddenly that this is something I can talk to Luke about. I can ask him about Evie and H. J., because Luke knew them when he was alive.

Outside, the rain turns to snow before our eyes. It falls halfway to the ground as droplets, then morphs into clusters of stars. Growing up, I didn't see snow until I was six. Even when we first started coming back to Rabbitbrush, it was always in the summer. I can remember not completely believing in snow, the way I didn't completely believe in dinosaurs, or Santa Claus. I hoped it was real but couldn't be entirely convinced. It still seems like magic to me, in the first moments it begins to fall.

"Hey," I say. I know what I'm about to tell her will feel out of the blue. At the same time, I think that probably Evie will understand. "My dog died last night."

Her face rearranges itself in three quick, visible phases—shock, memory, then sympathy. "Oh, God, Tressa," she says. "I'm really sorry."

"Thank you," I say. My eyes fill up with tears, but I realize that's okay. Dr. Reisner would say it's appropriate.

"Listen," she says. "Come with us on Saturday, promise? It can't make it better, I know. But at least it will take your mind off it."

"Sure," I tell Evie. "I'd love to go skiing with you guys."

We clear our lunches and say good-bye a little awkwardly. I head to my locker to collect my books for
French, and it must just be a Burdick kind of day, because
I see H. J. and Mr. Tynan standing outside Mr. Tynan's
classroom. I am the only student in the hallway, and they
don't notice me, not at first. I wonder if I should wave or
say something about Evie inviting me to ski on Saturday.
But Mr. Tynan's voice is uncharacteristically stern and
sharp. Usually he moves gently, wearing a wry smile.
But talking to H. J., his face looks drawn and angry. I hear
the word "inappropriate." "Massively inappropriate,"
Mr. Tynan says.

I open my locker, and the two of them turn their
heads at the metallic ping of the latch. I expect H. J.'s face
to look penitent. But it doesn't, only calm and composed.

"Hi, Mr. Burdick," I say, though in my head I call him
by his first name. Before H. J. has a chance to answer,
Mr. Tynan grabs him by the shoulder and propels him
inside his classroom, looking back over his shoulder, still
frowning—as if he means to protect me.

A couple nights a week I can get away with eating at my
grandparents' house. The rest of the time, unless Mom
and Paul go out (and my mother is still too committed to
keeping a close eye on me to go out very often), I have to
conform to this temporary family unit—Paul, my mother,
me—at least until the baby comes, and I leave, and the
future finally takes the shape Paul always dreamed of.

In my stepfather's house, upstairs on the third floor, my room retains something of the spirit of our old life, my mom's and mine. The eaves slant, the floorboards sway a bit. My maps are tacked onto the walls, and the furniture is a hodgepodge of relics from my grandparents'. I still use the old farm quilt I've been hauling around since we first came back to visit. I think that Francine may have actually given it to me, back when I was just a little kid and she hadn't quite admitted my mother was a threat. My upstairs room is not fancy but frayed and worn in a cozy and familiar way.

Downstairs, on the other hand. The downstairs at Paul's is modern and luxurious. It's not ostentatious unless you know how much they spent on that sideboard in the dining room, or the brand-new energy efficient washer-dryer in the laundry room. When I was a kid, my mother used to haul our laundry around in old pillowcases. I have seen her stand on the street in front of Laundromats, begging strangers for quarters. Now she shuffles her pregnant self with surprising grace around a state-of-the-art kitchen. She bastes a roast chicken. Biscuits made from scratch wait patiently in the warming oven. Paul walks in and starts setting the table, and Mom asks me to toss the already prepared salad. I watch Paul lay out three wineglasses, and wonder if he will pour me a glass or if that third is just a nod to symmetry.

Paul tries to smile at me as he pulls a bottle of white

wine from the refrigerator and I pick up the wooden salad spoons. "This is a perfect winter dinner," he says to my mother, or me, or both of us. The last, I think. Paul rarely says anything directly to me. It is not just since Luke and I fell in love that things have been awkward between us, and it is not just since Luke died. Ever since Paul first discovered my existence, I have been his chief competition and an unavoidable remnant of my mother's escape. If it weren't for me, he could pretend that she had always lived here with him, playing Barbie to his Ken in their mountain Dreamhouse.

It may seem like I hate Paul, but I don't, not exactly. I respect the love that he and my mother have. Although I don't see much of Luke in him (in looks and mannerisms Luke seems almost entirely Francine's), I recognize pieces of Luke and me in Paul and my mother. There is something about their rapport that indicates a long, intense, and destined-to-be-repeated history.

My theory about Paul is that his good looks have ruined him. Born beautiful and athletic, he never had to develop much of a personality or make an effort to charm anyone. I guess the same could be said of my mother if it weren't for all that nervous energy. Mom is too self-conscious to be believable as Barbie. She's too fluttery and—in her heart at least—too much of a flake.

Paul, on the other hand, fits Ken perfectly. Like a plastic doll, he barely feels the need to speak at all. He just pulls his good-looking sweaters over his good-looking head and lets them hang from his good-looking shoulders. His good-looking face has weathered in a good-looking way, and there is good-looking gray at his good-looking temples. He never needs to pick up the phone to call the world, because he knows the world will call him. The only thing in Paul's entire life that ever eluded him now bustles around his kitchen, domestic and pregnant and basting chicken.

I carry the salad to the table as Paul fills his glass with wine, then pours spring water for both my mother and me. Of course. He is not the sort to give liquor to the pregnant or the underage. I have searched his eyes for some sort of twinkle, some sort of spark, and have never found any. The only things extraordinary about Paul are his bank balances and my mother. And of course Luke.

I take a sip of water and say, "I got invited to ski in Telluride on Saturday."

"Oh, honey, that's *great*," my mother says immediately.

At the same time Paul asks, "Who with?" Their voices meld together, one bright and overexcited, the other suspicious and thrown off its game.

"Evie and H. J. Burdick," I say, and both Paul and Mom stop their movements for a moment.

The first words out of my mother's mouth are, "The poor Burdicks." And then she says, "The boy, too?"

"Yeah," I say. "Both of them."

My mother scoots past Paul to take her seat. He shoots her a good-looking frown as he begins to carve the chicken. "H. J.," Paul says. "Wasn't he in Jill and Katie's class?"

Mom nods, but really, how would she know? Then she fesses up, saying, "I haven't seen H. J. since he was a little boy. He used to look so much like Jenny. Remember, Paul?"

At Paul's silence my mother looks toward me and tilts her head to one side and then the other, as if considering, as if this is something she needs to weigh before granting or denying permission. Probably they are both wishing I could go skiing with some normal kids, not people sullied by tragedy like me.

"Mom," I say. "I don't have to go, if you don't want me to."

She reaches out and touches my hand. "No," she says. "Of course I want you to go. But it's a mom's job to worry, right?"

She tilts her head, and I tilt mine in the opposite direction. I like it when she asks this sort of question, her tone ironic enough to admit she knows her current persona is partly an act. Over the summer I had enough therapy to understand the unfairness of my disliking her attempts at Happy Homemaker, when while I was growing up, that was all I ever wanted from her. I know Mom wants me to rediscover the joy in life (thereby continuing to live). But she's also visualizing me skiing into a tree, on purpose, at full speed.

For no particular reason I think of H. J. in the hall at

school with Mr. Tynan. *Massively inappropriate*. I feel as if I've heard that phrase before, possibly in connection with me and Luke. "Tressa," Jill once complained. "He's my *brother*."

"But he's not mine," I told her—compliant in every other area of my life, but defiant in that one.

Paul passes out plates laden with chicken and potatoes. He takes a sip of wine. "Well," he says, as if after briefly considering he has come to a decision. "I think that will be fine, for you to go skiing with the Burdick kids."

My mother moves her hand from mine to touch Paul. They smile at each other, so pleased in their joint parenting that for a second I want to tell them that I've changed my mind and won't go skiing after all.

After dinner I take my time. I clean up the kitchen while my mother gets off her feet and Paul answers e-mail in his study. Instead of going upstairs to my own desk, I spread my books across the dining room table and work there. I do my homework carefully, double-checking, studying much longer than I need to for tomorrow's Human Behavior quiz.

When my finished work is stored in my backpack, I take out a fresh piece of paper and draw a map of the kitchen. Drawing maps is the one thing I haven't been able to stop doing. Something about visualizing the place where I am, and not just drawing it but *charting* it—the process stops my brain from worrying. It calms me down. You couldn't use my maps to find your way anywhere. I'm no cartographer, and they're not exactly to scale, or even anything like accurate. But drawing them makes me feel like I know where I am. When I was little, I used to love imitating those maps at malls, with the little arrow. YOU ARE HERE. Even in the hospital I couldn't stop myself. I drew maps of my room, the courtyard, the cafeteria. The mountains that I could see through my window but never got to explore.

Now I let my pencil flutter over the page. It's almost like I'm using a Ouija board, just letting the pencil guide me. My oil pastels are upstairs, so for now I content myself with this sketch. A chicken on the table. A spatula represents my mother, standing at the stove—I draw dollar signs for its burners.

About thirty minutes later I make myself a cup of tea and head upstairs to the "kids" room—where Jill and Katie used to play, and after that, Luke. Where the new baby will play. I sit down with my map at the old art table and run my hand over a black Sharpie mark. Maybe Luke is the one who left it there. This makes me picture him standing outside, staring through my window as if he's the outsider. I wish, for the thousandth or millionth time, that we could trade places. Then I color in my map of the kitchen with chalky whites and steel gray.

As I work, I think about Evie, and after a while I put the map aside and turn on the computer. The only people who e-mail me are my old friend Isabelle and my sisters—Jill from Denver and Katie from LA—so I don't bother checking e-mail. Instead I do something I haven't done in a million years, not since I first got home from the hospital. I log on to Facebook. It's not exactly something that brings me back to glory days. It probably sounds crazy, but I never even had an e-mail account until I was sixteen, and I've never been in the running for a popularity contest. In fact, I have exactly three Facebook friends, the same people who send me e-mail. Mostly I used my account to store photos, as a backup to my computer files. Luke and I were never friends on Facebook, because our mothers monitored our accounts—a pretty easy task, in my case, though I imagine Luke had plenty of traffic on his page. I wonder how his wall must look now. I imagine all the notes people must have posted after he died.

I go to the search bar and type in "Evie Burdick." When I find her, I hit Add Friend and then stare for a while at her profile picture, which was taken from a chairlift. She's skiing down a very steep run, looking like a pro, and I suspect I won't see much of her on Saturday.

For a moment I think about typing in Luke's name. I wonder what would come up, what I'd be able to see. I remember the sad look on Kelly Boynton's face today, walking down the hallway with Francine, and I find myself typing in her name instead. When I get to her page, her profile picture is just a shivering stand of aspens. Considering how pretty she is, this modesty impresses me, even though I realize that, like me, her parents might not allow her to post a public picture of herself.

I navigate over to Amazon.com and look up Evie's book, *Lover of Unreason*. It turns out to be about a woman I've never heard of named Assia Wevill, who was, according to the subtitle of the book, "Sylvia Plath's rival and Ted Hughes's doomed love." I know about Sylvia Plath vaguely, from a couple poems in English class. I know she committed suicide. According to the synopsis on Amazon, this woman Assia Wevill committed suicide too. So of course Evie would try to hide that book from me. I wonder if that impulse stemmed from not wanting to remind me of my own suicide attempt, or from self-protection—not wanting to confess her own preoccupation, given her family history. Probably, I decide, a little bit of both. I click Add to Cart and charge the book to Paul's account. Then I go into Jill's room to search her bookshelves. There it is, right where I remember seeing it—an old, frayed copy of *The Bell Jar*. I open it and read the first few lines of the introduction.

It says that Sylvia Plath committed suicide a month after the book was published. It also says that she had two little kids and was separated from her husband, a poet named Ted Hughes. I read a little further, till I find out she was diagnosed with clinical depression.

At the hospital Dr. Reisner used those same words to describe me. He said that in addition to suffering from acute post-traumatic stress disorder, I was clinically depressed. I snap the book shut and tuck it under my arm.

Upstairs, getting ready for bed, I take care not to rush my preparations. There can't be any hurrying the night. I know this because I used to try. After dinner I would hop to my feet and slam my dishes into the dishwasher, then plead a headache and rush up to my room. I would brush my teeth and pull on my nightgown, then crawl under the covers and wait, sitting up, hugging my knees to my chest.

Now I know my mind needs to be quiet. I need to move slowly, as if I don't expect anything. I wash my face very carefully. I floss and rinse with Listerine. I sit up in bed reading awhile. Plath's novel, I know, is autobiographical, and I search her words for something of myself. I like the differences between me and her protagonist, Esther Greenwood—the disdain for love, the disgust with her tubercular boyfriend. I keep reading until I reach a scene where Esther dances with a man who tells her, "Pretend you are drowning."

I close the book abruptly, planning to collect myself and then go on reading. But a dreamy tiredness settles itself around me, and the next thing I know, at some nameless time of night—the sky completely dark and the trees rustling outside my window—my eyes flutter open. *The Bell Jar* rises and falls on my chest, and I know Luke will appear at any moment.

But he doesn't. I sit up in bed, wondering how I could be wrong. Not that I haven't expected him and been disappointed before. But there's a very specific feeling to his arrival, and I know this time that I'm not wrong. It's like when you're waiting for someone's car in the driveway; you may think you hear it a million times, but the second those wheels actually hit the gravel, you know that this is it, now, finally that person has indisputably arrived.

I push the covers aside and go to the window. I push it open and lean outside. In the short time I slept, snow began to fall again. It gathers in my hair as I search the ground for signs of Luke. I have never looked for him outside before. I don't even know if he would leave footprints.

And then I see it—written on my windowsill in the fresh snow. Clear, printed capital letters that must have been written moments ago—already the snow gathers in their grooves, obscuring the words:

MEET ME AT THE RIVER

Instantly, without thinking, I use the bare flat of my palm to sweep the snow and its message off the sill. As soon as it's done, I bury my hands in my hair. "What did you *do*?" I ask myself, too loud. There on the sill, a message from Luke, something he'd written. And now it's gone, and I can never get it back.

But I'm not just talking to myself. Because Luke must know—how could he not—that even though I know the exact spot where he'll be waiting, I can't possibly meet him at the river.

Rabbitbrush has creeks and rivulets and streams by the tens. But whenever anyone says "the river," there's no need for explanation. The Sustantivo River wends its way through four hundred miles of Colorado, New Mexico, and one corner of Utah. Our piece of this water-way is one of the town's few hopes for tourists, with fishing and kayaking and white-water rafting. The Sustantivo curves along rocky red banks; it bisects my grandparents' land, winding through their prop-erty. The trek would require long underwear and snow pants, gloves and a scarf and hat, my Sorels, or maybe even cross-country skis. I would have to trudge through miles of snowy darkness, and then back again, past all sorts of nocturnal wildlife, through freezing tempera-tures.

None of which is the reason I slam the window shut and crawl back under the covers, my palm tingling with the melted frost, my shoulders shaking, my hair damp. It's painful, physically painful, to crouch still in this way while Luke waits for me at the one place on earth where I simply cannot go. Because even though the river runs slowly this time of year, even though at this moment its banks are covered with freshly fallen snow, its lazy pace preventing it from freezing into stillness—one sight of those frigid, running waters, and I cannot promise anyone that I could keep from hurling myself into its current.

(6)

LUKE

My mom got married for all the normal reasons. Love, plus security, plus she wanted a houseful of kids. Thanks to my dad she had a head start on that last part. Katie and Jill went to another wedding. They walked down the aisle, two little blond kids dumping rose petals. As far as they were concerned my mom was their mom. She took them everywhere. They'd go with her to the grocery store and gas station and library. She drove them to school and summer camp. She fed them, tucked them into bed, helped them with their homework. All the usual mom things.

But back to the wedding, my mom and dad's wedding. This friend of theirs read a poem. Probably it's been read at a hundred other weddings, but this one line stood out to me. *Now there will be no more loneliness.*

Mom's face looked shiny. It looked young. I think she believed that was it for loneliness. She felt the way my dad probably felt when he married Hannah. Too bad it wouldn't take him long to crush Mom the same way Hannah crushed him.

It makes me feel guilty, watching the wedding, because I feel like I should at least *want* to warn her. But I don't. I stand back from the crowd with my hands in my pockets. Even though I know how this will turn out, I want it to happen.

Their groovy minister doesn't bother with the speak-now-or-forever-hold-your-peace part of the ceremony. And even if I said something, no one would hear me. But I *wouldn't* say anything, no matter what. For one, I can't stand the idea of squashing all that happiness. Just because it won't last doesn't mean it isn't worth something.

And another thing. I want to live.

I've watched the wedding a few times. It's interesting, how everything I always heard turns out to be more or less true. And I like to see my dad trying, which is more than I would have expected. I can't think of anything he could've done different in terms of Hannah, at least not at that point. He loved her, and she left him. He waited for her to change her mind and come back, but after a while he figured he couldn't wait forever so he got a divorce. He found a new wife. He had me. Another kid. His only son.

* * *

And then, eight years after Hannah left, she came back. It was summer. Dad was at work. The twins were at school. I don't know where I was, maybe upstairs in the playroom. Downstairs in the kitchen Mom wiped off the same table where Hannah had left her good-bye letter. I can almost see the shape it left behind, like an invisible scar on the table. My dad used to sit there and drum his fingers on that very spot.

When Hannah showed up she didn't knock. She just walked through the back door, slamming the screen like she'd never left. Mom froze. She knew Hannah the second she saw her. Mom pulled herself together and stood up straight. She walked over to Hannah. I think she wanted to look confident. She wanted Hannah to see who belonged where. But when she held out her hand, her elbow looked too stiff, weirdly unbent.

"Hello. I'm Francine Kingsbury." Her voice got a little louder on that last name.

Hannah didn't look surprised. She just looked tired. "Hi," she said. "I'm Hannah Earnshaw." My mom relaxed a little. Hannah didn't look like much of a threat. Her skin looked broken out and her eyes looked red. Her legs were bony and covered with scratches. She had her hair in a ponytail that looked tight enough to hurt.

My mom was so wrapped up in looking at Hannah that it took her a minute to notice the little girl, standing outside the screen door.

* * *

Sometimes I get tired, looking back. It takes so long for everything to happen. But that's the day it starts again, and I can't help watching. Me and Tressa standing in the backyard by the butterfly bush. My mom and Hannah watching the two of us like regular moms at a regular playdate. Like reasonable, civilized adults who won't wreck each other's lives.

And then my dad comes home. The sun's very bright. I see him park his car in the driveway and get out slowly, slamming the door. He's not in any kind of a hurry. I can tell from the way his shoulders slump that he's had a long day. I watch him walk up the hill toward his wife and the woman he thinks is a stranger.

And then he recognizes her.

He recognizes her, and everything changes. He doesn't look tired. He doesn't move slow. He drops his briefcase and breaks into a run, until he realizes what he's done and stops short. It's too late. Mom's face has fallen and won't ever go back to normal. Hannah's body relaxes. I think I even see her smile.

Don't get me wrong. Nothing is official. Hannah's still got plenty of disappearing left to do. But that's the day my mom figures things out, and she'll never forgive him. But you know what? I kind of do. Forgive him, that is. At least for that one second, when I see him run up the hill.

Because I understand. I know exactly how he feels. I can't stand to watch. I want to live.

(7)

TRESSA

For three nights in a row I open my window to find
the same message written in the snow. It looks to me
like an accusation, which can't possibly be how Luke
means it. Never once, in all the times he has visited, has
he shown any sign that he blames me for anything. But
tonight when I push my window open to face the cold
air instead of his warm presence, I feel angry. Angry at
Luke for the first time since he died. How could he ask
me to go to the river, when I am trying so hard to stay
alive?

Once again I sweep the message away. The snow
falls to the ground below with a shuffling whoosh. Then
I lean out the window and yell, "Don't you get it? I can't
go there!"

It feels weirdly like the same kind of fight we used to

have, and the second the words are out of my mouth, I regret them. Not because Luke might stop coming back. I know him, and the two of us, and a few angry words won't separate us when even death can't.

But my mother—she'll have heard, and she'll come running, endangering her baby by taking those steep steps too fast, and she'll fling open the door and I'll be caught. I'll have to find new ways to convince her that I'm okay. That I'll never do any of it again. I jump back into bed, pull the covers to my chin, and stare at the ceiling. I wait for her frantic footsteps, and after a while I guess she hasn't heard.

It takes a long time for me to get back to sleep, so when I do hear Mom climb the stairs, it's to wake me in still-dark, early morning. H. J. and Evie have arrived to take me skiing. I sit up in bed, startled. Evie wasn't at school on Thursday and Friday, and neither was H. J. When I walked past the classroom where H. J. usually teaches freshman English, I saw Mr. Tynan through the window, waving *Lord of the Flies* in his left hand. Later that day, after my English class, I stopped to ask Mr. Tynan, trying to sound disinterested: "Where's Mr. Burdick today?"

"On leave," Mr. Tynan said, his voice stern and final with its withholding of detail. I could tell, though, that H. J. had probably been fired for his *massively inappropriate* actions, and I assumed in the wake of this mishap that he and Evie would forget all about our plans to ski.

Mom goes downstairs to tell them I'm getting ready, and I can hear H. J. talking to her. His voice sounds deep and thoughtful—grown-up. Probably after everything he's been through, losing a job doesn't seem like a big deal. I root through my drawers for glove liners and wonder again how he and Evie could have endured so much, and not have it show in their every word and movement.

"Sorry I'm late," I say, walking into the kitchen. H. J. sits at the table, his coat off, a mug of steaming coffee in front of him. Evie slumps in the doorway, coat still zipped, apparently not the sort of girl who rejoices in conversations with adults. My mom takes my ski jacket from under her arm and holds it out to me.

"Honey," she says. "Here's your coat. Paul's putting your skis on their car."

"We already got your boots," H. J. says. Whereas Evie looks even paler than usual, with dark circles under her eyes, H. J. seems downright breezy. He stands up and puts on his coat, thanks Mom for the coffee, and then sidles past Evie out the door.

"Here," Mom says. She thrusts an oversize plastic baggie into my hand. It's stuffed with PowerBars, an apple, and the kind of aluminum juice bag you would give a three-year-old. I look up to say *Thank you*, and see that she is looking at my face with more than the usual worry and concern.

I place my hand on her belly and say, "Thanks, Mom."

"Have fun, sweetie!" she says, and I promise her that I will.

"Your mom's a hottie," H. J. says as his ancient, wood-paneled station wagon rumbles through the dusky, snow-covered morning. People have been telling me some version of this statement my whole life, and I never know what I'm supposed to say. Thank you? Luckily, Evie rescues me.

"H. J.," she says in a shaky voice, as if she can't stand another second of embarrassment at his hands. "That is not an appropriate remark."

"Sorry," H. J. says, though he doesn't sound sorry at all. He is driving, while Evie rides shotgun. I sit in the back, eating a PowerBar. I'd like some juice, too, but would feel too silly sipping from that babyish straw.

"Do you know your mom and our mom were friends?" H. J. asks.

"Yes," I say, sitting up. "I remember that." The car winds its way through Ophir, heading down into the Telluride valley. When we pass the road that leads to Alta, I expect to want to look away, but I find myself staring up the snowy path. Luke and I used to park at the bottom, cross-country ski up to the deserted mining camp, and commune with ghosts in the abandoned cabins. Cross-country skiing was something I could do well enough—you didn't have to start when you were three to become moderately proficient. You didn't have to be a native. I used to love drawing maps of Alta—guessing at the significance of different buildings—but I threw them all away after Luke died.

I glance in the rearview mirror and catch H. J. looking back at me. Behind his glasses his eyes crinkle a little bit in a sort of smile. The kindness surprises me enough to make me smile back, though I don't know why it should. Surprise me, that is. Maybe because I've only ever seen him from a distance, and he always seemed like such a shaggy and preoccupied presence.

"How are Jill and Katie?" H. J. asks.

"They're fine," I say. "Katie's in LA trying to get into movies."

"Is she having any luck?"

"A couple horror films. She won't let us see them."

H. J. laughs. "Cool," he says. "Good for her."

I remember suddenly that one summer a good ways back, H. J. and Katie were both counselors at the Youth Center drama camp. Katie complained about him so much that Jill accused her of having a crush on him. It didn't help that the previous spring, Katie had kissed H. J. in the school's production of *Dead End*, possibly the first kiss of her life. "I do *not* have a crush on H. J.," she promised Jill. "He stands too close and he *looks* too hard. It's not comfortable."

H. J. drives with his shoulders slightly hunched—bundled up in his parka, occasionally clearing the fog off his glasses with the butt of his palm. I think about him acting in that play and wonder if he would have gone to California too, or New York, if his parents hadn't died.

Out of nowhere H. J. says to Evie, "It looks like your friend is too polite to ask why I'm on leave."

"Oh, H. J.," Evie says. She sounds more exasperated than anguished, and I step in quickly to try to help her out.

"It's okay," I say. "You don't have to tell me."

"Come on," H. J. says. "Aren't you curious?"

"No," I lie. "I'm really not."

Evie turns around in her seat and faces me. The look on her face makes me feel guilty, as if she can read my morbid curiosity through my protests. "If you must know . . . ," Evie begins.

"I mustn't," I say, and H. J. laughs again. "I mean," I correct myself, "you don't have to tell me."

"It's about Kelly Boynton," Evie says. For a moment my blood stops pumping. I've been thinking about Kelly so much lately that the mention of her name feels like a weird invasion of privacy. My bite of PowerBar goes down painfully, sharp and cardboardy.

"Well," Evie goes on. "It turns out she's a cutter. And do you know who she decided to tell about this cutting? My brother. She showed him the scars on her poor little arms. And you know what he said, my brilliant brother? Instead of sending her straight to Mrs. Kingsbury, like any normal human being?"

This time Evie realizes she has lobbed a hand grenade of a name. She flushes slightly, and stops. H. J. takes over for her. "I told her to just cut a little bit," he says.

This is so contrary to what I expected that I burst out laughing, even though I know it's not funny at all. I picture poor Kelly, her tortured and tear-streaked face. I wonder if H. J.'s advice surprised her as much as it does me. I wish I could ask her about it.

Evie frowns at me, then turns back around in her seat. "I'm sorry," I say to the back of her head. "I don't know why I laughed. It's definitely not funny." I can see Evie's face in the side-view mirror, staring out the window. She looks earnest and very young, little wisps of hair escaping from her wool cap.

I sit forward and place my hands on the back of Evie's seat. She and H. J. ride silently, as if an argument to be continued later has been put on temporary hold. But I don't want it to be on hold. I want to know, urgently, if Kelly told H. J. *why* she cut herself, if it had something to do with Luke. Did she start cutting when she and Luke broke up? Or when Luke started going out with me? After he died? Or maybe she started cutting for reasons completely un-Luke?

I think of Evie's description, "poor little arms," and I want to take the tubes of Mederma my mother keeps buying me and slather the lotion on Kelly. When I was at the hospital, Dr. Reisner told me that a lot of mental health professionals didn't take wrist-slashers seriously as suicidal personalities. They saw it as just a bid for attention, not an honest attempt at death. "Especially now," Dr. Reisner said, "with all the teenage cutters."

H. J.'s brown hair curls messily over the back of his collar. I'm impressed that he doesn't seem upset at all. There is something insouciant about him that I admire, as if the worst happened so early in his life that he's committed himself to moving forward casually. I imagine H. J. counseling Kelly, and how he probably shrugged, and smiled a little, as if cutting were the most insignificant thing in the world. "It's okay," he would have said, unimpressed by the raised, red, crisscrossed wounds that she expected would horrify him. "Just do it a little bit."

Just do it a little bit. I am healthy enough to recognize the words as bad advice, but still. I can't help liking the sound of them. They sound, somehow, like forgiveness. Like hacking into your own flesh is not sick but perfectly understandable. *Just don't do it too much.*

"Do you know," I ask, trying to sound nonchalant, "why she did it?"

The two of them glance at each other, as if my question were intrusive. H. J. throws the question back at me. *"Why?"* he says, making the word sound ridiculous. As if there could never be a good reason for hurting yourself. I imagine Kelly, newly glassy-eyed from antidepressants, talking to a therapist—maybe even Dr. Reisner—who tries to convince her of different, more complex reasons than what she knows as the simpler truth.

"I was just wondering," I persist. "I mean, I know there's no good reason. But I saw her in school the other day, and she looked so sad. Do you know when she started? Cutting, I mean."

"I wish I could tell you," H. J. says. By now we're on the last bit of road leading into Telluride, alternating ragtag horse farms and afterthought trophy houses. "But it doesn't seem right. You know? Maybe you could ask her yourself. I'm sure she'd appreciate the concern."

From someone who went even further, he doesn't say.

I sit back a little in my seat. Through the window I see snow-covered pine trees, and up ahead the winding, icy trickle of Bridal Veil Falls. Luke used to say he liked looking up at the waterfalls because their beauty reminded him of his own insignificance. I'm not sure if they have the same effect on me. What I do know is that I feel more natural around these two—Evie and H. J.— than I have around anyone, for what seems like the longest, longest time.

H. J. takes the chair ahead of us, and Evie and I ride up together. "What does 'H. J.' stand for?" I ask her. Our feet dangle heavily beneath us, and even though Evie's not much taller than me, her skis are about a foot longer. I feel slightly embarrassed and inadequate with my stumpy beginner's skis. Both she and H. J. wear blue jeans, Evie's with giant holes that show off pink long johns. It's the kind of outfit you'd only wear if you knew you wouldn't fall. Meanwhile I'm wearing all the state-of-the-art waterproof gear my Mom bought for me right after she and Paul got remarried and she felt giddy with new credit cards. Which is just as well, since I'll probably spend most of the day on my butt.

"It stands for 'Haskett Jenkins,'" Evie says. "They're the last names of my mom's grandfathers."

"Fancy," I say, and Evie nods. She can throw out those phrases, "my mom," "my dad," so casually. I haven't said Luke's name aloud to anyone since I got out of the hospital.

"'Tressa' is an unusual name," Evie says. "Where did your mom get that?"

"I'm named after my father's mother," I say, and then I add, "not Paul."

"I know," Evie reminds me. Something about her openness makes me want to give her more information. So I do something I pretty much never do. I tell her about my father, how my mom dated him for a little while when she lived in Ireland. They weren't together long, and Mom came back to the states when I was a baby. I tell Evie how his mom—my other grandmother— was with her at my birth and helped out those first few months. She showed her how she could use a dresser drawer as a cradle.

"I never saw her again, that grandmother," I tell Evie. "But I've met my dad a couple of times. He came to visit once or twice, but he's lived in Wales ever since I was little."

"Is he Welsh?"

"No," I say. "Irish. But he married a Welsh woman and moved there."

"Do you hear from him much?"

I remember the letter my father sent while I was in the hospital. It was tentative and careful, like something you'd expect from a polite and distant relative. It made me sad, the sight of his handwriting—crowded close together on the page, unsure and filled with apology.

"Once in a while," I say.

"Does he have other kids?"

"No. He doesn't."

"I bet he thinks about you a lot," Evie says. "Maybe you can go to Wales and visit him someday." This suggestion seems so obvious, it shocks me that the idea has never once in all my life occurred to me. Evie looks ahead, squinting into the glare off the snow, and I suspect she wishes that visiting her own father were as simple as a plane ticket to Wales.

The chair slows down, and Evie lifts the bar. I have the strange sense of extra cold air coming toward me, and a little bit of stage fright as we push off onto the snow. I reach forward with my poles, getting my balance unsteadily. As soon as I slide off the lift, I lose control, skidding down the snow and landing in a heap. H. J. has been waiting for us, and he skis over. Evie's not far behind.

"I see we have our work cut out for us," H. J. says. He wears goggles over his glasses, a Carhartt jacket, and a bomber hat, flaps down. The look wouldn't fly in Aspen, but for Telluride his rugged dishevelment is right in vogue.

"Sorry," I say. "I told you I'm not much of a skier." Evie holds out her hand and helps me get to my feet. The strength of her tug surprises me. "Let's do See Forever," she says. "There are some nice mellow stretches."

"All right," I say. I push myself over to the blue sign at the beginning of the run and let Evie and H. J. go first. I think of a scene from *The Bell Jar*. Esther goes skiing, and stands at the top of the run looking down. *The thought that I might kill myself formed in my mind coolly as a tree or a flower.*

Evie and H. J. whoosh down onto the run, so I bend my knees and push off, following. Despite my klutziness it feels good to be active, the cold air on my face and the sun climbing high enough in the sky to warm the slopes and the top of my head. I resist the urge to fight it— feeling good. Strangest of all, I find I like this new idea of going to Wales. The notion feels so odd and foreign, it's like trying on someone else's clothes and discovering that they don't quite—and may never—fit. Unless I somehow, someway, manage to grow another inch.

The three of us ski together until a little after noon,

and then we head to Gorrono Ranch Restaurant. It's crowded, the Saturday after the first big snow, and the sounds of voices and clanging silverware echo through the high-ceilinged space. Evie piles her tray, and because I have been exercising all morning, I allow myself to do the same. We all crowd together at a round table in the center of the way, with steaming chili and huge hunks of crusty bread. Across the way I see the family I used to babysit for, the Cummingses, and I sit down with my back to them, hoping they won't see me.

H. J. and Evie both wear the kind of gloves Luke used to—thick wool mittens covered by leather farming mittens. Luke swore it was the warmest possible system, and looking at their hands—rosy and flexible, I think he must have been right. Must *be* right, I correct myself. I press my bare hands against my hot paper coffee cup and take a sip. The warmth feels good going down my throat. I barely listen to H. J. and Evie's conversation about a pair of movie stars who sit bundled up and scarfing chili a couple tables over. Evie announces that the pair are Scientologists, which somehow segues into a book about palmistry that H. J.'s reading.

"I think it's all a load of crap," Evie says. "Don't you, Tressa?"

I shrug, not thinking much one way or the other but not wanting to offend either of them.

"Evie's a nonbeliever because she has a very short life line," H. J. says. "I keep telling her not to worry. Mine used to be short too, but then it grew."

"That can happen?" I ask. It must be unsettling to have a short life line, especially for them.

"Sure," H. J. says. "Your future's always changing, depending on the paths you choose. Here." H. J. reaches across the table, toward me. "Let me see your palm."

Instinctively I pull my hands away and place them in my lap. My thick Gore-Tex gloves with the liners still inside them lie on top of the table, and I curse myself for taking them off.

"No, thanks," I say. "I don't believe in that stuff."

"Ah, but when Evie asked, you shrugged. That means you're still open to possibility. Let me make a believer out of you." H. J. pushes his glasses up on his nose, then holds his palm out for me to see. "See how my life line snakes all the way around my wrist?" he says. "It used to end right here." He points to the center of his palm, and I peer into it politely. He has big hands, wide and chapped. I find myself thinking he'd be good to have around if a jar needed opening.

"Come on," H. J. says, tugging at my sleeve. "Let me see your palm."

"H. J.," Evie says, her voice full of warning. "Tressa said no. Didn't anyone ever teach you that 'no' means no?"

Apparently not. H. J. reaches down to grab my hand. He tugs it insistently and a tiny bit roughly toward himself, acting like he doesn't know that I'm supposed to be dealt with very, very delicately. Maybe he considers his own history worse and so doesn't care.

H. J. stares down at my palm. My sleeve is in the way, and he pushes it up in one big sweep so that it bunches at my elbow, revealing a bare stretch of white wrist polluted by red scars. I haven't seen my scars this way—publicly, under bright light—in a very long time. They look raised and screaming. They climb upward, like an invasive foreign species—kudzu vines—and I think how they reveal way more information than the lines on my palm ever could.

I feel more naked than if I'd pulled my whole shirt over my head. But H. J. doesn't say anything. He just stares intently at my palm, his brow knit in concentration. With the tip of his index finger, he touches three spots on my hand, then says, without looking up at me, as if he's still contemplating, "You have a mystic cross. Look. It's right between the head line and the heart line." He touches both these lines as he speaks, a light and gentle touch. His fingers are surprisingly warm—another point for Luke's mitten system.

"What's a mystic cross?"

"You see?" he says, pointing again. "It's that little *x* right there. It means you're in tune with the occult, the spiritual. Yours is very prominent. In fact, it's the deepest one I've ever seen."

I lean my head in closer and say, "What else?"

H. J. still doesn't look up at me. One of his hands holds my upper arm, his fingers closing around my sweater sleeve. The other hand hovers above my palm. He points his index finger again and this time lets it land on my wrist, right on top of my scars. Then, as he didn't do with my palm, he begins to trace them with his fingertips.

"You have a death wish," he says.

The room falls away beneath me. I sit there, completely frozen. Not because I hear Evie gasp a little, or because I feel her kicking H. J. under the table. Not even because of the words H. J. used, or the fact that nobody since the hospital has ever mentioned my scars, and even there nobody touched them. Nobody has touched my wrists since the doctor in Durango sewed them back together with dissolving thread, and nurses swabbed them with disinfectant when they changed the bandages.

Everything around me disappears. Nothing exists but this astonishing discovery: I can't feel H. J.'s fingers.

I can feel his hand, closed around my upper arm like he's testing my blood pressure. I can feel the edge of his knees, knocking ever so slightly into mine as he continues to lean toward me. But I can't feel his fingers at all. I can't pick up any sensation whatsoever. Not warmth, not skin, not anything.

Just like when Luke touches me anywhere else.

I pull my hand out of H. J.'s grasp. "Thanks," I say. I can feel my face, burning with possibility. Probably H. J. and Evie mistake it for embarrassment.

"H. J.," Evie moans. "That was so inappropriate."

Massively inappropriate, I want to say, but I would say it with a smile, and I know H. J. would smile back. He picks up his hot chocolate and takes a sip, staring at me over the brim.

I laugh, a short tremulous burst. "It's fine," I say, finally able to speak. "I don't mind at all."

Evie looks worried. "Are you sure you're okay?" she asks.

"I'm fine," I say, trying to contain my jubilation. H. J. smiles, but the tone of that smile is inscrutable. Not that I care about what he's thinking. This time right now means nothing. The time over the next hours—the afternoon of skiing, dinner with Mom and Paul, the quiet nightfall in my bedroom, will be endured. None of it has any importance, none of it matters until tonight—when I will see Luke.

And I will see him, no matter what I have to do, even go to the river. Because now I have stumbled upon this most important key.

(8)

TRESSA

I can't remember when I started drawing maps. It's just something I've done, for as long as I can remember. We don't have any of the ones I did when I was really little—Mom never kept anything like that. But my grandmother did, so we've got a good collection of the ones I drew starting at six or so, silly little crayon lines, with square houses and stick figures. Grandma of course liked the ones of Rabbitbrush, or her house, or rooms in her house. She's got her favorite one framed and hanging in the front hall. It's the very first thing you see when you walk in the front door.

At some point I got old enough to save the maps myself, and I've got a pile of accordion folders brimming over with them. My favorite ones I tack onto the wall, but I don't frame them like Grandma, because I always have a new favorite. I like having a record of all the places where we've lived.

Sometimes when you read articles about famous actors, it will say their parents were in the military, or academia, or some other profession that made them move a million times, and that's what shaped them. They had to learn to be a class clown or a charmer or a chameleon, so that they could fit in quickly in different places. But that's not what happened with me. I was shy, no good at acting, more comfortable in solitary pursuits. As a kid I always felt the need to observe the customs awhile before understanding them, and by the time I figured out that it wasn't cool to wear your backpack over both shoulders—poof! We'd move again, and at the new school nobody but me would be carrying their bags lopsided, plus the black nail polish that had been de rigueur for my old classmates made all the new ones think I was a creepy Goth. So I stopped trying. My mom never connected to my sadness over my perpetual loner status. "What do you care what those kids think?" she would say with a wave of her hand. I wonder if she liked the way it heightened the sense of her and me being the only ones who mattered, and she never had to worry too much about yanking me away from a school where I didn't have friends anyway. It didn't matter—except when she grabbed me away from Luke.

Luke didn't care how I wore my backpack or what color my nails were. From the very first second I ever saw him, he just . . . liked me. That sounds so simple, but I don't know how else to say it. With Luke, even as a tiny child, I felt an instant recognition. Oh, *there* you are, as if we'd been together before and I'd only been biding my time till we could be together again.

The summers my mother brought me back, or times I spent with my grandparents—Luke had all the friends I had ever wanted, but he had no problem leaving them behind for me. He would try to give me all the information I'd missed out on. He taught me how to ride a bike in the parking lot of Paul's real estate office. We swam in the freezing community pool, and in the trout-stocked, man-made lake past the Mackenzies' sheep farm, those fluffy white herds dotting the hills. Once as we hiked up the Franz Lubbock trail, a rattlesnake stopped us in our tracks. We reached out and grabbed hands, quietly backed up a few steps, and then turned and ran— screaming—down the path toward home. We would climb on top of Sturm and Drang and just sit there, hanging on to the horses' manes and enjoying the improved view while they munched the grass with no intention of taking us for a ride. Luke and I knew every inch of my grandparents' property, every square foot of this town, and we knew it together.

And then after the summer Luke and I were twelve, my mother didn't want to come back to Rabbitbrush for a long while. I had a weird, uneasy feeling that it had to do with the way Luke's and my feelings had shifted—how we'd become aware of each other in a slightly different way but not knowing how to admit it. Until that summer our relationship had been defined— made special—by our inability to categorize it. We weren't just best friends, because we were family, but at the same time we weren't family—not siblings or even cousins. It felt to me like, when we got to see each other, we formed our own little bubble of family, away from all the others. The four years between twelve and sixteen, years that Luke and I didn't see each other once, felt like both a waiting and a changing. Time apart in our separate cocoons.

When Mom and I came back to stay for good, Luke had changed, and I had changed. But I never felt the barest moment of awkwardness. We just looked at each other a long moment, and then we were off and running again. Everything felt more elemental that year. It's true that I showed up at school stupidly hoping I might fit in. But when I didn't, I had the best consolation, something I'd never had anywhere else. I had Luke.

The first time it snowed, he taught me how to cross-country ski. With snow falling all around us, we trudged through the forest, our breath coming out in happy, visible gusts. And then, when I attempted to go down a small hill too fast, and ended up crumpled at the bottom of it, Luke whizzed down behind me, intentionally falling on top of me, the two of us laughing and then—all of a sudden—kissing. We lay there in the snow, the back of my head damp and freezing, layers of clothes preventing any kind of real contact. We just kissed and kissed and kissed until our bodies, unlike our lips, were too frozen to continue.

Now it's after midnight. I tiptoe down the stairs, past Mom and Paul's tightly closed bedroom door, past the old playroom, through the kitchen, and into the garage. I take my mom's wax-less cross-country skis instead of my own; I don't know the proper color wax to use. I haul the gear back through the house and out the front door— the electric garage door would make too much noise.

Outside, I snap my boots into skis and pull my hat down over my ears. The night exists in dozens of still layers, most prominently three: the glaring blanket of snow, the twinkling ceiling of stars, and the glassy blackness in between. I move forward, my skis breaking through the perfect, untouched crust of snow. At first my body protests this activity after a day of downhill skiing. But then it succumbs to the hypnotic rhythm, the swoosh, swoosh of my skis drowning out whatever rustling wildlife watches my progression. I don't feel cold at all. The pump of my blood keeps me warm, and although I am already sore from Telluride, I don't mind this different movement, as if by stretching my muscles in another direction, I will reverse whatever strain occurred during the day.

I take the back way, through my grandparents' woods.

I don't care about safety, just that it's faster and doesn't involve going past the Burdicks' house.

Now I can hear the river. I almost want to say, *Finally I can hear the river*, but that doesn't reflect my feelings, not exactly. Since this afternoon in the ski lodge, I've been overcome with happiness. In this context—rushing toward Luke—happiness is entirely allowed.

The river sounds different, a more tentative rushing than last spring. The water has obstacles now—icy layers, fallen branches, its own frigid temperature. Still its sound is louder than anything else the night provides. I glide through the trees, into the opening glen, and I know I won't have to wait. I can't hear them, not the barest sound, but immediately there they are. Because it's not just Luke. It's Luke and Carlo, a hundred yards away from me, walking up the riverbank.

Carlo sees me first. He stops for a moment, his black fur gleaming in the wintery night. His ears perk up. And then he breaks into a run—the sort of young, unhindered run I haven't seen from him in ages. He porpoises through the snow with the most gorgeous agility, and finally leaps through the air to place his paws on my shoulders and tackle me backward into a snowbank.

And I can feel him. I can feel him! I can feel his rough dog paws and their too-long nails on my neck. I can feel his tongue on my face and earlobe. As quickly as I can, I wrap my arms around his neck, and pet his chest. I can feel his fur and his corporeal thickness, his bones.

I plunge my fingers into the glorious, familiar softness.

In a minute Luke stands over us. He puts his hands into his pockets and stares down, smiling. He's not dressed right for the weather, in jeans and a flannel shirt over long underwear, but of course he doesn't look the slightest bit cold. His eyes are the kindest, widest, darkest color imaginable, and his cheekbones slope sharply. His lips always look like he just got done eating a pint of blackberries. Around his neck is a tiny silver peace sign with pearl inlay. He's worn it on a leather string for almost as long as I can remember.

"Luke," I say from underneath the quivering, overjoyed dog. I reach my left hand up to him. "Touch my wrist," I say. "Touch the scars."

His smile fades into solemnity and he sinks to his knees. I can't feel the hand that he lays on my forehead. I can't feel when he moves that hand beneath my elbow and raises my arm toward him. I can't feel his fingers, peeling back the sleeve of my coat and sweater.

But his lips. When he presses his lips to the inside of my wrist and kisses the terrible scars—I can feel them. I feel their warmth, and their softness. I can see Luke's eyes widen in happiness and relief, but he doesn't draw his mouth away to speak. He just keeps pressing his lips to my wrist and kissing, kissing; just like that time, it seems a thousand years ago, when we kissed in the snow. And for the first time in six months and nine days, I am truly, completely, and happily alive.

* * *

We walk along the river. And I don't feel sad! The heavy, aching cloud that has weighed me down for so long has vanished into thin air, and I can almost float. Luke has his hand closed around my left wrist—that's where the most prominent scars are, because I slashed it with my stronger hand. That sounds morbid, I know, but it doesn't feel morbid at all, because I can feel the warm inside of his palm, pressing against my wrecked skin. I think again about all those Mederma creams my mom keeps giving me, and I almost laugh out loud, so glad that they were useless.

Carlo runs beside and around us in happy circles. I have taken off my skis, and Luke carries them over his left shoulder. I carry my poles over my right. After a while we veer away from the riverbank and head toward Paul's house. I don't know for certain how far Luke will be able to accompany me, but it turns out to be a good long while. We take the road this time, and though by now dawn stirs with rustling bird wings and rays of light, I see nobody to witness our slow, sauntering progression—none of us particularly wanting to reach our destination, but only to stay as we are, walking together.

When the sun begins to rise in earnest—its burgeoning curve above the eastern slope—Luke stops. "This is as far as I can go," he tells me. Reluctantly, one finger at a time, he releases his grasp from my wrist and drops my skis by the side of the road. I kneel down and hug Carlo, then stand and face Luke. He brings my wrist to his lips and kisses me one last time, then turns and walks away, into the woods. Carlo follows him, and I stand and watch the two of them go, graceful boy and graceful dog, until the trees behind them are too thick and they disappear down a snowy rise—or perhaps just into mist.

I step back into my skis and climb the last bit of road before Paul's house. From the end of the driveway, I see a police car parked in front, its red and yellow lights silently whirring. My stomach seizes up, terrified that something has happened to my mother and her baby. I pick up speed, climbing up the driveway, and to my relief I see my mother and Paul, wearing heavy coats over their pajamas, talking to a police officer. My mother looks past them and sees me. The transition in her face cuts me in half. I see her movement from desperate hysteria to profound relief to sheer rage.

"Tressa," she yells. She pushes past the police officer and marches over to where I now stand. She grabs both of my shoulders, as if making sure I'm really there, really whole. Then she looks down at my feet, and back into my face, and shakes me—hard.

"Skiing?" she says. "You were *skiing*? Are you kidding me? Are you fucking kidding me?"

I don't know how to react. The thing about my mother— she doesn't get angry, not like this. Not at me. Paul and the police officer—Officer Sincero, whom I unfortunately know by name—step forward to intervene. As Officer Sincero steps between us, Paul puts both arms around my mother and pulls her close.

"I'm sorry," I say, peering around the policeman. From the car his radio chatters, its staticky conversation making everything seem too serious, too dire. "I couldn't sleep."

"You couldn't sleep!" my mother shrieks. "You couldn't sleep." She tries to step out of Paul's grip, and I duck back behind Officer Sincero, certain she'll hit me if she breaks loose, even though she's never so much as raised her voice to me, not once in her entire life.

"Here," Officer Sincero says, taking me firmly by the arm. "Let's get you inside while your mother calms down."

Thirty minutes later the four of us sit around the kitchen table. It feels bizarre, the lack of coffee or food, but my mother is too shell-shocked to offer. Paul glowers at me across the table. *Haven't you done enough,* his eyes accuse. I hate the way Paul tries to act like he knows my mother better than I do, or cares about her more, and I can't help but feel that he looks slightly happy, a tiny smile twisting below the look of concern. As if this one moment of anger could ever separate my mom and me. Distinct from how I feel about the way Paul treated Luke—the way he came between Luke and me—is the persistent little-girl feeling that I've always had toward my mother's boyfriends: *You may think she's yours, but I know she's mine.*

Because she *is* mine, the main reason I'm still here, and I hate seeing her so angry and upset. We sit there, staring at each other across the table, neither of us actually hearing the gentle lecture delivered by Officer Sincero, about how I need to be careful with my parents, and myself, and remember how everybody worries about me. For no particular reason I remember a time in family therapy when Mom told Dr. Reisner she'd never felt like the twins were really hers. "Maybe it was because I was so much younger, but I just felt so distant from them, like they had nothing to do with me. By the time Tressa was born, her father was already out of the picture. She always had everything to do with me, and only me. I always knew that she was mine." Mom wept at this admission, and Dr. Reisner handed her a box of Kleenex.

"Do you think," he said, "that after the twins you may have been suffering from postpartum depression?"

Mom shrugged this idea away. She never liked unromantic explanations. As incriminating as it may have sounded, she preferred to think that it had to do with me, some special bond between the two of us.

From the way she and I stare at each other across the table, Officer Sincero probably realizes we haven't been listening to a word he's saying. He stands to go.

"Now, you call me if you need anything," he says to Paul and my mother.

We sit there quietly while the door closes behind him. His car door slams and the engine starts. Then tires pick up speed over snow-covered gravel. My mother leans forward. Her hair looks too blond, almost white. Artificial. Her face looks craggy and pale. She lifts one finger and points it at me.

"You can't do this," she says to me. "Not now. You can't just disappear in the middle of the night and scare everyone to death. To death!" she yells, as if she finds it liberating, shrieking that taboo word right at me.

My body starts to shake. Not only do I feel sorry for my mother, but I have committed myself to staying alive, in this world, for her benefit. I love her. Really, I do. I love her second best of anyone in this entire world.

So it's confusing to feel so guilty and at the same time so electric, so energized—like every raw nerve ending is exposed and open for business. All this drama, all this forbidding. All of it, so immediately familiar. It's just like when Luke was alive. Which of course makes me feel that he *is* alive. And just like when he *was*. I will not let any sense of duty come between us.

It doesn't matter what they want or what they expect. They can make me promise never to leave the house at night again. But I *will* leave the house at night, if leaving brings me to Luke. It is, all of it, the very least I can do for him. Because I know, absolutely, that *we* are alive—even if Luke is not.

(9)

LUKE

A couple months before Tressa's and my eighth birthday, Hannah came back to Rabbitbrush. She stayed with her parents a little while, then took off again. This time Tressa stayed behind, and that's when she started showing me her maps. She'd already been drawing them for a while. Even the ones from when she was super little, like five or six, look like maps. They never look like just drawings. I can't explain why. Something about the way she lays it out on the page. What Tressa would do was choose a place that meant something to her. It could be a room, or a whole building, or a town, or a state, or maybe just a view from a window. She would draw it in pencil, with funky little pictures for the things she liked best, and then she'd color them in with crayons. Later on she started using those Cray-Pas kind of crayons, or sometimes she'd do watercolors.

But the first map I saw was colored in with crayon. It was Arapahoe Road. For the Burdick house she drew a big blue box with flowers all around it, and for her grandparents' house she drew a giant yellow sun with a couple of huge horses standing next to it, plus a black dog and two kids that I could tell were her and me. The map had this line of butterflies streaming up the road toward the Earnshaws, and more butterflies flying all around us. Tressa colored in every single little detail, her blond hair, my black hair, plus every wing on every butterfly, every flower, and every piece of sky. I couldn't believe I knew the person who'd made it. I reached out and ran my hand over it because I wanted to see what all that color would feel like. Tressa pulled it away from me like she thought I'd ruin it, then right away looked guilty for maybe hurting my feelings.

A few days after that we had our birthday together, the only time that ever happened when we were kids. Mrs. Earnshaw baked a cake in the shape of a heart and we decorated it. When Tressa leaned over to blow out the candles, I thought her hair would catch on fire, so I blew as hard as I could to keep that from happening. Afterward Tressa gave me the map of Arapahoe Road, rolled up in a little scroll with a ribbon tied around it.

That's not the most important thing that ever happened, but I like watching it. If I have to live my whole life over again in this weird way, I wish I could just stick to happy times. It's interesting to watch the sad moments that I can't remember, or that I wasn't there to see, but the ones I *can* remember I try to avoid. It's bad enough I had to live through them. But sometimes I can't help myself, like picking off a scab, and I end up going back.

Take for instance the summer we were twelve. Hannah and Tressa showed up in late spring. This time Hannah said they were going to stay, but nobody got too excited because she'd said that before. The second I saw Tressa I knew something had changed. There's not much point describing the way a twelve-year-old girl changes. You've seen it yourself. Not to mention a twelve-year-old boy.

I get it now, much more clearly than I did back then. One thing I don't mind watching is Tressa, sitting on the porch of her grandparents' house. She's playing her guitar and singing. Given how her speaking voice is kind of musical you'd expect her to have a good singing voice but she doesn't. It's terrible, reedy and off-key. Still, I like listening to her. If she had a good voice it wouldn't feel so private. By now she's got brown hair and her arms and legs aren't so skinny. I guess Hannah's gotten smarter about the guys she chooses, figuring it's better to go for the ones who can at least feed them.

I couldn't have thought this when I was alive. I definitely couldn't have thought it when I was twelve. Back then I would've noticed things like her bra that I could see through her shirt. When did she start wearing a bra? I would've noticed the superlight hair on her arms, and the dark freckle on her throat.

But now instead of all that, the physical stuff, I watch Tressa play guitar and I have this strong sense of both our lives. Tressa used to be younger. She used to be a little kid. Before long she'll be a teenager. And then I think about everything that will happen without me, all the years I'll miss. Tressa at college. Tressa as a mother. Tressa as an old woman.

It drives me crazy that I won't be there to see all that. Even if I can stay in the after-Luke, I won't be able to hear a word Tressa says about her new life. I won't see the new maps. And what if she leaves Rabbitbrush? What if the way she looks changes so much that I won't be able to see her?

She must worry too, but we can't talk about it. Just like when we were twelve and couldn't admit anything had changed. Instead we hung out the way we always had, running around Rabbitbrush. We rode our bikes, and hiked around her grandparents' property with those huge horses following us like dogs. Tressa spent a month at Rabbitbrush middle school. She didn't have much luck making friends, but I thought maybe that would get better in the fall. When school got out, we went swimming at Silver Lake. We went for walks along the river. We pretended everything was just exactly the same.

*   *   *

On the morning it happened, I figured I would eat breakfast and then head over to the Earnshaws' like I'd done every day of the summer so far. Mom handed me a plate of scrambled eggs and said she wanted to drive into Telluride and hike up the Jud Wiebe Trail. I told her she had to be crazy. It'd been very hot, over a hundred degrees all week, and as far as I knew, that day would be the same. Not exactly my favorite hiking weather.

But Mom had made up her mind. "There's so much shade on that trail," she said. "And I feel like I've barely seen you this summer." She'd just cut her hair short. It barely covered her ears. I couldn't get used to the look of it and neither could she. She was always reaching up to push away hair that wasn't there.

"Can Tressa come?" I asked. I started to get up so I could call. My dad came into the kitchen. I saw him frown at Mom.

"No," she said. "Not this time. Today I want you to myself."

Dad poured coffee into his thermos. This is almost the part I hate the most. None of us knew this was the last time things would ever be normal. Dad kissed the top of Mom's head. "I'll be home before dinner," he said.

Mom and I hiked slowly. The day got hotter and hotter. We kept stopping to sip from our water bottles. At the top of the trail we barely took in the view. Instead we ducked below the treeline and walked downhill along the creek. We didn't speak much on the drive home. Mom looked like she had something to cross off her to-do list. Quality time with her only son, check. When we got home, I didn't even bother going inside. I just grabbed my bike, slid my water bottle into its cage, and yelled, "I'm going to the Earnshaws'!"

The house looked deserted, no cars in the driveway except for the old hay bale truck. Sturm and Drang weren't around either, which meant Tressa could have been on a walk with them, or she could've gone somewhere with her grandparents. I went inside anyway. Nobody in Rabbitbrush locked their doors. I'm not sure the Earnshaws even owned a set of house keys. They kept car keys in the vehicles, either right in the ignition or on the floor of the driver's seat.

I ran up the stairs toward Tressa's room. I could picture her lying on her bed with a book from the summer reading list that I hadn't even looked at yet. Just as that picture formed in my head, I got to the top of the stairs and heard a low groan.

For a second I thought I had made that sound. I stopped short, suddenly hoping Tressa *wasn't* at home so she wouldn't have heard me. Then I heard someone laugh, and whisper. Then another moan, plus a noise that sounded a little bit like someone crying.

Did I mention it was a hundred degrees outside? Now it felt like two hundred. I knew exactly who and what I was listening to, even though I'd never heard it before. The sound came from behind Hannah's closed door. The polite thing to do was turn around, walk down the stairs, leave the house, and bike away. And after that, keep my mouth shut forever.

But it made me so mad. My *dad*. And Tressa's *mom*. Just that morning I'd seen Dad kissing the top of my mom's head. I wanted to yell, *Seriously? Are you kidding me?* But I didn't yell. I just kicked Hannah's door open and walked right into the worst and strangest moment of my entire life.

Hannah and my dad. Naked. It was hot so they were on top of the covers. When I came in, they jumped off opposite sides of the bed and grabbed at the quilt. There was this second or two where they had a little tug of war. Then my dad let her have it. What a gentleman! Once she covered herself up, he grabbed the sheet for himself, but by this time it was a little late.

"Luke," he said when he got the sheet around his waist. "What are you doing here? You should have knocked."

Like my rudeness was the problem with this situa-tion. "Why?" I said. Mad as I was it took me by surprise, how loud I said it. "Why should I have knocked, Dad? So I wouldn't see you fucking Hannah?"

Both of them sat back down on the bed. Hannah put the quilt over her face, and I thought I heard her say "Damn." Dad reached out and kind of patted her like *she* was the one he needed to worry about. I looked around the room for something to throw at his head.

I didn't have a chance, though, because Hannah took the quilt away from her face. "Luke," she said. "You don't have to tell Francine, you know. It would only hurt her."

"No," I said. "I'm not the one who's hurting her."

There wasn't much else to say, and I couldn't stand being there anymore, like I was a part of this whole thing. So I turned around and ran down the steps, then jumped onto my bike and pedaled home. As far as I know my dad didn't try to stop me.

And I may have been just a kid, but at that point I knew the score exactly. My dad wanted Hannah. He wanted her so bad that he didn't care if I knew, or if I told Mom. In fact, he probably *wanted* me to tell Mom so she would pack up, get out of the way.

Which is just what she did. She moved out of his house and took me with her. What Dad didn't bet on was Hannah, who had a lot more practice running away. She grabbed Tressa and left my dad, and me, and didn't come back or send word for the longest four years in history. And I don't think Dad ever forgave me for that any more than I forgave him. At least not till after that day at the river.

(10)

TRESSA

Silver Lake has frozen solid. Last week Mr. Zack drove his Land Cruiser straight across the ice, to the very middle, to prove to nervous mothers that it was safe to skate. So when I find the message written in the snow on my windowsill—*Silver Lake* is all it says—I know to throw my skates over my shoulder. I also bring two hockey sticks and a puck.

The lake is closer than the river; I only have to hike the back way through Paul's property, barely half a mile down a steep incline. Coming home will be a little more difficult, but I don't mind. And I'll be quick. I don't want the drama of getting caught or making anyone worry about me. But I have to go.

When Luke sees the hockey sticks, he laughs. I toss the puck onto the ice, and Carlo runs after it, sliding across the surface on his bare paws, trying to get his mouth around the slippery black disc. Luke already wears his hockey skates, the Stealth 15's his mother bought him last Christmas. I have no way of knowing if the same skates still lie on the shelf of sports equipment in Francine's garage, and it strikes me that I don't know what she's done with Luke's things, if she's sold everything on eBay, or given it to Goodwill, or kept everything in its same old place, as if he could one day come back and use it. Maybe that's exactly what he did this evening—stole into his mother's garage and took the skates, then brought them out here. I ask him, but he just looks perplexed, the question too tied to his death and everything afterward.

I sit down on the old pine log, take off my boots, and lace up my figure skates. I never got good enough for hockey skates. We don't glide out onto the ice right away, but sit on the log for a while, Luke's hand wrapped around my wrist. Every so often Luke lifts my hand and kisses me. It is huge and wonderful to feel him, but already I can't stop myself wanting more than his lips on my wrist—like his lips on my lips, for example. Luke must want this too. He smiles and runs his fingertips over my hair, a phantom gesture, and right away I feel a knot in my stomach, a wish to *feel* his hands in my hair. Instead of making me grateful for feeling him at all, being able to feel him on that one spot makes me want every other spot. I know this is greedy, I know it, but I can't help what I feel, and that's the urge to tackle him right there in the snow and kiss him, kiss him, feeling every single molecule of his body against mine. The way I used to.

But that's not possible, so we stand up and glide out onto the lake. At first we try to play hockey in earnest, but I can't skate fast enough, and Luke beats me so easily every time that it hardly seems worth it. So after a while we just skate around and around, and then play keep-away with Carlo, who runs and slips and slides across the ice like a sleek black polar bear cub. I can hardly believe Carlo was ever this *young*, this full of movement.

Sometimes in winter, during the day, Rabbitbrush seems very stark and bleak. The light goes flat and still, and if no snow has fallen for several days, the sky becomes gray and weary with the absence of moisture. Apart from the conifers, bare branches abound, everything sleeping too soundly beneath the soil.

Oddly, the night never feels bleak but—like Carlo—full of dark, pretty movement. I love this delicious air, the possibility that lurks around every corner. It's so much better than the two of us sitting up in my room. It feels less safe, more like life. Perhaps, despite Mr. Zack's efforts, the ice could crack beneath my skates. I imagine looking up from the frozen water, Luke kneeling above me, his hand placed flat on the ice, peering through.

But the ice stays firm. After a long while we skate to the edge of the lake. We both change into boots. I hadn't noticed his Sorels, waiting with mine by the makeshift bench. We both tie our skates together and drape them over our shoulders.

"I guess I have to go," he says, his voice deep and wistful.

"I wonder what would happen," I say, "if I tried to come with you."

He stares at me a long moment, as if what I said has not computed. Then he takes my wrist, and we both stand. We walk through the woods together, Carlo at our side. I recognize the path where we're headed—the river—and I know I will find myself alone at that shore. That there will be one definite way to follow him, and it won't be simply walking by his side. I try to imagine what that transition would look like, how long it would take for me to travel—like my dog—from damaged to dead to perfect, wandering this mountain range not only with Luke and Carlo but as one of them. I can't picture it, though, without picturing Luke—his floating body, his funeral, the sorrow left in his wake and then my own. I shake my head sharply, and we both stop at the same time, Luke and I, still managing to operate as one person, the same instincts, the same reactions. Still holding on to me, Luke says, "I wish I could keep you safe."

We both know I will have to walk home through the snow—by myself, in the dark, among too many nocturnal creatures to name. I say, "I don't care about being safe." Luke looks troubled by this. My eyes close for the barest second—just a blink, I could swear. When I open them, he and Carlo are gone.

The long trudge toward the place I'm supposed to call home takes a good, long while. My complete lack of fear makes me feel eerily close to the end of this place, this world. It's the kind of feeling Dr. Reisner would call a warning sign, and I try to remind myself how I made a promise with the best and sincerest intentions.

But I can't stop the voice in my head. *Come out, come out*, it calls—to the mountain lion that prowls these hundred acres. To the black bear that overturns my grandparents' garbage. *Come and find me.* I imagine my own white bones, the remnants of this body finally left behind so that the rest of me can go where it belongs—where I belong, with Luke.

Last year, when Mom and Paul decided Luke would corrupt my purity and ruin my future, they installed an alarm system. This was ridiculous and embarrassing in a town where nobody even bothered to lock front doors. At night, when the alarm system was engaged, if any door or window opened, it would sound a siren that connected directly to the police department. During the day, when the sirens were turned off, the alarm spoke in a tinny mechanical voice whenever we opened a door. "Front. Door," the alarm would announce through speakers on the first and second floors, and most notably in Mom and Paul's bedroom. A sultry but urgent female voice alerting us. "Kitchen. Door." "Garage. Door." It annoyed even my mother and Paul. After Luke died, they had it disconnected.

The afternoon after skating with Luke at Silver Lake, the security system truck is in our driveway when I get off the bus. I have to step around the uniformed alarm guy to walk into the kitchen. Mom stands at the refrigerator, staring into its contents like there's some code she needs to break. When I say "Hi," she jumps a little.

"Oh, hi," she says, and then gestures a little too dramatically at the refrigerator. "I'm starving, but there's nothing I can stand to eat."

She closes the door slowly, like maybe something will jump out and catch her eye at the last second. Then she turns toward me. Her belly seems to get bigger on a daily basis, and sometimes it shifts. Today it looks weirdly pointed toward the left, and she'll probably have to do another round of maternity clothes shopping. Her popped-out belly button is visible through the strained front of her turtleneck sweater.

"What's with the alarm?" I say.

She crosses her arms over her stomach and says, "What do you think?" She's been a little less careful with me since the incident with Officer Sincero. Dr. Reisner would probably call this a healthy sign. Maybe she's not quite so scared I'll jump ship. I worry for a second that she knows I went out last night. But then, the alarm guy has to come all the way from Durango, so it probably took a few days to get the appointment.

"Well," I say, trying to sound lightly sarcastic. "It'll

feel like old times having that lady back. Telling us which door is open."

"I chose a male voice this time," Mom says, the sternness completely shed from her voice. She's always had that quality, the ability to abandon discomfit and become cheerful in an instant. "He gave me a whole list of options, and I picked a male voice with an Australian accent."

I narrow my eyes. It's the kind of joke she would have made in the old days, and I wonder if my escape the other night somehow jolted her back to the person she used to be.

"I'm totally serious," Mom says. The alarm guy, hearing our conversation, types a code into the panel, closes and opens the kitchen door. A male voice says, "Kitchen door is *open*," with a nice Australian accent, like after we close it, he'll invite us over for shrimp on the barbie. Mom and I crack up. The alarm guy tells her everything is set, and she signs a work order form so he can leave.

"Listen," she says when he's gone, making a sweeping gesture with her arm as if pushing the laughter aside. "This was Paul's idea, hooking the alarm back up."

This kind of statement—passing the buck to Paul—also seems very pre-them-getting-back-together. From out of nowhere I get this memory of the two of us, Mom and me, riding in the back of a pickup truck with a bunch of other people, new friends she'd just acquired. One of the warmer states, probably in the West. The dirt road was very steep. I must have been pretty young, because

I sat in Mom's lap, her arms tight around my middle. Every time we hit a bump, the two of us flew up a little and screamed, her breath right beside my ear. I knew it was dangerous, but I also knew she wouldn't let go. If we flew out of the truck, we'd go together.

A part of me wants to tell Mom there's no point in reinstalling the alarm system, because I'm a total expert in circumventing it. When Luke was alive, all I had to do was unlock Carlo's dog door and shimmy through on my belly. I may not be quite down to my original weight, but I'm close, and I don't think I'll have any problem getting out as much as I need to—which proves as much as anything that I'm my mother's daughter.

"Hey," I say, suddenly wanting to do something for her. "Is there anything you do feel like eating? I could go out and get it for you."

Mom glances over to the hook beside the door where she keeps her car keys. I see her thinking, weighing how she feels about me behind the wheel of a car.

"Let's go together," she says. I dump my backpack onto a kitchen chair, and we head out. "Kitchen door is *open*," the mechanical Aussie tells us, and we're still laughing as we buckle up. Except for the heated leather seats, my mom's pregnant belly, and the fact that we're bothering with seat belts, it feels like old times—the two of us laughing, driving away together. I tell myself that in this instance it's all right to feel happy, away from Luke, because I'm doing it for Mom.

(11)

LUKE

After everything blew up with Dad and Hannah, Mom and I moved into a two-bedroom house not far from the high school. At first she rented it and then when she got her divorce settlement she bought it. The two of us ripped up the carpet and installed white oak floors she ordered from Lumber Liquidators. We did our best, but I was just a kid and she was no kind of handyman. Walking across that floor in bare feet you could feel how the boards were uneven. Every crumb and mud flake settled between the cracks.

Jill and Katie went to college pretty much right after Mom and I left. I guess they wouldn't have lived with us anyway. But the way things timed out they didn't have to take sides. We went from a family of five to just Mom and me. Our entire house could've fit into Dad's first floor.

Dad didn't bother to act sorry that Mom and I'd left. All he cared about was Hannah, and guess why she was gone? Because of me. That's what his warped mind figured, anyway. When the time came for lawyers I said I didn't want any kind of visitation, not even once-a-week dinners. Mom tried to talk me out of it. "He's your father," she said. But Dad said fine. No problem. I imagined him walking around his empty house. Daughters, gone. Son, gone. Wife, gone. Worst of all, True Love. Gone, gone, gone.

Sometimes I'd see him around town. He looked sad, and not because he missed Mom and me. His shoulders slumped. He didn't have to pretend not to see me because he wasn't looking around at anyone—just down at the sidewalk, scowling.

Screw them all, I decided, the summer I turned thirteen. My mother said that I fell in with the wrong crowd and she was half joking, but I guess I kind of did. I went to parties where I drank beer and smoked some pot. Nothing major or extreme, nothing that didn't get boring very fast. Like I said before, sometimes I think about life, I watch it all happen, and I get very tired. It *looks* tiring.

After my parents got divorced I went ahead and woke up every morning. Mom and I got along fine, we ate breakfast and walked to school. When she caught me drunk, she grounded me. When she found pot in my drawer, she believed me when I told her it was a friend's, but grounded me anyway. Mom never made things feel like the end of the world, not even the divorce. Sometimes it didn't feel like we'd lost anything. It felt more like we'd moved on.

Roaming around old moments of my life, I stumble into tenth-grade Earth Science. Mr. Camacho is talking about the big bang theory. I wouldn't have thought this at the time, but now—listening to him—I get this picture in my head of Tressa and me standing at the edge of the universe, watching it all take shape.

But fifteen-year-old me doesn't think that. I'm probably not even listening to Mr. Camacho. Instead I'm thinking about Kelly Boynton, who's sitting next to me. She just moved to Rabbitbrush from a little town in New Mexico. She's repeating ninth grade but she's my age and in a couple of my classes. Kelly looks boyish, skinny with short hair. But pretty. She's wearing a skirt, her bare legs look pretty great, and I'm wishing I could touch them. I remember that it bothered me how Kelly fit in around here so quick when Tressa had such a hard time. She grew up by Angel Fire so she knows how to ski, skate, etcetera, etcetera. The things that end up making a difference can seem pretty stupid. Around here if you don't know how to ski, you might as well be in a wheelchair.

But I guess it didn't bother me that much, because I catch Kelly looking at me. I see her back then, and also now, watching it happen again. What I do next makes me cringe a little because it seems like stealing from Tressa. I draw a map of the classroom. It's a very lame drawing, all stick figures and squares. The only faces I draw are for Kelly and me, and I give us big smiles. The fact that the picture looks like something a five-year-old would draw doesn't stop me. I crumple it up and toss it onto Kelly's desk. She uncrumples it and irons it out with her hand. Then she turns beet red. After a couple seconds she smiles and looks over at me, biting her lip a little.

Another summer rolls around and I turn sixteen. So does Kelly. I should go back and watch. Remember how I said I used to hold back with Tressa? Well, I didn't do that with Kelly, and it all blew up pretty bad. Her parents found out, and they hit the roof, they wanted to have me charged with statutory rape. The one thing my dad did for me between the time I was twelve and that day at the river was talk them out of it.

Kelly's parents told her she couldn't see me anymore. You wouldn't think she'd be so obedient but that was the end of it. We saw each other at school and nowhere else. In my head we'd pretty much broken up by the time Tressa came back, but Kelly told me that seeing me and Tressa together broke her heart. She said she always thought we'd get back together once everything settled down. I didn't want to be my dad. So I told Kelly the truth—we would never get back together. I wanted to be with Tressa. That didn't go over too well.

I want to watch what happened next, but here's what I see instead: Tressa. She's twelve years old, standing in a field. Maybe Rabbitbrush but it could be anywhere. She picks up a dandelion spore and blows the seeds and watches the fluff float away. I don't have to guess what she wished for because I already know. Those years when I tried to forget about Tressa, she remembered me every day. She remembered, and waited, until we could be together again.

If Tressa hadn't been living with him and Hannah, Dad probably wouldn't have known about us. It's not like he bothered keeping tabs on me. In fact, the day I walked out of my house and found him standing on the sidewalk, I was surprised he knew where I lived.

"Hey, Paul," I said, mostly to piss him off. In my head I still thought of him as Dad. It must have been December because I remember exactly where I was going, to buy crayons for Mom to donate to Toys for Tots. Every year she put together a bag for them, and because of Tressa I always threw in some crayons and pencils and paper.

"I need to talk to you," Dad said. We were both pretty bundled up, with our breath swirling in the air around us. I knew right away what this was about. Dad had finally got the thing he wanted most. This time he wasn't going to risk anything scaring Hannah off. Like, for example, me sleeping with Tressa.

I just stood there on the sidewalk, staring at him.

"You're seeing Tressa now?" he came right out and said. "Is that the new thing? You're *dating* her?"

I shrugged, not wanting to say yes or no. On the one hand it was none of his business. On the other hand I liked anything that made him squirm. Like him, I finally had the girl I wanted. Unlike him, I didn't have to worry about her bolting, ever.

"Do you really think that's appropriate?" Dad said. I'm still not sure what he meant. Was I supposed to think it wasn't appropriate because of our families? Or because of what happened with me and Kelly? It seemed like the real reason it bothered him had nothing to do with inappropriate and everything to do with inconvenient.

So I said, "Yeah, Paul. I think it's totally appropriate. You know what wouldn't be appropriate? My mother having to look out the window and see you standing here. So maybe you should get on your way."

Dad raised a finger and touched me for the first time in over four years to poke me in the shoulder. Now that I think of it, it was also the last time he touched me. I wonder if that ever occurs to him.

"You're not going to do with Tressa what you did with Kelly," Dad said.

I looked him straight in the eye and said, "Huh. Thanks for the morals lesson, Paul." Then I turned around and walked down the sidewalk. The only way I know he looked more scared than angry is that just the other day I went back to look.

But you know what? I don't have any reason to blame him. Whatever else he did, the after-Luke is not Dad's fault. Let's say that instead of trying to keep me away from Tressa he slapped me on the back and passed around cigars. That still doesn't mean we wouldn't have walked Carlo by the river that day. We had done it a thousand times before. We would have done it a thousand times again.

Here's how it went. Tressa came back to Rabbitbrush. She didn't fit in. It bothered me more than it bothered her. That's what Tressa said, anyway. And it did drive me nuts. It was so stupid, the things people didn't see. Tressa may not have been able to ski, or talk about the things other kids did. But she had this cool way of speaking. And this cool walk, with a very straight spine. She looked like she came from someplace else, which may have been the whole problem. The girls at school thought she was stuck up.

But Tressa wasn't stuck up. She was just this very particular combination of experiences. Once in the Mountain Village restaurant two people walked up to Tressa and started speaking French. They couldn't speak English, they had some questions, they were having a hard time getting around. In a room full of about two hundred people, they looked around and saw Tressa and walked straight over to her. They didn't even bother with *"Parlez-vous français."* They just saw all the things about her that drove other kids away, and they started talking.

The Kelly thing didn't help Tressa make any friends. Kelly was popular, and whenever Tressa and I showed up together, she'd start crying. For example, at Tom Knudsen's keg party, the August before senior year, out in the woods behind Silver Lake.

I don't go back to see this. I don't like remembering it but I can't help it. We had a fight because Tressa didn't want to go to the party. She told me to just go without her, but I wanted her to come. Finally she said okay, but she still didn't want to, so she was already jumpy when we showed up. Kelly saw us and ran into the woods crying, three of her girlfriends taking off after her. I could tell from Tressa's face that she didn't want to start fighting again, so she kept quiet.

I poured two beers and handed one to Tressa. She held on to it but didn't drink. It bummed me out, the way she just followed me around, not talking to anyone else. I thought, Could she at least try? Kelly and her friends came back, hanging out on the other side of the party, watching us and whispering. I pulled Tressa over to two girls, Ginger and Rachel, and tried to help her get into their conversation. Unfortunately they were talking about VH1, which I don't think Tressa had ever watched in her life.

"Oh, I know Christina Aguilera," Tressa said. "She's in my American history class."

Ginger and Rachel stared at her a second, confused. Then Ginger said, "Tressa, that's Christina *Guevarra*. Christina Aguilera is a famous singer."

They weren't trying to be mean, but they laughed. I wished I had listened to Tressa and come by myself. Maybe then I could've enjoyed the party. And I wouldn't have had to see Tressa, her face turning red. She swallowed her first sip of beer, probably ever, way too fast. I guess she just wanted an excuse to get away, so she downed the whole thing and went over to the keg for a refill. This repeated itself several times until I had to walk her home. She was stumbling, hanging on to my arm for balance, and then she puked all over the front steps.

That's how Hannah found us, Tressa puking on the WIPE YOUR PAWS welcome mat and me with my hand on her back. For the first time since that day at her parents' house, back when I was twelve, Hannah stopped looking embarrassed.

"You can go now, Luke," Hannah said. "I think you've done enough for one day."

And after that pretty much everybody, even Tressa's grandparents, got on board for the anti-Luke campaign.

It wasn't so unusual. The same thing happens every day all over the world. Parents lay down the law for reasons of their own. Before I brought Tressa home drunk and puking, there was already the fact that everyone figured we were having sex. And in our case maybe they were a little trigger happy, since us being together weirded everyone out in the first place. Nobody wanted any kind of bridge between the chopped off sections of our family. They wanted to keep us separate. It made it easier to have a definite excuse, a reason to keep us apart.

When Kelly's parents told her not to see me, she listened. But Tressa looked her mother straight in the eye and said no for the first time in her life. She snuck through a dog door in the middle of the night. She left notes in my locker, with the best places and times to meet her.

I know how she must feel now. She takes everything harder than anyone else. I should've thought ahead. I should've stopped myself from running by that river.

But I didn't and now here's what I see. Tressa, picking up that dandelion. I see her do it at twelve and sixteen. I see her do it at ages she's never been, twenty-two, thirty-three, forty-four. Sixty. Ninety. I see her make the same wish over and over. I don't see Kelly, not once, and not because I never loved her. Not because Tressa is prettier or smarter or better to anyone else except me.

The thing is, Kelly, and my sisters, and my friends. Even my mother. They'll be okay. They'll make other wishes. They might not do it quickly. It might take a long time. But once that long time's over, they'll settle into the after-Luke as the natural order of things.

But not Tressa. And that's why I can't leave. Why I won't.

(12)

TRESSA

Kelly Boynton hasn't been in school for a week, but today when I walk into the cafeteria, I see her across the room, sitting with a boy I don't know. He has short blond hair like hers, and they lean their heads close together, creating a cheerful kind of symmetry. From a distance it looks like the sort of conversation that would make you smile, if you happened to overhear. The boy has a tray of cafeteria food, but in front of Kelly sits a crinkled brown bag. When they pull apart, Kelly laughs. She has nice, white teeth that I can see from all the way across the room. The smile breaks her face into an entirely different shape—diamond, sparkly.

I step backward into the hall and head to the main exit door. I don't want anyone to see me watching, least of all her. For a second I imagine myself carrying a tray over to their table, sitting down, joining in. It's one of those visions that seems too improbable, even for fantasy, and I shake it out of my head. Instead I think of the map I could draw of the cafeteria, and all the tables. In the corner where Kelly and that boy sit, I would draw the happiest images possible, like a pair of sunflowers, or maybe sea otters—circling and tumbling, playing and smiling, not a single care or worry in the world.

When I get home that afternoon, just after the electronic Aussie has announced the kitchen door opening, Mom says, "You'll never guess who called today."

For a moment I freeze, certain she'll say *Luke*. I almost want to say it out loud.

"Give up?" Mom says.

I nod, my throat full of insane hope.

"Isabelle Delisle!"

I sit down at the table, my hands shaking a little. I'm so stupid.

The prospect of talking to Isabelle should make me happy. She's the daughter of the Frenchman my mother ran away with the very last time we left Rabbitbrush. Hugo is independently wealthy but amuses himself with a bar and restaurant in the Marquesas. Tending bar was always one of my Mom's default positions—"You can always get a job if you can make a decent margarita," she'd say—and she had been working at a club in San Francisco for just a few weeks when Hugo strolled in and they drummed up a romance, which eventually led to the two of them, plus me and Isabelle, living sometimes on Nuku Hiva but mostly sailing around French Polynesia on Hugo's forty-foot Baba. *Halcyon*, that boat was called. During those three years, the longest she ever stayed with one person, Mom became proficient at sailing and occasionally tended his bar, but mostly she worked as a professional sunbather. Hugo paid for everything, including the tutor who taught Isabelle and me from textbooks issued by the French government.

"Aren't you going to say anything?" my mother asks. I'm surprised to see her so happy at word from the past that she generally pretends never existed. I haven't heard her mention Hugo or Isabelle or even the South Pacific since she remarried Paul.

"Where was she calling from?" I ask. Not long after my mom and I left, Hugo enrolled Isabelle at an all-girls boarding school in Connecticut.

"She's in Telluride!" my mother says. "She and Hugo are staying at the New Sheridan. She wants you to go out to see her tomorrow." Mom hands me a slip of paper with a phone number scrawled across it. I can tell from the slant of her handwriting that she was excited when she wrote it down. I remember living on the boat, when communication between us and this mainland was next to impossible.

"Are you going to come with me?" I ask my mother.

She glances toward the ceiling, and I guess that Paul is working in his office upstairs.

"I better not," she says. "But it would be fun for you, right? You and Isabelle were so close." Mom turns and starts digging through the utility drawer. She pulls out an extra set of keys to her Lexus SUV and drops them into my hand. I stare down at them. When I got my driver's license, I inherited her old Jeep, but when I returned from the hospital, it had disappeared. "It hasn't snowed all week," Mom says. "The roads are nice and clear. Do you feel all right driving?"

I cock my head. "Do you feel all right with me driving?" I ask her.

Mom puts her hands on top of her belly. "Tressa," she says. "I wouldn't give you the keys if I didn't."

"Okay." I can tell by her face that she doesn't *truly* feel all right, and likely never will. But she's so pleased at the thought of me seeing an old friend—my only old friend—that she's willing to risk the worst, and can't wait to hand me these keys, which I won't even need until tomorrow morning. "Thanks, Mom," I say, and then, "I promise I'll be careful."

Upstairs I check my e-mail for the first time in more than a week, to see if Isabelle has sent a note about her visit, but all I have is a note from Katie, probably asking what I want for Christmas. I don't open it but just sit there staring at the screen, thinking about how Isabelle and Luke never met. How much fun would it be to bring him into Telluride to meet her? I imagine the three of us sitting around a table, me and my only two friends.

Instead of reading Katie's e-mail I log on to Facebook and type in Kelly's name. Her parents might not let her post a profile picture of herself, but they haven't checked her privacy settings. When I click on photos, I'm able see her albums. And even though it feels like spying, I sift through photograph after photograph, trying to find a picture of her and Luke. I want to see what the past looked like. I want to see what the present—the future— *should* look like, if I had never come back to Rabbitbrush.

There are pictures of Kelly on vacation with her family in a tropical place, and pictures of her with kids I know from school. There is photo after photo of a dog, some kind of pointy-eared heeler mix. She also has a series of pictures with a little girl, either her sister or someone she babysits for. Of course, this is Facebook, so in every picture Kelly looks happy, smiling, idyllic. No one looking at these photos could imagine her face streaked with tears or her arms scarred and injured.

But what strikes me most is that in all these pictures— hundreds of them, the computer counts for me—there is not a single one of Luke. Even though the photos date back several years, spanning the time she and Luke were a couple. Maybe she deleted them after they broke up. I imagine her destroying all evidence that he ever existed. And I imagine her regretting that now.

* * *

Late Saturday morning Isabelle Delisle stands waiting for me in front of the Village Market. Although the sun shines brightly enough that I wear a fleece jacket over a long-sleeved T-shirt and jeans, she has bundled herself into a thick black parka, mittens, a gray cashmere hat, and a matching scarf wound around her neck. When I called her disposable cell phone—not allowed at her boarding school and useless on the water, but purchased for this trip—Isabelle told me she had no interest in skiing. Raised on tropical climates and weighing about ninety-three pounds, Isabelle hates the weather at her boarding school and has zero fondness for winter sports. She may be looking at Colorado schools, but I bet she ends up in a place with a balmier climate.

I can feel the air whoosh out of her parka as we hug hello. Even at my thinnest Isabelle always made me feel like an elephant. She is naturally skin-and-bones, breast-less, built on a narrower scale than the rest of us.

"*Bonjour*, Tressa," she says, kissing me on each cheek. She's so fluent in English and French that both are almost without accent.

"Hi, Isabelle," I say, wanting to speak English. These days the whole world feels enough like a second language.

Isabelle looks just the same, with blunt-cut brown hair and pale freckles across her nose. She's a year younger than I am, and those three years of close quarters coupled with her own vagabond history make her feel more like a sister than either of the twins. Nights on the boat, we would lie on the deck and stare up at the stars, searching for the Southern Cross. Isabelle barely remembered her mother, who died when she was three; we would imagine the departed Madame Delisle gazing back down at us. We talked about anything and everything. So it doesn't take me aback now when she reaches for my wrists and pulls them toward her.

"Let me see the scars," she says.

Isabelle pushes back the sleeve on my left arm, then peers down, squinting. "Ooh la la," she says. "It looks worse than I imagined. Did it hurt?"

"I took a lot of Vicodin when I did it," I say. "But it hurt afterward, when I woke up. Quite a lot."

She lets go and hooks her arm through my elbow. Without either of us mentioning a destination, we begin walking up toward Colorado Avenue.

Armed with Hugo's MasterCard, Isabelle hits a few stores where she stocks up on winter gear. "You won't believe how cold it gets in New England," she says. "It's worse than here. Very damp." She insists on buying me two sweaters and a pair of jeans. "Hugo would want to get you something," she says with a wave of her hand. Eventually we make our way to The Steaming Bean and sit down across from each other, shopping bags piled up high around us.

"So," Isabelle says, as if she's been waiting to say it

these past couple hours. She takes a moment to blow delicately on her café au lait. Not so much a purist as Isabelle, I have a sugar-free vanilla latte.

"*Ça va?*" Isabelle says. "You're all right now?"

"*Oui,*" I say automatically. "*Ça va.* I'm fine."

She narrows her eyes at me, not quite believing. I try to make my face look honest, convincing. I remind myself that saying "I'm fine" does not constitute a lie, because in fact, I do feel fine, and hopeful, and—most important—willing to stay in this world. As long as I can keep seeing Luke at night.

"I didn't hear about what happened until nearly a month later," Isabelle says. "Hugo forwarded a letter from your mother that said you were okay. I sent you an e-mail, but you didn't answer." She looks down at her coffee. For a moment I take her pause as an apology for the complaint, but then she says, "When you didn't answer, it made me feel like you were gone. Like, gone as in really gone. You know? Even though I knew you weren't."

"I'm sorry." There's never anything else to say.

She picks up her spoon and gives her coffee a few needless stirs. "I'm not trying to make you feel bad. I'm just trying to tell you what it was like for me. Hugo and I spent the summer on the boat, and I would lie on the beach and look up at the stars, and I would imagine you up there looking back at me. Even though I knew in my head you were safe and sound in Colorado."

"I'm sorry," I say again, wondering if the words sound as stale to her as they do to me. If she wants me to know that what I did affected people other than myself, she can rest assured that that has been taken care of. I don't say this, though. I understand that Isabelle needs to do this, chastise me, and my job is to let her.

"Don't do it again," she says, clanking her spoon back to the saucer. Her voice sounds stern enough to settle the matter. I look out the window of the café. The snow piles along the side of the road in dirty clumps. The sky looks flat and gray. I remember being on the boat with Isabelle, how her company eased that time away from Rabbitbrush. I take a sip from my fake-sweet latte, staring longingly at Isabelle's huge piece of chocolate cake. Half an hour ago she ordered it enthusiastically, but as far as I can tell, she hasn't had a single bite, only taken it apart with the side of her fork and spread the crumbs around on her plate. I remember this style of non-eating from our years on the boat and decide if she can be forthright, then so can I.

"I'll tell you what," I say. "I promise not to commit suicide again if you promise to take five bites of that cake."

Isabelle mashes her fork down on a piece of cake heavy with frosting. She frowns at her food. Even though I've been dying for something authentically sweet, I wouldn't want to eat her cake after the mess she's made of it. But then I realize it's my wording that has thrown her off, not my command. She reverses the direction of her fork and places it into her mouth, her brows knit together in concentration. She wants me to amend myself, say "attempt" instead of "commit." But I don't do it. If all these mini lectures have taught me anything, it's that suicide is something that's committed whether you succeed or not.

A week ago the book about Assia Wevill, the one Evie was reading, arrived from Amazon.com. Assia Wevill killed herself, successfully, along with her four-year-old daughter. Though I find this information frightening, it's also a kind of perverse relief. Somebody did something worse than me. I understand there's no way to commit suicide without taking others down with you, but at least in my case the others were only metaphorical.

As Isabelle attempts my demanded five bites, she looks so pained that I do the only thing a real friend could: take my spoon out of my coffee cup and help her out. I close my eyes to savor the exquisite, melting frosting, and when I open them, I am immediately punished for this brief second of earthly pleasure.

We have been here, sipping our coffee drinks and not eating cake, for nearly an hour. I sit with my back to the door, which has opened and closed twenty times or more, always with a jingle. I don't know that I have turned around once at this sound. But the breeze that enters with Luke's mother alerts me somehow, a shift in the room's atmosphere, the bell shaking differently—with a slight tone of warning. Isabelle has never seen Francine, or Luke for that matter; she wouldn't detect the resemblance. But she lets her gaze follow the sharp turn of my head that Francine doesn't register at first. She strides past our table, down jacket zipped to her chin.

Isabelle follows my gaze, looks at me questioningly.

"That's Luke's mother," I say. I could swear my voice comes out in a whisper. But Francine's head swivels as if I shouted the words across the room. She looks at me, blinking, almost as if she's forgotten who I am, then puts her hands into the pockets of her jacket and walks toward us. It is the first time she has made eye contact with me—let alone approached me—since before Luke died.

My hands slide off the table and into my lap. I'm not sure if I'm allowed to look back at her. I refuse to let myself hope for any sort of olive branch as Francine stops just beside our table.

"So," she says. Her face looks uncharacteristically pale, her strong jaw set. I see that the gray is gone from her hair. She has rinsed it out, and for some reason I feel a slight jolt of relief, as if this might be a good sign. She stands there, hovering over me. Then she says, "Do you have something you want to tell me?"

I stare up at her, completely flummoxed. My mind flashes to Silver Lake, and Luke's new hockey skates. The two of us, slamming the puck across the frozen white surface. Could someone possibly have seen us?

"No," I say, my voice cracking slightly on the word. I think that I have never sounded more like a liar.

Francine bends one knee and scrapes the toe of her boot across the floor. "I ran into your mother this morning," she says, "at the Safeway. She's looking very pregnant."

My brows contort, and I nod. This can't be what Francine means. Everyone knows my mother is very pregnant.

"She told me about your dog," Francine says. "She seemed to think I already knew."

Isabelle reaches across the table and takes my hand. Francine makes a motion that mimes batting her hand away, though she is not bold enough to actually touch a girl she doesn't know.

"Don't hold her hand," Francine snaps, then looks surprised that she has said it out loud. I'm surprised too, not that she thinks I don't deserve any kind of comfort, but that she feels it so strongly that she can admit to it. Isabelle doesn't reply, but tightens her grip around my fingers.

"I'm sorry," I whisper, easing my hand out of Isabelle's so Francine can see that I agree with her. I don't deserve this café, this friend, or even this wrecked chocolate cake. I don't deserve the air around us.

"Tressa," Francine says. Her voice shakes with the effort of achieving balance. "I know you're hurting. Don't you think I know that? But couldn't you have told me yourself? So I wouldn't have to find out like that, all of a sudden, in the middle of the supermarket?"

It hasn't occurred to me until this moment, but of course I should have told her. I should have at least written a note, even an e-mail. A stale, floundering survival instinct wants to argue with her. *But you won't speak to me*, it protests. *How can I tell you anything if you won't speak to me?*

Instead I say, "I'm sorry." The same old stupid, useless words.

Francine brings her hands up to cover her face. She says something, muffled, behind them. "What?" I say, not because I want to hear but because I want her to take this chance—this anger allowing her to look at me—to say whatever she needs.

She doesn't take her hands away but opens her fingers so her words might be more audible. "I don't want to be cruel," she says. Her eyes fill up with tears.

Isabelle speaks up in her sharp colonial voice. "Then don't be. Can't you see she's sorry? Tressa lost him too, you know."

Francine drops her hands. Her face looks so pale, so drawn and conflicted.

"It's okay," I say quickly. "You're not cruel."

She nods her head and looks toward the window, out at that slushy snow. Wipes a tear away. I want to cry too, but use all my might not to. Because even though my regret could fill a lake, an ocean, and a very particular river, all it can do is hurt Francine more. She lost the one thing in the word that can't be replaced. It seems unfair that Luke comes back to me and only me. I wish I could tell Francine, *He's not really gone,* and invite her to join us, but of course I can't. So I just sit there, silently, until she says, "The flowers."

I raise my eyes to hers, tense with endless apologies.

"Thank you for stopping," Francine says. Then she walks away from my table, out of the coffee shop, whatever she came in for unclaimed, her hands returned to her pockets and her eyes to the cold winter ground.

"How did Isabelle look?" my mother asks at dinner. "Has she gained any weight?" She passes me a bowl filled with rice pilaf, which I push across the table to Paul. The questions about Isabelle come fast and furiously, but Mom doesn't mention running into Francine. I don't know if this omission is for my benefit or Paul's.

"She looks the same," I say, trying to imagine the confrontation between the two Mrs. Kingsburys, whether it *was* a confrontation or just a strained, polite exchange. I picture the two of them facing each other in the harsh lights of Safeway's produce aisle, the automatic sprinklers buzzing intermittently with their summery spray. I hate that in addition to everything else Francine has to endure bumping into the woman who is her predecessor and successor—my mother with her three living children and another on the way. If only Mom had run away and taken me with her after Luke died, Francine would never have to see either of us again.

After we eat, I clear the table and wipe down the counters, then walk outside. Clouds gather overhead as if the sky is gearing up for another big snow, and in my heart I feel low and lonesome. Something tells me Luke will not appear tonight. And if he *does* appear, I won't be able to talk to him about what happened with his mother at the coffee shop. But that doesn't matter. What matters is Luke, his face in front of mine, the tips of his fingers on my wrist. The sorrow in Francine's voice continues to rattle in my brain, jarring all my nerve endings.

I walk through the kitchen and into the garage to grab my mittens, jacket, and skates. "Mom," I call when I come back inside. "I'm going to walk out to the lake and skate for a bit."

In about two seconds Mom appears in the kitchen, the world's fastest middle-aged pregnant woman. "Now?" she says. "It's already dark. I don't think that's safe."

"I'll bring a flashlight," I say. "And I won't be long. I want to get some exercise."

Mom sighs, not ready to agree to this but not wanting an argument. Then she says, almost to herself, "Maybe we need to get you another dog."

I frown, thinking uncharitably of all the various replacements she has provided throughout our life together. Reading my expression, Mom holds up her hands, defensive, and stops me before I can say anything.

"I'm sorry," she says. "I know we can't replace Carlo. I just meant that I always felt so much safer when he was with you." She pauses, then adds, "I miss him too, Tressa, and I worry about you."

Mom's voice sounds breathless. Her skin looks mottled, and I know the "him" she misses is not necessarily Carlo.

"It's okay, Mom," I say. I reach out so that my fingers just barely brush her belly. Then I promise for the millionth, zillionth time, like my body isn't my own but some vessel I've been unwisely trusted with, "I'll be careful."

Mom's face doesn't merely cloud; it contorts. It crumples as if she might cry, not only at the thought of me out at night but at the thought of arguing with me about it. Understanding how it feels not to be able to face what's just around the corner, I take off my mittens in surrender and throw them onto the counter. If I'm living for her benefit, it makes sense to comply with her wishes.

"Okay," I say. "I'll go in the morning." Mom's face relaxes. She waits until I've left the kitchen before she exhales, but I can hear that breath—its frantic relief, a bullet dodged—as I head up the stairs.

Just as well, I tell myself. Maybe I'm wrong, and tonight Luke *will* come to me. Maybe, I think as I climb the stairs, if I stay indoors, the world will know how much I want and need him. And he will come to me.

* * *

But he doesn't. In the morning my room is infused with flat, empty Sunday morning light. Everything settles into its place with heartbreaking sameness. My book on the nightstand where I left it. My worn, woven rug lying flat and undisturbed, waiting to protect my same bare feet from the cold floor when I get out of bed. My mother clanking around downstairs in the kitchen, a domestic and predictable creature, nobody needing to wonder where in the world she might be. The ukulele Grandpa gave me sits in its still-unopened case. If I accepted his invitations for lessons, if I took out that miniature instrument and learned to play, would it be enough of a change to prevent Luke from seeing me? Better not to risk it, to instead keep everything as close as possible to the way he remembers.

"Tressa!" Mom says when I walk into the kitchen. She has done this since I was a little girl, exclaimed over the sight of me, as if I were the last person in the world she expected and the first person in the world she wanted. If only the twins could have experienced this greeting, maybe they wouldn't be so angry at her all the time.

"I'm making waffles," Mom says.

"Thanks," I say, "but I'm not that hungry. I think I'll go skating instead."

She pauses as if to protest, but then seems to remember her victory from last night. "Sure," she says. "You go skating. Work up an appetite. I'll save the batter."

Waffles. Private college. A new dog. The things people try to float toward me, to make life tolerable. Walking out to Silver Lake with my skates slung over my shoulder and my boots sinking into the snow, I understand the sadness accompanying their efforts, how they all know only one impossible thing could ever make me happy again. Sometimes I wish I could tell them, *It's okay. You don't have to worry. I have this time I get to spend with Luke, and that makes me happy.*

For a moment I try to imagine what it would be like, a different dog walking beside me. I picture Kelly Boynton's, its gray spotted coat and funny pointed ears. So much smaller than Carlo, it would struggle through this deep snow on the hill, its front legs scratching the surface of the incline. The image fades quickly. He looks like a nice dog, but he belongs to someone else, he doesn't fit.

At the top of the hill I slow down. I can hear skates scraping across the ice, gliding and stopping. When I get to the edge of the frozen water, it turns out to be H. J. He doesn't see me at first, and I watch him speed skate in graceful circles, his hands behind his back, his legs kicking out behind him. I like to skate, and I can manage slow, rhythmic circles, but I can't go fast or even backward. The part of me that feels persistently embarrassed about this deficiency wants to turn around and tiptoe back down the hill. But before I have a chance, H. J. catches sight of me and skids to a neat, expert little halt. I don't want him to feel badly about chasing me away, so I sit down on the log to put on my skates.

"Hey," H. J. says. "Fancy meeting you here." He glides over and sits next to me as I ease one foot out of my boot.

"Hey," I say, trying to sound friendly. Normal. Despite the weirdness of our last interaction—the palm reading—I like H. J. well enough, and also feel somewhat indebted to him. If it hadn't been for him, I might never have figured out about my scars.

"Guess what," H. J. says. "I got fired on Friday. I mean, I knew it was coming, but they made it official. I haven't told Evie yet. I thought I'd work off some adrenaline and tell her this afternoon, so she doesn't hear it at school tomorrow."

I stop tying my skate and sit up. H. J. isn't wearing his glasses, which makes him squint a little. His eyes are the same hazelish brown as his sister's. I try to read his face so I can know how best to respond. He doesn't look sad exactly, just weary. It doesn't surprise me that he burst out with this personal information without a lead-in. I have figured out that he doesn't bother with small talk. I've also figured out that I like this about him.

"That's too bad," I say. "I bet you were a good teacher."

H. J. shrugs. "I was okay. Maybe I would have been good eventually, if they'd let me keep going." He sounds more wistful than sad, and I imagine that he has learned to put things into perspective. He knows how to sort out disappointment from tragedy. I feel myself relaxing, not wanting him to go away anymore. "Anyway," H. J. says. "It was pretty stupid, how I handled it. Probably they're right to keep me away from school-age children."

I laugh a little. Kelly is about the same age as me, and I don't exactly think of myself as a school-age child. "I guess," H. J. goes on, "that I didn't realize how serious it was. Cutting. I thought she was trying to shock me, and maybe if I wasn't shocked, she would just . . . stop."

"Can I tell you something?" I say. A low cloud blows over the lake, giving the early morning a sense of gloaming. H. J.'s face looks sweaty and cold at the same time, pink blood rushing under skin that's been whitened by chilly air, and I'm surprised by the youngness of it. He doesn't say anything, or even nod, but I go on. "If I were Kelly. I mean, if I were a cutter." I close one hand around my wrist, where H. J.'s eyes immediately flicker. I remember Katie saying, "He stands too close and he *looks* too hard. It's not comfortable." But I don't feel uncomfortable, so I keep talking.

"If someone said that to me, what you said to her, about just doing it a little bit? It would make me feel better. Like what I was doing wasn't so sick. So horrifying. You know? Maybe you gave her permission to do it so she felt less ashamed. Maybe that's what gave her the guts to admit it to someone who could really help her. It got you fired, which is awful, but maybe it also saved her."

"That's a nice thought," H. J. says. "I would like to save someone."

His voice catches on this last word, and we both sit for a moment, thinking—I think—of the various people neither of us have managed to save. Then I say, "I saw Kelly in the cafeteria on Friday, and she looked happy. She was laughing."

"Laughing is good," H. J. says. But he doesn't smile. He puts his hands on the log, on either side of his thighs, as if bracing himself for something—a gust of wind, an unwelcome emotion. I think about asking again if Kelly told him why she was cutting, if the reason—as far as she was concerned, anyway—had something to do with Luke. But as soon as Luke's name forms in my mind, I get this picture, as if I'm looking at myself from across the lake. I see myself sitting on a log with a guy—a *man*—having this very personal conversation. H. J.'s shoulder doesn't exactly touch mine, and neither does his leg. But both hover close enough that I can feel their molecules, the tiny breadth of space between us. And suddenly I want him to go away, even though I feel more myself with him and Evie than I have with any living person since last spring, even Isabelle. Even my mom.

The thing is: I'd rather feel uncomfortable. I may be obligated to stay alive, which to some extent means fighting against misery, which means going toward the things that make me happy, which I have completely forsworn. It's an impossibly vicious circle, and suddenly

I feel exhausted. The only thing that ever gives me a break is Luke, and suddenly he won't come.

Sitting out here on the log, chatting with H. J., feels like creating a friendship, something new. In other words it feels like the thing I refuse to ever do, which is move on. What if someone came upon the two of us, sitting on a log and talking? Even though H. J. is essentially someone's dad, he's not *that* much older than me, and it could easily look like . . .

No. I get this horrible feeling of the whole world watching us from behind every one of these bare branches. My mother behind that tree, Francine sitting on that rock. Paul watching too, and my sisters and my grandparents, and worst of all Luke—standing in the middle of the lake. What would he think? I imagine him turning to walk away, Carlo at his side, the two of them disappearing into gray skies, finally gone forever, while I run after them, yelling in vain: *No! Stop! It's not what you think!*

My fingers act before I make a decision. They unlace the one skate I've managed to put on. "You know," I say, without looking at H. J., "I feel really cold all of a sudden. I think I'm just going to go home." I can feel him looking at me but keep my eyes on my skates. If I've hurt his feelings, I don't want to know.

"But you'll warm up once you start skating," he says. "Come on. It'll be fun. We can race."

"I'm a crappy skater," I say.

"That's okay," H. J. says. "I just like your company."

I yank my Sorel back on, then try to tie my skates together as I realize my fingers are shaking. I don't want him to like my company. I don't want to skate with anyone except for Luke.

"I'm sorry," I tell H. J. "I have to go."

Once my boots are on, it takes all my might not to run down the hill toward Paul's house. I can feel H. J.'s bewildered gaze on my back, and then I think maybe he's not bewildered at all. Maybe he understands completely. And I don't know how to feel about that. I don't know how to protect myself from becoming so sad again, so sad that I want to die; and at the same time I don't know how to protect myself from returning too fully to this world.

Because how can I possibly face it, the rest of my life? What am I supposed to do? Grow up? Go to college? Have other boyfriends? That last idea is the wrongest thing I can possibly ever think, and I feel so lost, so hopeless. I wish that forest ranger had never found me at Alta the day I slit my wrists. I wish I hadn't told Luke to meet me at the river. Most of all I wish that I had fallen down the bank instead of Luke. Leaving *him* on the bank, helpless in that moment, and sad—yes— but so much better equipped than me for everything. Especially life.

part two

staring down before

(13)

LUKE

It happened toward the end of May. Paul and Hannah had this plan to send Tressa back East to be a counselor at a girls' summer camp. Tressa took it hard but to me it seemed pretty temporary. In June we'd be eighteen. In August we'd both head to Boulder, something Dad and Hannah didn't know. I told Mom to tell Dad that I only got accepted at Greeley. I admit it was kind of hard, letting him think I wasn't smart enough to go to Boulder. But we had to make sure they didn't try to send Tressa someplace else. The main thing was, soon they wouldn't be able to do anything about us.

And you know what else? Part of me looked forward to the summer on my own. I could go to parties and hang out with my friends. That doesn't mean I didn't love her. It doesn't mean I don't remember the V of her

T-shirt coming down a little lower than she probably realized. It's not like I didn't want to be with her. But I also knew how to wait. I'd had a lot of practice.

I walked through the woods past the old, rusted-out school bus to meet Tressa. She was right where she said she'd be, sitting with Carlo in a stand of aspens by the river. She stood up. I could see she'd been crying; her face was swollen and red.

"What's wrong?" I said. She stepped forward and hugged me hard. Her cheek felt wet. She said something into my neck that I couldn't understand, but I could guess.

I stepped back and put my hands on her shoulders. "It's just the summer," I said. "Eight weeks. And then this whole part of our lives will be over."

"Or else we could run away," she said.

I laughed. Tressa stood there looking at me, completely serious. "I mean it," she said. "I've got my Jeep. We could just leave. We could drive away and never see their faces again, and we could be together."

"That doesn't make any sense." I tried not to sound annoyed. We both knew summer would be so much easier on me, here in Rabbitbrush. "Look," I said. "We've got one more month of high school. Two months of summer. It would be crazy to run away now. We just have to wait it out."

Tressa looked away, toward the river. "I guess you're right," she said.

I put my arms around her waist and kissed her. She dropped Carlo's leash. We stood that way, kissing awhile. I really liked the way those jeans looked, and I slipped my hands into her back pockets. In the river, sticks and leaves rode the current downriver. Carlo lay across Tressa's feet. Finally she pulled away. We held hands and walked by the raging water.

Carlo went trotting ahead in his lopsided old-dog way, his leash dragging behind him. One of us should have picked up that leash. He'd slipped down the bank before, and once he almost landed in the water. But neither of us did. We just held hands, nothing to be afraid of, walking along the Sustantivo River.

(14)

TRESSA

How could you do it, to people who love you?

Nobody ever asks me that question in words. I see it in their faces. I hear it in my own head, insistent and accusing. After all, I knew what it felt like, to lose someone. I saw everyone else—parents, sisters, friends, acquaintances—and how that loss laid them low, the empty space it left behind. The disbelief, the horror, and the impossible, unavoidable longing to stop time and wind back the world. Please, please, let me do this over. Let me do it right this time.

How could you do it to your grandparents? How could you do it to your dog, Carlo, who trusted you, who made protecting you his life's work? How could you do it to your sisters, who had just lost their little brother? Worst of all, how could you do it to your mother, who chose you again and again—who not only loved you but needed you?

My only answer—there didn't seem to be any choice. Once as a kid I burned my hand very badly in a campfire. I remember the squirming agony of that burn. It hurt so much, I couldn't stop moving my feet or my shoulders, like I had this instinctive need to wriggle out of my body and escape the pain. Multiply that times a hundred, and you get how I felt after Luke died. My stupid, stupid impulse to cling to him had clung him right into those freezing waters. Now I wanted to go back. Was that so much to ask? Let me go back and not leave that note in his locker. Let me go back and greet him with a smile— *Yes, I will endure one last separation. I will be as strong as you.* Let me go back and not bring Carlo along, or at least let me hang on to his leash, keeping him safe and sure beside me.

It seems like such a paltry request, to go back minutes in time. But then the minutes turn to hours and days and weeks, all time that you have to live with this burning regret and sorrow and loss. How could I live with myself? How could I live without Luke? I needed to see him. It felt so urgent, so imperative. I had things to tell him. I had forgiveness to procure. I couldn't stand the pain a second longer, without doing something to stop it. So I sat down at the kitchen table, the same place my mother had written her fateful farewell note, years before Luke or I was born. There were a million things I could have written. A million words for my sadness, none of which even began to cover it. So I wrote down the simplest part, the most elemental truth:

I'm sorry. I have to see him.

The day Luke died the ground was soggy because the crust of ice had just melted. A few leaves and shoots tried to break through, but they didn't stand a chance, not at this altitude. One last storm could still come along and cover them with snow. But on that day, for a few hours anyway, we had spring. Birds chirped all around us. The river crashed fast and hard from all the melt-off.

Luke took my hand. The two of us walked beside the river. I knew I should pick up Carlo's leash but I didn't. What could go wrong—an old, obedient dog. I want to go back and shake myself, hard. *Don't you remember how he loses his footing? Stupid, stupid girl.*

Because after all the yelling and rules and the alarm system, here's what finally managed to keep Luke and me apart—a rabbit. It burst out from behind a tree, and Carlo—forgetting his age and arthritis—gave chase. Luke and I laughed at the same time, the exact same noise, blending together so that it sounded like a single sound from a single person. Sometimes I think I made up what I said next, that I've created this memory as a way to make myself feel better. But at the same time I know for certain my exact words when the laughter stopped. I said, "Oh, my God, Luke. I love you so much."

Luke would have gathered me up and kissed me, except that as soon as the words were out of my mouth, we heard the splash. Neither of us saw the fall itself, Carlo tumbling down the bank. The next thing we saw was his sleek black head bobbing above the water, his paws in a frantic dog paddle, his body hurtling downstream the way we'd just come.

Luke and I ran along the bank of the river, calling to Carlo. I still can't describe the panic I felt, watching my dog go. After a while he seemed to stop struggling. We couldn't see his paws, just his head, occasionally—terrifyingly—sinking below the water, then bobbing back up.

"Hold on," we both yelled to the dog. "We're coming."

Luke hurtled ahead of me, until after a while I couldn't see him. He had escaped down the path, running like an action hero, his dark head rising and falling on shore the way Carlo's rose and fell in the river current.

And then another slip. From my distance around the bend, I heard it, a foot sliding in the mulchy leaf litter. I heard the sound of a tumble, and a splash, and suddenly it was me running like an action hero, faster than I would ever have imagined possible.

The forest ranger and the EMTs said he must have struggled. The current was too fierce. If only he had given up, the way Carlo did—which is why the river finally released the dog, just around the next bend a quarter mile or so down, as it came upon a beaver dam. The water pooled and almost stilled. When I reached that point, my chest heaved and my air emerged in honking gasps. Carlo managed to pull himself out of the river, soaked through to the bone. He shook himself off and sprayed me with water before he collapsed onto the bank in an exhausted heap. While Luke floated facedown, still traveling downriver but painfully slow.

I ran forward, splashing into the calmer water, all that ice-cold, melted snow. I turned Luke over so that his face pointed toward the sky. I pushed wet hair and leaves off his face and placed my lips on his, trying to breathe for him, but I couldn't get enough traction. So I moved behind his head and looped my arms under his shoulders. I dragged him onto the bank and beat on his chest and blew air into his lungs, amazed at how exactly Hugo's course in CPR came back to me.

But Luke. He did not come back to me. What I labored over, it was only his body. He himself, Luke, had already made his exit, somewhere upriver, while I had run after him with my useless, pounding feet.

In the hospital, before Francine arrived, they let me go into the room with his body. I opened the door and walked on tiptoes across sterile linoleum. The nurse stood next to him and lifted up the sheet. My heart swelled with the most illogical burst of relief, almost joy. Oh, I thought. It's not him!

This reaction went beyond wishful thinking. Despite Luke's beautiful face, his shiny black hair, the peace sign with the bit of pearl hanging from its leather thread. A body just doesn't look like itself when a person no longer inhabits it. Luke without Luke no longer looked like Luke. He, Luke, had left the building. And if he wasn't there, he must have been somewhere else. Right?

I tried to continue, to move forward, to stay alive. The devastated faces of Luke's father, our sisters, his mother, showed me exactly what would be wrought if I did what I wanted and followed him.

"Let's go away," I said to my mother one night when she walked into the living room, a book under her arm. Paul was over at Francine's collecting his share of Luke's ashes. I couldn't stand the thought of him walking through the door, carrying those split-in-two remains.

"Tressa," Mom said, her voice appalled, as if she and I hadn't run away together a million times.

"Why not?" I said. "There's nothing keeping us here anymore."

"There's Paul," Mom said. "My parents. This house. Our life." We stood in the living room, next to the red velvet love seat. I pushed her hard on the shoulders, and she sat down. The heavy book fell to the floor.

"Mom," I said. I didn't yell. My voice sounded more furious than if I had yelled. It sounded strained and broken. How could she not get it? Who had taught me that the best antidote to anything was getting into your car and pressing down on the gas?

"I have left for you again and again," I said. "You've dragged me away for your own purposes, and now I am telling you, I need to get away. I need to get away now!"

"Tressa," Mom whispered. Her face clouded, sad, and hopeless, and she picked the book up off the floor and held it up for me to see. *What to Expect When You're Expecting*.

I stared. My first thought—stupid, stupid!—was to tell Luke. *You won't believe it. Another sibling that we half share.* But I couldn't tell him anything, not ever again, and I sank to my knees and sobbed in my mother's lap.

"I'm sorry," she said, running her hand over my hair. "I wish I could. But I can't. I just can't."

I have seen the regret in her face every day since. If only she had granted my wish and taken me away. Because on my own in Rabbitbrush—the town where Luke didn't live anymore—I could only think of one place to go. One thing to do. Over the next week an urgency mounted. I had to escape, to get away from all these feelings. Never mind the mourning, grieving faces all around me. They'd be better off without my face to remind them of everything they'd lost. Only one person in the world could grant the forgiveness I needed to continue living. In the absence of that there was simply one thing to do, and nothing else:

I'm sorry, I wrote. *I have to see him.*

(15)

LUKE

I can't see it like it's happening, and I can't remember because I wasn't there. I know what she did but I can't talk about it. The words don't come together. I only know it in the foggiest kind of way, like waking up from a dream where you remember the feeling but not what happened.

I want to take the whole thing off Tressa's shoulders the same way I want to wave my hand over her wrists and make the scars disappear. But then I remember what's bringing me back and letting me touch her (according to Tressa, anyway) and I get confused.

I get confused. I need to rest. It's too much to think about, Tressa and me wanting different things. Before when we wanted different things they were pretty insignificant, like a party, or her going to summer camp. But in the after-Luke there's this. I want to live and she wants to die. Which sounds like the same, even though I can't shake the feeling that it's not.

TRESSA

That night I hung on to Carlo for the longest time, my face buried in his fur. "I'm sorry," I whispered again and again. "I love you. I'm sorry." I knew I couldn't bring him with me, because he wouldn't let it happen. He would bark and whine and howl for help. And then I'd be gone and he'd be deserted.

My mother had a bottle with five Vicodin left over from her last miscarriage. I had already stolen them from her medicine cabinet. I had also stolen an X-acto blade from Paul's toolbox. Back then I still had my Jeep. I bundled up. Nights were cold. I didn't want to be uncomfortable. I didn't want to hurt myself. I wanted the pain to *end*. For everyone. I wanted to see Luke. I wanted to tell him about everything that had happened since he'd been gone.

At the funeral I had watched the different faces and the various reactions. There was Francine, front and center, unable to look my way. There was Kelly, weeping in the back pew. There were all Luke's friends, buttoned into coats and ties, looking pale-faced and shell-shocked and tearful. The whole town was there, and I sat in the front pew with Mom and Paul and my grandparents. My sisters sat across the aisle with Francine as if it were a wedding, one side bride, one side groom. And all the places I hadn't belonged had nothing on that moment— me sitting in the front row, supposedly a star mourner, when all I wanted to do was spare everyone the miserable, guilty sight of me. I would rather have stood before a firing squad than in front of the entire town, acting as if I had any right to even grieve.

The night I left I carried a backpack with the knife, the Vicodin, and a bottle of Paul's red wine. I chose the one that looked cheapest. I just wanted to make it possible, what I had to do. I locked the dog door and closed the kitchen door carefully behind me, pushing Carlo's nose back inside, sliding my arm through the barest crack so he couldn't wriggle through and follow me. In the rearview mirror I watched the windows to see if any lights came on, but none did. I was safe, driving out of Rabbitbrush, down the highway toward Ouray, and Alta—the abandoned mining town. I don't know why I chose Alta except that the place always seemed so rife with ghosts. When I finally arrived, I sat for the longest time in my car, which I could drive all the way up to the buildings now that the snow had melted.

I don't know what I expected. Maybe I thought I'd be able to see those ghosts, the people who used to live there, going about their business. The miners' wives would stop to chat with each other as they hauled water or chased children. Maybe I'd see the whole community, all of them, walking to the large common building for a town meeting. Maybe some of them would be wearing headlamps, shining toward me through midnight, letting me know what I could expect, just around the corner.

I didn't know what to look for. I'd never seen a ghost before.

For hours I sat there, seeing nothing but the night, the moving trees, the falling-down buildings. Darkness masked all the years of graffiti by hikers and skiers and tourists, but the town didn't look any more inhabited than usual, or anything more like its former self. Like Luke, Alta wasn't in Alta anymore. Everything that mattered had gone.

I took a sip of the wine, wincing. I had never developed a taste for alcohol, especially since my one experience had ended so badly. Tonight I drank for purely medicinal reasons. After the first few sips it tasted fine, warming. My head began to spin a little, but the hole in my heart still gaped open.

Wisps of light rolled over the horizon, this mountaintop one of the first spots touched by sunrise. The gas gauge read almost empty. I turned off the car. I opened up the Vicodin bottle and swallowed the five pills one by one, sipping the wine to wash them down. I knew the combination wasn't enough to kill me. I only wanted to block the pain so that nothing would prevent me from doing what needed to be done.

I left the half-drunk bottle of wine on the road beside the car. I carried my pack, though I only needed one thing inside it. I chose the closest building, a family cabin probably, the old fireplace in its center ground down to nothing but a pile of bricks, the staircase crumbling, leading up to nowhere.

I had learned from the Internet that slicing vertically works best. Every single resident of Rabbitbrush knows what happened next. There's barely any point in telling. How my strong young heart worked overtime, pumping more blood to compensate for the loss. I couldn't stop it from doing so; I had passed out. I had forgotten to tell my body that I had no more use for properly functioning organs.

Still, my plan would have worked. My mother didn't find the note inside the bread box until after I'd been brought to the hospital. Even if she had found it, chances are slim they'd have figured out in time where I'd gone. Naive method or not, I severed an artery. The blood was flowing, I lost consciousness, I was on my way out. But a park ranger decided to have his breakfast at Alta, sitting in his truck, watching the sun rise and the ghosts evaporate. He saw my car and the wine bottle beside it and set out searching. He found what should have been my body but was still me, and he ripped apart his own shirt to stop the blood.

Life assaulted me by continuing. Instead of oblivion and possibly Luke, I got a blur of sirens and white coats and two days in the state mental hospital, followed by four weeks in the private one paid for by Paul. At the time I thought he'd spend any amount of money just to have me gone an extra month. Now I realize my lack of gratitude, considering. And all I can say is I'm sorry, truly sorry, for all the expense and worry, all the pain and grief that I caused, beginning with killing Luke and ending with trying to kill myself.

I understand, believe me, all the ways I need to atone. But in the meantime I am grateful for the one thing that persists, my last acceptable solace—which is Luke and me, together again. I will take that in any shape I can, however limited or brief or fleeting. Please believe me when I say that I regret everything. And still I would do whatever I needed, anything in the world: to bring him back to me.

part three

getting through the after

(16)

TRESSA

Luke stays away. He stays away well into early December, while my mother grows so large that she has to walk with her legs waddled wide apart, as if she's balancing a bowling ball between her thighs. I'm in a fog the last weeks of winter term. At night I lean out my window and trace messages in the snow. Sometimes I write, *I love you*. Sometimes I write, *Come back*. Sometimes I write, *Goddamn it, Luke*, or *Where the hell are you?* The snow sifts inside, piling up beneath the window. My mother wonders why the floorboards have started to buckle.

School lets out. The snow falls and falls, and still Luke doesn't come. I send in the last of my new college applications to Stanford and Colorado College. I use the same essay I wrote last year, about my years of wandering and how they affected my character and what I learned about the world and myself. Blah, blah, blah. I do not consider for the barest second writing a new one about everything that's happened since last May.

My grandfather brings us a Christmas tree cut from his Western hill. He will not look at Paul when he delivers it. He barely even looks at my mother. He offers me ukulele lessons again, and I hate saying "No, thank you," because he looks so disappointed. My sisters— our sisters—come home mid-December and plan to stay a full three weeks because the baby is due. My mother goes into labor a few days after they arrive. Paul and she go to the hospital together while Jill, Katie, and I wait at home by the phone. We get a call around midnight.

I have dozed off on the couch. Katie crosses the living room and picks up the phone in the kitchen. I hear her voice, matter-of-fact and not particularly celebratory. Jill listens along with me, a few feet away in the red velvet armchair. The twins both have blond hair, like our mother, and her same pale blue eyes. Jill is built on a thicker scale than Mom, more like our grandmother, with broad shoulders and strong legs; Katie was like this originally, but since moving to LA she has lost the twenty pounds her agent demanded and looks unnaturally thin. They both wear their hair long, but contrary to what you might expect, Jill's always looks perfect—combed and loose and glossy—whereas Katie usually pulls hers back in a ponytail or messy bun. Katie would never admit that the desire to be a movie actor is a piece of wildness inherited from Mom. I wonder what she looks like in the horror movies she won't let us watch. I've never seen her with the barest stitch of makeup.

Jill and I listen to Katie's low voice until she replaces the phone onto the receiver with a gentle click. She comes back into the room. She wears checked flannel pajamas and looks much younger than twenty-four.

"Hannah is fine," Katie says. Neither of the twins ever call her Mom. "Everything's fine. They ended up doing a C-section, but that was pretty much expected because of her age. It went well. The baby is fine."

"What is it?" Jill asks.

"A boy," Katie says. "A healthy baby boy. Seven pounds." I nod, surprised by the relief I feel. It hadn't hit me, not consciously, the worry that something would go wrong, until I hear that everything has gone right.

"Why do they always tell you the weight?" Jill says.

"Because," Katie says, "if the kid only weighed two pounds, that would be bad news. But seven pounds, that means he's okay."

"What did they name him?" I ask.

Katie crosses the room and sits down on the couch with me. "His name is Matthew," she says.

Jill stands up and walks over to the window. She peers into the darkness and taps on a pane. For a strange moment I think maybe she sees Luke and is trying to get his attention. But then she says, in a flat voice, "Dad loves those apostles."

Katie and I look at each other. She puts a hand on my knee. "Well," she says. "We have a brother again. I guess we can all go to bed now."

Climbing the stairs behind my sisters, I concentrate on how happy my mother must be. Finally, a boy. I wonder if Paul feels scared, or grateful, or both—at everything he has to do over again, and hopefully get right this time.

In my room something about the air has changed—it feels like a barrier has constructed itself around the walls, the window. This new being in the world, this new sort-of brother. I sit on my bed and remind myself that this baby was planned—conceived even, implanted—before Luke's death. He was never meant to replace him. Now I can only hope he won't prevent Luke from coming back.

I hear footsteps on the stairs, one of the twins. Before the knock I already know it's Jill, who moves much more assertively than Katie. She doesn't wait for me to answer her knock before she cracks the door and pokes in her head.

"Tressa?" she says. "Are you all right?"

I grab a pillow and hug it to my chest, realizing as I speak that the gesture may seem to contradict my words. "Fine," I say. "I'm happy for Mom."

Jill crosses the room and sits at the foot of my bed. She says, "I'm happy for her too. I want to be, anyway. The whole thing still feels so surreal." She scratches her nose with the back of her hand, three or four brisk rubs. Then she flattens her hand on my quilt, Francine's old quilt. I wonder if Jill recognizes it.

"I guess I keep waiting for it not to be hard," Jill says. "Hard to think of having a little brother that's not Luke. Hard to believe she'll take care of a kid this time. Which of course I want her to do, but then I think, if she does, then why couldn't she do that for Katie and me? And for you."

This last is just a polite attempt to include me. But I say, "I know what you mean. It's a little weird. The milk-and-cookies mom."

"Or even a mom at all." Jill has every right to feel the way she does. But I don't want to betray Mom—who is *Mom* to me—by agreeing with her.

"Anyway," she goes on. "It's very weird. The whole thing. On so many levels. I keep wondering what Luke would say." She raises her chin and stares at me with clear, faintly challenging eyes, then moves her gaze back to the quilt, picking at a loose thread. "You know," she says. "I know Katie and I weren't here for you and Luke. I feel bad that I never said anything to Dad, to try to help you two out more."

"Oh," I say. I recognize this as a chance to grant what I want most—forgiveness—and jump at the chance.

"Don't worry about that. It wouldn't have done any good anyway."

"Maybe not. Who knows? I guess what I'm trying to say is, I've been thinking about it a lot. It's very hard coming home and having him not here. When I'm in town, I can't stop expecting to see him when I turn corners." She picks harder at the quilt. "I wake up in the morning and I think I should go over to Francine's and see him, and then I remember. I feel sad all the time about him being gone, and at the same time I keep forgetting he's gone. You know?"

I lean forward and put my hand over hers. She looks down at our two hands and says, "I have to admit something to you, Tressa." I hold my breath, slightly scared of whatever she'll say. "It wasn't just laziness or distance that kept me from helping you two. The truth is, I never wanted you together, partly because it was weird—my sister and my brother. But the other part . . . it wasn't that I agreed with them, that Luke would corrupt you. Honestly I didn't even care if he did, because what would it amount to? A couple of beers? Lost virginity? Big whoop, right? But still I just thought it would be for the best if you weren't together, because I felt sure you would break his heart."

This idea is so bizarre, so apart from anything that ever could have happened, that all I can do is point to my chest. "Me?" I say, as if she could mean anyone else. "Break Luke's heart?"

Jill nods. "I guess, in my own weird way, even though it wasn't your fault, I always thought of you as running away. I saw myself in Luke. That's what I realize now. I saw myself in Luke, and Hannah in you, and I thought you'd do to him what she always did to me."

"Jill," I say, my voice a little twisted, a little hoarse. "That never would have happened. Not in a million years."

She smiles sadly. "But we'll never know," she says. Tears have started streaming down her face.

"*I* know," I whisper. "I would never have left him. I promise you, Jill. I would never, ever have run away. Not from Luke. Not ever."

Jill wipes the flat of her palm over each eye. I try to imagine my sister's daily life. She lives in Denver and works taking care of plants in large office buildings. Such a loving job, tending and nurturing, but also solitary. It probably gives her way too much time to think about these past months and what they've done to our weird and fractured family.

She flops down on her side, lying across the foot of my bed. I pull my feet away and cross my legs. Jill lies there for a long time, the two of us looking at each other, until her eyelids start to droop, and her breathing slows. I watch her sleep, light freckles dusting the bridge of her nose, fairy-princess hair spread out across the bed. Asleep, she looks more adult than she did awake—less restful than worried, drained. Another wounded one of us.

Part of me feels disappointed that she's fallen asleep there, knowing that her presence will keep Luke away for yet another night. Another part of me hopes even more strongly—if it's possible—that Luke *will* come. I imagine myself waking Jill. *Look who's here*, I would say. And then I could sit back, giving them room, watching the joyful reunion.

The next day, when my sisters and I walk into Mom's hospital room, she's sitting up in bed, alone, her head turned and gazing out the window. Paul's not here, and neither is the baby. I can hear squalling from the nursery, and from adjacent rooms, but in here feels like a little bubble of quiet.

"Hannah," Jill says when Mom doesn't turn to look at us.

She snaps her head in our direction, as if we've startled or woken her. Her hair is pulled back, and even though she looks tired, the harsh lights don't seem to be doing much damage. Instead of a hospital gown she wears a lavender nightgown that I've never seen before, with a high, ruffled collar. She looks pretty. I walk over and give her a hug, then climb onto the bed next to her. "Hi, girls," she says to the twins, once I've settled in.

"Where's Matthew?" Katie says. The two of them still stand just past the threshold of the room.

"He's in the nursery," Mom says. "I wanted to rest. Your father went down to get the paper and some coffee."

"We're going to go see the baby," Jill says. She grabs hold of Katie's elbow, pulling her toward the door.

"Sure," Mom says. "You can bring him back here, if you want."

"I doubt they just hand babies to anyone who asks," Jill says.

"Oh, right. Well, tell the nurse she can bring him here, if she has time."

When they've left the room, Mom puts her arm around my shoulders. "I'm glad to see you," she says. "I was worried about you."

"Worried about me," I say. "Can you please be the one who gets worried about? Just this once? With the whole baby-operation thing?"

She smiles and leans her head back on the pillow. "What's he like?" I ask.

"He's very small," she says, and sighs a little. Then, by way of apology, "I'm really tired, Tressa. And taking painkillers. I'm not myself."

"You're fine, Mom. Don't worry."

A nurse who looks exactly like Meryl Streep comes into the room, carrying a squirming bundle. Jill and Katie trail in behind her, followed by Paul. The nurse leans over the bed, about to land the baby in Mom's arms. "Give him to Tressa," my mother says.

The nurse halts in midair. "He'll want to eat," she says, slightly scolding.

"In a minute," Mom promises. "Let his sister hold him."

I glance apologetically at Katie and Jill as the nurse matches the numbers on the baby's bracelet to one that Mom's wearing. Then she lowers the baby into my arms. She's so used to doing this for novices that she doesn't need to give me instructions, just mimics how I should cradle him—his head supported by the crook of my elbow—as she lowers him down.

And suddenly I'm holding this squirming being. He wears a little blue skullcap, and his eyes are a murky gray color. As his mouth opens and closes, he makes weird bird noises—a cross between gulping and chirping. He looks red and scrunched and tiny and strangely perfect. I reach down to touch his tiny hand—fingernails!—and he closes his fist around my finger.

"Wow," I say. "Look at you."

Paul settles into a chair next to the bed, a paper coffee cup in one hand and the newspaper across his lap. The baby opens his mouth and starts wailing, the most insistent sound I have ever heard. Mom reaches for him, and for a moment I resist her taking him from me. Then I hand him over. I guess there must be some kind of flap in her nightgown, because in a second she's nursing the baby without unbuttoning it. Somewhere in the process his cap has fallen off, and I reach across Mom's body to touch the top of his head. It feels unbelievably tender, downy.

"Now, Tressa," Jill says with a laugh, from where she and Katie still stand, in the doorway. "You have to promise not to date this one."

I can hear an intake of sharp breath from both Mom and Paul, but I take it as I know Jill meant it, as a joke, and I laugh too. So does Katie.

How weird, and surprising—new life. I'm glad I got onto the bed with Mom, because I hadn't been at all prepared. For this feeling flooding me, from the tips of my toes to the top of my head.

"I promise," I say, letting my hand rest on the baby's stomach. It covers his whole tiny self. "But I do love you," I tell my new brother. "I really do."

Days pass. Mom and Matthew come home. The house becomes so full that it's teeming, brimming. Filled with bustling, exhausted life—the constant sound track of that baby. The distracted air Mom had in the hospital seems to have vanished. She carries Matthew with her everywhere, she sleeps with him on her chest, she is up at all hours tending him. I would have expected to feel relieved that her attention has finally been diverted from me, or maybe even a little jealous, but I don't feel either, not exactly. A couple times a day I manage to wrest Matthew away, usually once he's fully fed. I find a place to sit down with him in my lap, and I stare at his little face. Every once in a while he does this startled movement, both fists pumping into the air above his head. When he yawns, he looks like a baby hamster. I love the way the top of his head smells. "You're the best pet I ever had," I tell him, and immediately

I'm floored, realizing that I've forgotten Carlo for a full minute.

Maybe that's why he and Luke stay away; they sense the pressure, from everywhere, to make us all move on. Sometimes at night when the baby wakes, when I hear the crying from downstairs, I walk to the window. I've given up on my messages, but I stare out across the snow. I know I won't see him, standing in the moonlight. I know he won't be moving behind that tree, or within that shadow. But still I look. I feel mournful and lonesome, but not desperate the way I did last spring. Think of that baby. Miracles occur. Luke will return. It's only a matter of when.

Come tonight, I beg through the window. *Come now. Come soon.*

The snow on the sill sits, pure, untouched, and silent.

One morning after New Year's, not long before school begins again, I look in the bathroom mirror and am amazed to see what looks like my old self. My face has lost most of the pale puffiness that marked me as a recovering mental patient. My collarbones have returned, along with my cheekbones. The skipped meals and late-night roaming are returning me to my former size, but it's more than that. Against all odds I've started to look like me again.

I put on a robe over my nightgown and go downstairs. Jill has gone back to Denver, but Katie doesn't seem in any hurry to get back to LA. She and Paul sit at the kitchen table drinking coffee. Matthew sleeps in a little chair in the middle of the table. He wears a one-piece pajama set and a striped cap. My mother is nowhere to be seen, asleep I suppose, and I know it's only a matter of moments before this calm is shattered by his waking and crying for her.

"Good morning," Paul says, unnaturally bright. He always makes an effort to be nice to me in front of the twins. *Look!* he's saying to his daughters. *I have taken in my true love's troubled child! I consider her my own! I show her daily kindness, welcoming her into my kitchen!*

"Hey," I say, heading straight for the coffee.

"We were just talking about you," Paul perseveres. I open the refrigerator and hunt for the half-and-half, bracing myself.

"Here," Katie says. She picks up the small carton of cream, which sits on the table between her and the baby. I walk over, sit down, join them. Before pouring the cream, I reach out and touch Matthew's little toes through his footie pajamas.

"Don't wake him," Paul says, then tries to make up for the sharpness in his tone by smiling a little too kindly. Katie pours the half-and-half for me, and then my new brother betrays me by waking up and proving Paul's point. He doesn't cry, though, just makes a little cooing noise. His eyes roam the room thoughtfully, trying to focus.

"It's funny," I say. "He doesn't look like any of you."

Katie and Paul both lean forward to examine the baby. Paul frowns a little. I think that for all his robust and persistent handsomeness, he does not have particularly strong genes. The twins look like my mom. Luke looks like Francine. And this baby must look like the egg donor. Paul reaches out and touches Matthew's hand. The baby closes his little fist around Paul's finger, as if to make up for my callous observation.

"Tressa," Katie says. "What Dad and I were talking about is, I've decided not to go back to California. I mean, I'll have to go back to move. But I'm done with all that."

"You are?" I say. "What about being an actor?"

She pushes her hair out of her face. "I'm done with it," she says again. "Maybe if I'd had any real roles, it would be different. But I've been bludgeoned and strangled and axed and shot. My whole life last year was about nothing but death. I can't take any more violence. I need to think of something else I'd be happy doing."

"You're coming back to Rabbitbrush?"

"No," she says. "I was thinking Boulder. Dad said he'd pay for a place to start while I figure out if I want to go to grad school, or something like that. We were thinking, if I get a two-bedroom, then you could live there too. When you start college."

The two of them watch me, waiting for my reaction. "I can't," I say after a minute. "Freshmen have to live in the dorms."

"We could probably get a waiver for you," Paul says. He doesn't say why.

I don't want to think about this right now, the impossible future. Instead I say to Katie, "But you always wanted to be an actor."

"Well," she says. "Sometimes 'always' changes. You know?"

I stare into my coffee mug, at the swirling cloud of cream that looks vaguely curdled. *No*, I think to myself. Always never changes. It's always always.

Katie touches my elbow. "It might be fun, Tressa," she says. "We've never really had a chance to live together, you and I. Jill could bring us plants."

She looks soft and intent. I think of all the reasons she has to resent me, and I marvel at her kindness. Still, I don't feel ready to give in. I know the reaction I'll get if I say I might not go to college at all but just stay here in Rabbitbrush. So instead I say, "But I may not end up at Boulder. I applied to a few more places. I might be in Colorado Springs, or California."

Katie and Paul exchange glances, and I wonder if the family has already ruled out these possibilities. "Let's cross that bridge when we get to it," Katie says. "For now just promise me you'll think about living with me, for next year. We could take a weekend and look for a place together, if you wanted."

"Okay," I say, though there's no way I would leave even for a weekend in Boulder. Later on, a way out of this will present itself. For now Paul and Katie sit back in their chairs, exhaling with an air of accomplishment. Matthew starts crying, but Mom—newly psychic— swoops into the kitchen before anyone can reach for him. She picks him up and cradles him for a moment, rocking him back and forth, cooing at him with a face of such total absorption that the rest of us could easily vanish, disappear, and she wouldn't notice. And I have this weird realization, that even if I'd succeeded in dying at Alta last spring, this scene would still be playing out exactly the same way. Katie would be sitting here at this table, giving up her career. Paul would be staring at Mom, who'd be rocking her baby. They'd miss me, sure, but life would continue in more or less the same way. Just as it has for them since Luke.

Stop, I want to yell at life sometimes. *Stop continuing!* It doesn't seem right. It doesn't seem respectful.

Matthew keeps crying, his toothless little mouth gaping wide. And I think how I bear the exact same relationship to this baby as I did to Luke. Matthew is Paul's biological son, my sisters' biological brother, but not my biological anything. My brother, but not my brother. It makes me feel strangely left out, not having any real claim to him.

When the phone rings, I startle everyone by jumping up to answer. It's Evie, asking if I want to cross-country ski on the Ethel White trail. "Nobody's been out there since the last snow," she says. "We can break trail."

I hesitate for a moment. My eyes roam around the kitchen, from Paul's face—his fake joviality toward me changing into honest affection toward his son, my mother's disappearance into the baby and motherhood, Katie's concerned gaze fixed on me, coupled with a kind of puzzlement, the kind I'm used to. She doesn't really know me, not at all. How could I possibly leave the place where Luke remains in order to go live with her?

"Sure," I find myself saying to Evie. "I'd love to."

(17)

TRESSA

At the beginning of the Ethel White trail a sign reads WARNING. YOU ARE IN A MOUNTAIN LION'S HOME. The sign tells us to travel in groups. It says not to approach the mountain lion (as if we would) or to run away from it. STAY CALM IF YOU COME UPON A LION. TALK TO IT IN A FIRM VOICE IN AN EFFORT TO DEMONSTRATE THAT YOU ARE HUMAN AND NOT ITS REGULAR PREY.

Evie must have seen this sign and others like it a thousand times. But while I take my skis out of my mother's car, line them up, and step into them, Evie reads it carefully, her brow furrowed in concentration as if memorizing the words.

I glide to the opening of the trail to wait for her. She adjusts her hat and casts an apologetic glance. "My mom always said I was just the right size for a cougar attack," she says. "She used to worry about it all the time, even though she skied here too."

I nod. I wonder if now would be a good time to tell Evie that I'm sorry about her mom, but I worry that too much time has gone by, and honestly I can't bear for the topic to segue into her dad. The last few weeks of school, the books on Evie's lunch tray all revolved around Sylvia Plath and Ted Hughes. I understand the impulse to explore what frightens you most—keeping it right there, always by your side, so it can never take you by surprise. Every time I see a new book on Evie's tray, I order it for myself. While I like sharing this with her, I prefer to do it secretly, knowing it myself but never discussing it.

I try again to remember Evie's mom, if she seemed like the kind of woman who worried about cougar attacks. In the old days my own mother never would have worried about such a thing, but now—since I managed to awaken every dormant shred of mother-worry—of course she would, or at least she would if she had time to think about it.

"Ready?" Evie says.

"Sure." I stand aside and let her go ahead. The trail has already been broken, but the snow is perfect—deep and powdery with a thick, crackling crust on top. We make our way uphill in silence.

"I bet you miss your dog on days like this," Evie says after a long while.

"I miss him pretty much all the time," I say. "But he was kind of old for this kind of thing by the time we moved back here. I wouldn't have been able to take him with me."

"I'd really like to get another dog," Evie says. "But I'm going to college next year, and H. J. thinks he'll probably sell the house and travel."

"You used to have a dog?"

"Yeah," she says. "For a little while. A border collie. He died a few years ago. I really miss him."

I wait for her to tell me more. A few years ago, after all—that's when she lost both her parents. Did she lose a dog, too? Another burst of camaraderie explodes in my chest, but Evie says nothing, just glides forward in a steady, graceful rhythm.

"Do you know where you're going to school next year?" I ask her.

"I applied to all the state schools," she says. "Boulder, Durango, Fort Collins. Greeley. We don't have enough funds for me to go out of state, and my grades aren't that great anyway."

"Those are all good schools," I say.

"You still going to Boulder?"

"Maybe," is all I say.

From up ahead we hear voices, no doubt the early birds who beat us to break trail. In a few moments two other skiers, a guy and a girl, whiz down the hill we're about to climb. The guy swooshes neatly to avoid Evie, but the girl doesn't turn in time and crashes just in front of us. I hear her light laughter as Evie bends down and reaches out a hand.

"Oh, thanks," the girl says. Then she says, "Hi, Evie." And she looks up. It's Kelly.

"Hi, Kelly," Evie says. She looks back over her shoulder at me, her face filled with worry.

"Kelly's here," Luke used to say, warning me when we arrived somewhere to see his friends. Not because the sight of her upset me but vice versa—and then of course I *would* get upset, hating that my very presence sent someone else running.

"Hi, Kelly," I say now, bracing myself.

Kelly's companion—the boy I saw her with in the cafeteria—stays still and quiet. So does Evie. I hear a clump of snow fall from a nearby branch, and then another. Kelly and I stand there, searching each other's faces, waiting for the other to react. I wonder if this is how my mom and Francine might feel, facing each other after Paul died.

"Hi, Tressa," Kelly says. Her voice sounds calm. She doesn't run away, or cry. She just stands there, holding her ski poles, looking at me. I think of her cutting. I hope she has stopped, and I wonder what scars she has left over. I wonder if she would feel Luke if he touched her there.

"Well," she says after a bit. "I guess we better go."

"Okay," I say. "Bye."

"Bye." And then she adds, "Bye, Evie. See you later, Tressa."

Kelly and her friend head back down the trail, away from us. *See you later, Tressa.* It's probably what her therapist advised her to do, next time she ran into me. I could just picture the sort of advice Dr. Reisner would give me. *She's just another girl,* he would say. *All you have to do is say hello. And then say good-bye.* Hello, good-bye. The closest you can sometimes get to normal.

Evie and I don't talk much after that. "Are you okay?" she asks once they're out of earshot, and when I just nod, she understands that I don't want to go into it, I don't want to think.

So we ski for many hours, much farther than we'd planned. We ski beyond the trail, through the back of my grandparents' place and into the field that borders Evie's backyard. We stand in the almost-evening, not panting but cold and sweaty at the same time. I can feel every muscle in my body, from my ankles to my collarbones. There's no way I can ski any farther. I may not even be able to walk.

"H. J. can give you a ride back to your car," Evie says, remembering that I left it back at the trailhead.

"He doesn't have to. I can stay at my grandparents' tonight." I realize as I speak that this will require me skiing another half mile, and my heart sinks. As if bolstering myself, I add, "It'll be nice to sleep somewhere quiet for a change."

"Oh, right," Evie says. "The baby. I forgot to say congratulations."

We hear a rattling from a back window and look toward the house. H. J. is banging, beckoning us inside. "Want to come in?" Evie asks. I hesitate a moment. Above our heads the light, pushing toward late afternoon, already dims into dusk. I can see a fire flickering inside their house. Through the window the kitchen looks bright and cozy. We glide around to the front of the house and stick our skis into the snow by the porch steps. H. J. opens the front door before we get there. He wears a thick wool sweater and battered army pants. His hair is tied into a ponytail with a piece of white string.

"That's an interesting look," Evie says as she sidles past him.

"Why, thank you," H. J. says. Then to me, "Poor Evie heaps all the teenage embarrassment that should belong to our parents onto me."

I don't know what to say to this. H. J. moves aside so that I don't have to brush by him.

"You girls have a nice ski?" he asks when I've made it through the door. He follows me into the front hallway.

"Fine," Evie yells, I guess from the kitchen. She has left her snow-crusted coat, scarf, mittens, and hat on a wooden bench in the hallway, and H. J. immediately gathers them up. He hangs her coat in a hall closet and drapes the wet wool items over a metal coatrack by the door. I take off my gear and hang it beside Evie's.

"Come on into the kitchen," he says.

The Burdick house is dark and close and appealingly

messy. The walls smell just as I guessed they would, of wood smoke and exotic spices from H. J.'s cooking experiments. Evie sits at the kitchen table, a thick, wide slab of gnarled wood with benches on either side. A fire crackles in a woodstove in one corner, and a huge cast-iron pot steams on the gas stove, beside an empty skil-let, also steaming. Against one wall stands a battered, cozy-looking couch. H. J. sees me staring at it.

"Evie and I dragged that in here last winter," he said. "In eighteenth- and nineteenth-century houses there was always a couch in the kitchen. They spent so much time in here. We decided it seemed like a good idea."

At the moment it strikes me as such a good idea that I sink right down into it. The springs let out a little whoosh, like a welcoming but slightly put-upon sigh. I think I'd like to draw a map of this kitchen, and I decide to do exactly that when I get home. I can give it to Evie as a present.

H. J. starts to lay thick slices of bacon into the cast-iron skillet. They sizzle on contact.

"I'm making BLTs and tomato soup," he says.

"Like I told you," Evie says. "He's very into soup."

"It's winter," says H. J. "What's better than soup in winter?"

"Nothing," I have to admit.

"Well," he says. "There is one thing. Mulled wine. I've had a hankering lately for mulled wine. Will you come back tomorrow, Tressa, and help me make some?"

"Sure," I say, though I have no idea in the world what mulled wine is. The bacon happily sizzling, H. J. picks up a platter of cheese and crackers and offers it to me. I realize in that moment that I'm ravenous from the day skiing.

"How's life with the new baby?" he asks.

"Loud," I say after crunching into a rye-cracker-and-cheddar-cheese sandwich.

"Yeah," he agrees. "I remember that from when this one was born." He points at Evie with his thumb. "I didn't sleep between the age of seven and nine."

"Oh, please," Evie says. "As if you were involved."

"Who needed to be involved? I lived in the same house. You were not a happy infant, take my word."

My eyes roam around the kitchen, looking for a picture of the Burdick family. I try to imagine the house as it should be, inhabited by twice as many people, two of them bona fide adults. The two of them refer so easily to their parents, as if all that grief is in the past. I nod toward a crooked bookshelf, crammed tight with cookbooks and paperback novels.

"Is your palm-reading book in there?" I ask.

"Oh, that," H. J. said. "I've given that up. Moving on to secular humanism now."

I laugh.

"I ran into your sister Katie at the Mercantile this afternoon," H. J. goes on. "I was buying bacon. She seemed surprised that I know you."

"Really? What did you tell her about me?"

"I said that you were friends with my sister. That seemed to make her happy. That you had a friend, I mean."

"My family is always overjoyed at any indication I might be normal," I say.

"Because your brother died?"

"H. J.," Evie moans, her mouth full of crackers and cheese.

"He's not my brother," I say, shifting on the couch.

"Sorry," H. J. amends. "Your boyfriend, I mean."

I know that I should be offended by this flippancy, his making light not only of Luke's death but his relation to me. It's weird, how H. J.'s attitude doesn't infuriate me. It's a refreshing break from almost everybody else's refusal to discuss Luke at all.

"I think it predates that," I tell H. J. "My mother was such a flake, dragging me all over the country, and out of the country."

"You sound bitter," H. J. says. This surprises me. In my head I think of myself as Mom's defender. H. J. turns bacon with dark metal tongs. "Evie," he says, interrupting himself. "Will you slice that bread, please?" A loaf of homemade brown bread stands cooling on the wide table.

"I'm not bitter," I say. The words between us sound like confrontational banter, but I don't feel confrontational at all. I feel euphoric and matter-of-fact, liking that H. J. feels I can take it, these prodding statements of his.

Evie has made no move to slice the bread, so I stand up and walk to the table. I pick up a long serrated knife and start sawing into the loaf. "It's just that my life was very disjointed, very unusual," I try to explain. "And now it's kind of weird that my mom has decided to be all classic and normal just in time for me to grow up and move away."

H. J. covers a dinner plate with paper towels and lays slices of crispy bacon on top of it. "One day," he says, "that baby will grow up and be jealous as hell that he got the mom who went to PTA meetings while you got the mom who sailed around Tortuga."

"It was the Marquesas," I say. H. J. laughs, so I add, "I know I'm lucky in a lot of ways. But sometimes I kind of feel like I missed out on a normal childhood."

"Normal childhoods are overrated." H. J. carries the plate of bacon over to the table, then moves around the kitchen collecting dinner plates, then a head of lettuce from the fridge. Evie has finally started to help, slicing thick red tomatoes.

"This seems like a summery sandwich," she says, as if she hasn't been listening to our conversation at all.

"Praise jet planes and hothouses," H. J. says.

Evie hands him a plate full of the sliced tomatoes and proves she's been listening to us after all. "At least you have a mom," she says, her tone light.

The room falls silent except for the fire, crackling invisibly in the woodstove. The silence isn't awkward, just resonant. H. J. reaches over and touches his fingers to the top of Evie's head. It's a light and thoughtful touch, fond and connecting. Wanting to reach out to her also, I say, "You're right, Evie. I'm lucky. I know I am."

H. J. says, "Speaking of which, why don't you give her a call and let her know where you are? I'll get these sandwiches together."

He points me to the living room. Although I could easily dig my cell phone from my pack, for some reason I obey him and take the old-fashioned route. The Burdick living room is a low space crowded with furniture and dark wood beams overhead. It has a broad fireplace where an untended fire smolders dimly behind a brass fire screen shaped like a fan. I sit down in a red and white easy chair and place my hand on top of the telephone. On the mantel is the family photograph I've been looking for. Their father had brown eyes behind glasses, and hair the walnut color Evie's would be if she didn't dye it black. Their mother was dark-haired and blue-eyed. She had a deep, round cleft in her chin, and looking at her picture, I realize that both H. J. and Evie have that same dimple. Definitely she looks familiar to me, maybe because of memory, maybe because I've been spending time with her children. In the picture the four of them sit on the front porch, Evie little enough to perch on her mother's lap, H. J. around ten or so, with the same far-off, bemused expression he so often wears now. I imagine his mother's relief if she could know that these last few years have not erased that quality in him, the ability to find life odd and funny.

Here in this house I sense a kind of peace with grief that I can't imagine ever making myself. And then, out of nowhere, it hits me. They are my friends. H. J. and Evie. They like me, and I like them. I have managed to make friends, two of them, all on my own.

I pick up the phone and dial home. I know the house will be in disarray as Mom harkens to the endless cries of the baby. Absorbing and consuming though this may be, all the while she tends Matthew she will have one eye on the clock, thinking about where I might be. I know that whatever she's doing, when the phone rings, she will find a way to get to it before the machine picks up—as long as there's any chance that it might be me.

(18)

LUKE

I won't go away.

It should be easier with Carlo around. Less lonely. But he's starting to make me feel like maybe I shouldn't be here. The dog gets super happy when he sees Tressa but when we're not with her I can tell he wants to leave. Sometimes out of nowhere he'll just take off the same way he ran after that rabbit. Then he turns around like he wants me to come with him. He'll do that crouching thing dogs do, with his front legs flat and his butt way up in the air. Then he runs in the other direction, stops short, and looks back at me. Like he's waiting. I know he wants me to follow him but I can't. Tressa needs me.

I know she needs me, even though lately I can't seem to get to the house. Something's changed over there.

Carlo and I walk to the edge of my dad's property. We circle through the woods. Sometimes I can hear Tressa's voice. "Come back to me." But I can't get to her. The only thing I *can* do is stand in the woods with my hands in my pockets and stare at her window.

Carlo nips at my pants leg and I push him away. Dogs are supposed to be loyal. Especially this dog. I can't see why he'd want to leave. He must know how she's wanting us to stay.

Carlo and I walk past Silver Lake. We head up Arapahoe Road. In some houses I can see lights on. Every now and then a car drives by. I recognize Mr. Zack's truck and for a second I get this picture in my head of him pulling over and stopping. *Kingsbury,* he'd say. *What are you doing out here so late?* Half the people who drive by are people I've known my whole life. But nobody sees me so nobody stops.

Before I know it I'm on my way to the Earnshaws'. It happens this way a lot. I don't have to walk, I just picture the place and suddenly I'm there, standing in front of the house. It won't snow tonight; the sky's too clear. I touch Carlo's head. We look up, toward this other window of Tressa's.

I can feel her wake up. Even though I can't see her I know when her eyes open, and when she pushes off the blankets. She walks over to the window, slides it open, and leans out. When she sees us she smiles. Then she waves and closes the window.

I walk around to the front porch. Carlo and I climb the five steps and I sit down on the porch swing. I don't bother sweeping off the snow. Tressa opens the front door. She's got a down comforter over her shoulders and her grandpa's guitar in one hand. She's wearing sweatpants and sheepskin slippers. I brush the swing off next to me, clearing a spot for her. She can still feel the cold even if I can't.

She walks over and hands me the guitar. Carlo thumps his tail, and she scratches his ears and kisses the top of his head. Then she sits down next to me. I haven't held a guitar in a long time, and I strum one chord, then another. Before I know it, I'm playing a Neil Young song, "Four Strong Winds," and Tressa starts singing. I do what I always do when Tressa sings. I start in myself to drown her out. "Four strong winds that blow lonely, seven seas that run high. All the things that don't change come what may."

I could go on singing like this for days, but by the time we finish the song Tressa's shivering. So I put the guitar on the ground and wrap the down comforter around both of us. I can feel the blanket but not Tressa. I think of how it used to be different, back when I could feel her. How crazy it drove me sometimes. It makes me almost like it this way, without the whole physical thing to distract me.

"I wonder if we woke your grandparents up."

"I wish they would wake up. They could come out-side, and everyone could sit around listening to us sing." She puts her hand in my lap, and I close my hand around her wrist. "Hey," she says. "You've been gone awhile." I close my hand a little tighter. "I missed you," Tressa says. She touches my peace sign. I wonder if she can feel the metal.

"I always miss you," I say. She moves a little closer and puts her head on my shoulder. I wish I could feel her hair on my chin. We sit there, kicking the swing back and forth.

After a while, she says. "Do you remember the Burdicks?"

"Sure," I say. "H. J. and Evie. Known them my whole life." Tressa doesn't flinch when I say "life," but as soon as it's out of my mouth, I wish I hadn't said it.

"I remember their mother died of breast cancer," she says carefully. "And then their dad—"

"Yeah," I interrupt. Not sure why, but I don't want to talk about this. I don't want anyone to say the word. It took me so long to get here. I don't want to have to leave.

Tressa doesn't look at me. We swing back and forth a few times more. And then she says, "How did he do it?"

It takes me a minute to remember. "Their mother went really fast," I say. "It seemed like one day we heard she was sick, and the next day there was the funeral."

"Did you go?"

"No. But Mom did, and so did your grandparents."

"Then what happened?" Tressa asks.

I think for a second, trying to remember. "It was

about a year before you came back," I say. "Mrs. Burdick had been gone a few months, and everyone said Mr. Burdick was taking it really hard. One night he went out drinking in Telluride, and on the way home, where he should have turned, he just kept driving. He drove straight into that rock wall. The whole car exploded."

Tressa takes her head off my shoulder. She's not smiling anymore. I shouldn't have told her this story. She says, "He didn't have a dog with him, did he?"

"He did, actually. Now that you say that I remember he did. It was some kind of shepherd. I think it went through the windshield."

"Dogs don't wear seat belts," Tressa says quietly.

"It was sad." A major understatement.

Tressa says something, but I can't make out her words. I watch her for as long as I can stand it, but then I have to close my eyes. I wish she'd remember I can't talk about now. For a minute there it felt so normal.

Then she says something I understand. "You'd think there would be lots of ghosts."

"What do you mean?"

"You'd think," Tressa says, "that you would run into other ghosts. That Mr. Burdick would be walking around here with Evie's dog. You'd think you might run into each other now and then."

"Ghosts," I say. "Is that what you think I am?"

"No," she says. "I never think that. Isn't it odd?"

I kiss her wrist on the spot where she can feel it, but

I can't shake the feeling that that's how she thinks of me. Like a ghost. I pull back a little and the blanket falls off my shoulders. Tressa doesn't reach out to fix it but closes it around herself. Why not? What do I need with any blanket? I'm a ghost. I don't get cold.

Outside, toward the woods, the wind picks up. We look over at the swirl of snow. Carlo stands. I don't hear a jingle, and for the first time I notice that his collar and tags are gone. He trots to the stairs. Down on the snow he stops and waits for me.

"Don't go," Tressa says. "I love you so much."

I want to say *I love you, too*. But I can't, my meter's run out of time. I can't say anything else. I stand and walk across the porch, catch up with the dog. We walk away, into the night. I can't look back but I know that Tressa gets off the swing and walks to the edge of the porch. She holds the blanket around herself with one hand and rests the other one on the rail. I may be heading in the opposite direction but I can feel how much she loves me, and I know for sure I'll be coming back.

(19)

TRESSA

School doesn't start for another week, but Mr. Tynan, my English teacher, has agreed to meet me at the Rabbit-brush Café. I'm repeating his class this year because I like him so much, and he has rotated books so that I won't get too bored. But next semester he needs to concentrate on Shakespeare, plays he covered last year, so we've decided to figure out an alternate, independent study for me. I'm sure Mr. Tynan will feel relieved not to have me in class. All year he has pointedly avoided tragic books; it can't be easy to teach literature when you have to pretend life is cheerful.

The morning after soup and BLTs with H. J. and Evie—the morning after Luke tells me about their father—Grandpa has already left when I wake up. Grandma drives me to the trailhead where I left my mom's Lexus.

Lately, with my mother essentially housebound, the car belongs to me. I turn the key and let it warm up a little. It's a ridiculously luxurious vehicle, with a GPS screen that shows what's behind me when I back out. The seats have a musky lavender scent. It's my mom's scent, and I like the way it predates Paul's taming her. It dominates the spiffy leather interior, and I remember my mom from the old days, her restlessness and her tendency toward nervous, exuberant laughter. I remember all the ratty, rattly cars she's owned, scented with just this same personal perfume. I wonder if it's weird for her, cooped up in the house with a baby—the same house she fled more than two decades ago. I make a mental note to call her after I meet with Mr. Tynan, to see if she needs anything from civilization.

The day is increasingly bright. Downtown I pull into a parking space. The winter tableau of Rabbitbrush is fairly deserted. The main street gets plowed daily, but few cars make their way down the pristine pavement. Paul likes to say that dogs used to be able to sleep in the middle of Main Street, as if he's trying to illustrate how much things have changed. But the truth is, a dog could still have a fairly good nap, as long as the occasional car was willing to maneuver around it.

Inside the café a few scattered customers sit eating eggs and drinking coffee. A quick scan of the place tells me each of the ten or so customers is a local, including my stepfather and grandfather, in heated discussion at a corner table. I wave to Mr. Tynan, who is already waiting for me on the other side of the room, then go over to say hi to Grandpa and Paul. I can't exactly ignore them, even if they didn't seem to notice me walk in.

When Grandpa sees me approaching, he rearranges his face into a smile and stands up. He's so tall that he has to bend at the waist to kiss me. "Tressa," he says. "My girl. What are you doing here? Did you sleep well?"

I nod and then say, "Hi, Paul." He hasn't bothered to rearrange his consternation and looks up at me, still scowling. Grandpa and he must be arguing about that stupid drive-in movie theater.

"Hi, Tressa," Paul says. "What are you doing here? Are you all right?"

I wonder if everyone will always ask me this last question. My mother says that any time she phones her parents, the first thing they say is, "Where are you?" If I can't blame them for that, I guess I also can't blame anyone for that inevitable query directed at me.

"I'm fine," I say. "I'm meeting with my English teacher to talk about a project for next term."

Paul turns and looks across the room as if he needs to confirm my story. Being a former English teacher himself, Grandpa approves of this appointment. He pats my arm and says, "Good girl." Then he reaches into his pocket and pulls out his wallet.

"No, no," Paul says, also reaching for his wallet. "I'll get it."

"I have money," I tell them.

"Nonsense," Grandpa says to me, gently, and then not so gently he snaps at Paul: "Put it away," he says. "I'll pay for her breakfast."

Paul obediently puts his hand back on his coffee mug, and despite myself I feel sorry for him. Grandpa is a formidable opponent. He hands me two twenties, which at the Rabbitbrush Café is enough money to buy breakfast for me and five other people. I know the excess is partly due to generosity—he wants me over-loved, overfed—and partly to make a point to Paul. *We don't need your money*, the "we" referring not only to us, the Earnshaws—including my mother—but also to Rabbitbrush itself, the town whose land has enabled the son of ranchers, an English teacher, to spontaneously bestow green upon his youngest granddaughter.

"Thanks," I say to Grandpa. "I better not keep Mr. Tynan waiting."

Grandpa smiles at me. He doesn't sit back down but stands watching me as I cross the restaurant. When I reach Mr. Tynan's table, I wave at Grandpa. He waves back, then takes his seat. Typically, he never takes his eyes off me until he knows I'm settled, just like when he drops me off at Paul's, waiting in the car until he knows I've made it safely inside.

"Hi, Tressa," Mr. Tynan says. "How's your family?"

"Fine," I say. "My mom just had a baby boy. His name is Matthew."

"Yes, I heard," he says. "Congratulations."

"Thanks. It's funny how everyone says that to me. It's not like I did anything."

Mr. Tynan smiles. He's younger than Paul and Mom by about ten years, and he's not from Rabbitbrush originally. He says, "They're congratulating you because babies bring happiness."

I think of Matthew's scrunched little face, and his tiny fists flying up above his head. The other day I went with my mother to the pediatrician and saw another newborn do exactly the same thing, raise his arms up over his head in a startled jerk. It turns out that's called the Moro reflex. It bothered me to find out that all babies do this—the gesture had seemed so particularly Matthew's, his own little expression of gusto and surprise.

The waitress comes to the table. She graduated from Rabbitbrush High the same year as my sisters, so of course she has to ask how they are before she fills my coffee cup and takes my order for oatmeal and fresh fruit. When she heads back toward the kitchen with my ticket, Mr. Tynan says, "So have you thought about what you want to focus on for your project?"

"Yes," I say. "I want to write about Sylvia Plath and Assia Wevill. And Ted Hughes, of course."

Mr. Tynan doesn't say anything. We look at each other across the table. He has curly light brown hair, just starting in on its first streaks of gray. He blinks several times, then says, "Tressa. Do you think that's a good idea? Two women who committed suicide?"

The waitress returns with our breakfast. I stare down at my oatmeal and bananas—what passes for fresh fruit in the dead of Colorado winter—wishing it were a plate of greasy fried eggs and over-buttered toast like Mr. Tynan's. He watches my gaze and pushes his plate toward me.

"Here," he says. "Take a slice of bacon."

"No, thanks," I say.

"Come on," he says. "It will show evidence of wanting to live."

"Not if you consider the cholesterol."

He laughs and pulls his plate back toward him. "Touché," he says, and dips a toast tip into the runny egg yolk.

"Look," I say. "I know that I'm supposed to act like I don't even know suicide exists. I know everyone wants me to pretend life is rosy and never-ending. But truthfully, suicide's what I'm thinking about. Not in terms of committing it, but as a student. That's what interests me right now, that's what's on my mind."

Mr. Tynan doesn't look up from his plate. One of the reasons I like him is that he assigns work outside of the standard high school English canon. He doesn't shy away from books chock-full of profanity and sex. In his class last year we read *Written on the Body* by Jeanette Winterson and *Rabbit Redux* by John Updike. He assigns Tom Robbins and Dave Eggers. On the first day of class he always tells us that he doesn't grade on class participation. "I understand what it feels like to be a shy student," he'll say. "And I'm as likely as the rest of you to think, *I wish that asshole would shut up* when someone goes on too long." Mr. Tynan keeps a pair of old, battered couches in the classroom. Whoever gets to class early enough can sit on one of the couches instead of at a desk. He sometimes stops class discussion to play a relevant song on his CD player—anything from Gregorian chants to Lady Gaga.

I thought if anyone in the world would let me write a paper about Sylvia Plath and Assia Wevill, it would be him. So my heart drops in disappointment when he says, "I'm sorry, Tressa. I don't feel good about this."

I stick my spoon into my oatmeal and move it around without lifting it.

"It doesn't seem healthy," Mr. Tynan continues, "to dwell like that. I'd love to see you study something more . . . life affirming."

"Life affirming," I repeat.

He looks up from his eggs. His eyes look darker now. They won't quite rest as he tries to focus his gaze on me, and I recognize guilt in the way they shift. It occurs to me that Mr. Tynan himself would not have a problem with my doing this project. He might even think it's a good idea. But then what if I end up slashing my wrists again? Or what if I swallow a bottle of sleeping pills, and they find me dead on my bed surrounded by copies of *The Bell Jar, Ariel, Birthday Letters,* and *Lover of Unreason*? Mr. Tynan could lose his job.

He's thinking of H. J., I realize. I remember the two of them, standing in the hallway at school, the uncharacteristic sternness on Mr. Tynan's face. And I say out loud, almost before I can stop myself, "Just do it a little bit."

Mr. Tynan blinks again, startled. "What did you say?"

"It wasn't the worst advice in the world," I say, not just out of a renegade impulse to defend H. J., but because I believe it. I take a bite of oatmeal. Mr. Tynan puts down his fork.

"Tressa," he says. "I think you should make an appointment with . . ." He trails off, and I know that he was about to say, out of reflex, *Mrs. Kingsbury.* Instead he picks his fork back up and halfheartedly pokes at his eggs. I slide a piece of bacon off his plate in an attempt to convince him I'm willing to affirm life, even if our only school counselor can't humanely be expected to counsel me.

"Tressa," he says, trying again. "I hope you're still talking to someone. It's so much to go through. I really think you should have ongoing care. Of course it's not my place to say any of that. Or this. I hope you're not spending time with H. J. Burdick."

"Evie is a friend of mine." I say this sentence slowly, enjoying the way the words sound. "A friend of mine."

"Okay," Mr. Tynan says. "That's great. Evie's great. I'm glad. But the thing about cutting a little bit? That *was* bad advice. And I don't want him advising you similarly."

I wonder how H. J. could possibly do this. What would he say? Just kill yourself a little bit? Mr. Tynan looks across the restaurant toward Paul. He and Grandpa lean toward each other across the table. They almost look like a married couple, in the midst of a heated argument they don't want anyone else to hear.

"Look." I try to make my voice sound as calm and self-aware as possible. "The last thing I want to do is alarm anyone. This isn't a cry for help. I just don't want to pretend all that didn't happen, that it doesn't matter. That wouldn't be healthy either, would it?"

"I guess not," Mr. Tynan says, but he doesn't look convinced.

"So will you at least think about it?" I say. "Letting me do this project? I'm going to read the books anyway. It might as well be under your supervision, right?"

"I suppose so," he says. "But, Tressa. I hope you know that everybody—your parents, your teachers. Everybody. We just want what's best for you. We may not always say exactly the right thing, but we're rooting for you. We want you to be well."

"You want me alive," I say.

He smiles, but it's a very wry smile, and his eyes suddenly look damp. "Yes," he says quietly. "We want you alive."

I reach out and touch his hand. "I know," I say.

* * *

My mother doesn't answer her phone, so I head back to my grandparents'. Passing the Burdicks', I slow down, half hoping that Evie or H. J. will run out and wave me inside. I like the thought of being back in that living room. If I brought up their father's death, H. J. would talk to me about it. He wouldn't sugarcoat or pussyfoot. He would answer my questions, straight, no euphemisms or apologies.

Nobody emerges, and I actually stop the car and let it idle in the road for a minute. H. J.'s station wagon is gone. He and Evie must be off somewhere. I have a hard time getting my head around the story Luke told about their father last night. It seems so cruel, to leave two kids when they've just lost their mother. And then on top of that to take the dog along with him. I would never have hurt Carlo, would never have taken *anyone* else along with me. I think of Assia Wevill, who killed her four-year-old daughter when she gassed herself the same way Sylvia Plath did. This act seems so repulsive. No matter how I try, I simply can't connect it with anything I have done, ever.

I feel the same way about Mr. Burdick, but at the same time I also feel a little jealous of him, a little outsmarted. Why didn't I think of that, driving my car head-on into a stone wall? I remember something another patient at the hospital said, a boy who'd swallowed a bottle of Valium. He told me that wrist-slashing was a naive method of suicide. It hardly ever worked because it had to be done so precisely. "Next time you should hang yourself," he told me. "Do it right, and *SNAP*—there's no time for intervention. That's what I'm going to do."

It's not like hanging never occurred to me; it just seemed too heavy-handed, so blatantly an execution. Whereas Mr. Burdick was clever, original—engulfed in flames, instant escape, instant death, no window of time for park rangers and EMTs. For rescue.

When I get to my grandparents', Grandma and Katie sit across from each other at the kitchen table, holding hands. Katie lifts her face and blinks at me, and I see tears running down her mottled face.

"What's wrong?" I ask.

Katie wipes her face with the back of her sleeve. "Oh, I don't want you to feel bad, Tressa."

"What?" I say, my stomach clenching. "What happened now?"

"It's Francine," Grandma says, her voice an odd mix of sympathy and exasperation.

"What about her?" I say. "Is something wrong?" I hate to think of Francine, alone in that house, without anyone to take care of her. Luke used to heat up soup whenever she had a cold.

"Yeah, yes . . ." Katie pauses, as if unsure about saying the next words, but then goes for it. "She's in agony over Luke. And she won't see me or speak to me. She hasn't been taking my calls, and when I went by the house, she asked me to leave. She said it was too painful. She said we've taken everything she ever had away from her."

Katie starts crying again, and drops her face onto her arms. I look at Grandma, flummoxed. She reaches out and pats Katie's head.

Katie gulps before continuing. "I can see why she'd feel that way about Dad and Hannah. I can even see why she'd feel that way about you, Tressa—I'm sorry, but I can. But what does that have to do with me? Why do I have to lose another mother?"

"I'm sorry," I whisper. "It's all my fault."

Grandma and Katie both turn to look at me. I see that Grandma wants to say that it's not my fault, but she doesn't, waiting instead for Katie. Katie waits a minute and then, instead of contradicting me, wipes her eyes. She says, "H. J. Burdick called a little while ago. He said he invited you over there tonight."

I shuffle my feet, not sure how to respond, and try to imagine the conversation Katie had with H. J. Maybe she had a moment of thinking he was calling for her, and then felt let down. Or maybe Jill's teasing all those years ago was just that—teasing—and Katie never really had any feelings for him.

After a minute I say, "That's true; he did invite me."

"I don't think you should go," Katie says. Something suddenly hardens inside me. I've got my own resentments against my sister, who never supported Luke and me. Once she even called our relationship incestuous. I get the sudden, familiar flash—of my family, working to stand between me and possible happiness.

"Why?" I say, surprised at sounding so defiant when I feel so sincerely contrite about Francine's rejecting her, which really *is* my fault.

"H. J. is a grown man. Who was just fired for impropriety with a high school girl."

"You're making it sound like something different. It's not like he made a pass at her."

"Got the story from the horse's mouth, did you?"

"Girls," Grandma says quietly.

My first impulse, to say that I'm eighteen and that H. J.'s not *that* much older, sounds in my head like the wrong line of defense. So I say to Katie, "It's not like a date, going to the Burdicks'. Mostly I've been hanging out with Evie. She and I are friends."

"We're awfully glad for Tressa to have a friend," Grandma says. Her voice sounds so strained and hopeful.

"Still," Katie says. "I don't feel good about it. If Evie's your friend, why did H. J. call? I want you to call him, Tressa, and tell him you can't go."

I pause for a moment, remembering that cozy, smoke-scented house. Then for some reason I can't name— maybe loyalty, or simple tiredness—I nod. Katie narrows her eyes at the obvious reluctance of that movement.

"Seriously, Tressa," she says, her voice softening.

I think about how everyone wanted me to stay away from Luke. How they discouraged and dissuaded and finally forbade. Katie and Grandma stare at me, and I know they're sharing this odd sort of déjà vu.

"Fine," I say, giving in. "I won't go to the Burdicks'. And I'm sorry about Francine, Katie. I truly am."

"It's not your fault, Tressa," she says, but the words sound tired and weary, a mantra she's had to recite her whole life and never for one second actually meant. Then she stands up and crosses the room. She picks up a brown paper bag from the counter and hands it to me.

"Here," she says. "Before I left, I asked Francine if I could have something of his. She gave me this. I want you to have it."

I peer into the bag and recognize the garment instantly—a black turtleneck sweater that Luke used to wear with jeans when he wanted to dress up. Forgetting that Katie and Grandma are watching me, I stick my head into the bag as if trying to recover from hyperventilating, and breathe in the long-ago scent of sandalwood, snow, Luke.

"Thank you," I tell my sister. "Thank you."

I leave a message on H. J. and Evie's answering machine, saying that I can't come over. When I hang up, I can't help thinking that if I'd been this obedient last May, Luke wouldn't have been at the river.

For a long time I lie awake in my bedroom at my

grandparents', wearing Luke's sweater, staring at the ceiling. I don't change into my nightgown or read a book. I don't do anything but lie here, trying to imagine what the experience of nothingness might be, how total stillness would feel. I might be a tree, or a rock. I would enter a state of permanent semi-dreams, aware of the world around me only in terms of weather, a chill wind, a sideways rain, the hot sun beating down.

I'm not sure what time it is when I hear barking outside. The night has gone completely dark, and it has been a while since I heard Grandpa's and Grandma's quiet movements around the house. I get off my bed and peer out the window without opening it. It takes me a minute to register the dog, my dog, standing down there by himself. At the sight of me his tail wags ferociously, and he barks again.

When I come out the front door, Carlo doesn't run up the steps but barks again, so I go down to him. He trembles with happiness at the sight of me. I sit on the damp, snowy ground and cross my legs. He manages to wind his seventy-five pounds into an awkward circle and rest there in my lap, his head pressed up beneath my chin, just like he used to when we were both alive.

But you are *alive*, says a voice from somewhere, anywhere. Maybe it originates inside my head. Maybe not.

I am alive but Carlo is not. I know this despite how surely I can feel his fur, his warm doggy breath, his damp nose. I know it despite the clear, good smell that clings to him, like the dirt Grandpa tills in his south field, the one flat enough for corn. Carlo's fur contains the scent of each turn my life has taken, every place I've ever drawn a map of. It smells like Rabbitbrush, of course, and also the red clay of New Mexico, and the pineapple saltiness of the South Pacific, and the mulchy, mosquito-filled air of Marin County. Everywhere I've been exists and stands firmly within this dog.

I wind my arms around Carlo and hold him tight, burying my face in his fur and breathing in deep. Somehow I know that he has come to say good-bye. And I understand that I mustn't beg him to stay, even though I can't bear the thought of his leaving. My good, loyal, and obedient dog loved me more than life, and now he loves me more than death. If I asked him to stay, he would listen. Now is my chance to do it over, to make it right—the way I couldn't let him die when he needed to. A cold wind gusts over us, dusting both our heads with snow. As much as I love Carlo, as much as his absence will pain me, I understand that keeping him here would be wrong. It's time to let him go.

"Good-bye, my dog," I whisper. "Good-bye, my friend. Thank you for everything you gave me. I love you."

Carlo jerks his head from beneath my chin and licks my face. Then he gets out of my lap, takes two long lopes away from me. He pauses, quivering, then turns and comes back. He leaps through the air, lands with his paws on my shoulders, and knocks me backward. He licks my face and rubs his head against my chest as if he wants to leave his scent.

I hug him again, holding his body against me. When I let go, he bounds out of my arms. He runs down the hill, toward the river. He looks so happy, and so young. This time he doesn't turn back, he doesn't even turn his head for one last glance. When finally his sylphlike darkness has disappeared forever, and I know he can't hear me, won't ever hear me again, I whisper to him.

"I'll miss you my whole life," I say. Again the wind, cold and wet, mists me with icy, insistent snow. Winter at eight thousand feet.

How can I describe what I feel? Never mind knowing that I've done the right thing. This grief bubbles up inside me, so hot and liquid that I don't dare cry. My ribs feel like they might crack under the pressure, and I climb the porch stairs hobbled over, cramped and desperate.

Back in my room I lie across the bed. Staring at the ceiling as my chest rises and falls, I think of Carlo. I think of Luke, his too-big sweater draping my shoulders. All I want to do is sleep. It seems so unfair, how hard life is, just getting through every day. It's hard enough without these endless good-byes. Every sixteen hours the living have to close our eyes, all night long, just so we can recover.

(20)

LUKE

I'm ten. School just let out for the summer. The Sustantivo River is full of runoff from the mountains and we can hear it all over town. Every day I ride my bike to the Earnshaw's. I pedal up to their door and ask, "Is Tressa here yet?"

"Still no word, young man," Mr. Earnshaw says. "We're hoping to see her too."

To improve my mood I ride home no-handed. At the bottom of the driveway I pedal faster, picking up speed and heading down Arapahoe Road. When I think I'm balanced I lift my hands in the air. The bike starts wobbling. I don't make it a single yard before my body hits the ground.

I try five times, twenty, thirty. I can't do it. It's hot outside. I've been out here on the road for hours but I haven't seen a single car. Maybe the next one that drives up the road will be Hannah and Tressa. I picture Tressa's face looking out the car window. The next thing I know my hands come off the handlebars and the bike stays steady. I'm riding down the hill with my arms out at my sides.

About two weeks later Hannah brings her back. Tressa and I take one of the twins' old bikes from the garage and ride to the top of Arapahoe Road so I can teach her how to ride no-handed. She falls off her bike once, twice, ten times. Finally her knees are bloody and she wants to quit. But I'm not ready to let her just yet. I walk down past the Burdicks' while Tressa walks the bike up to the Earnshaws' driveway. Then I yell to her. "Look at me, Tressa. Think of me!"

The next thing I know she's barreling toward me, her arms outstretched, her bike balanced. She rides no-handed, her hair flying behind her like some crazy, rippling flag.

(21)

TRESSA

I wake to the sound of Matthew crying, and the noise enters my brain before I can open my eyes. When I do open them, I'm surprised to be at my grandparents' house. I pull the covers over my head and recite the names of my family members. Katie Kingsbury. Jill Kingsbury. Now finally, again, after all these years: Hannah Kingsbury. Matthew Kingsbury. I love them all, but I just don't belong over there with the Kingsbury clan. I am an Earnshaw. I want to stay here.

Downstairs I find Grandma walking back and forth in the living room with the wailing baby. Matthew's face is contorted, red, and screaming. He looks like he might explode. My grandmother holds him to her chest, walking with a strange lift in her feet. She bends and rises, chanting, like she's doing the Indian dance from the Peter Pan movie. All her effort does little good. Matthew just cries and cries.

Mom sits on the sofa, drumming her fingers on the armrest. When she sees me, she jumps to her feet. She looks agitated, wide-eyed, but strangely exhilarated. I notice that her stomach has shrunk back to approximately its original dimensions except for a little pouch, like she's back at the beginning of her pregnancy. She looks younger than I've seen her in a long time.

"Tressa," she says. "We got a phone call from your English teacher."

I run my hands over my face, which feels puffy with sleep. Mom and Grandma both stare at my clothes— Luke's black sweater, and jeans stiff with dried snow and dirt from Carlo's and my farewell.

"Tressa," Grandma says, practically shouting over the wailing baby. "Did you sleep in your clothes?"

"After doing some midnight gardening?" Mom adds. She doesn't sound admonishing but energized. I know this look. It indicates a change, an idea. It indicates flight. I've seen it a dozen times. The last time, she had just phoned Paul collect from a rickety phone booth on Nuku Hiva. "I'm coming home," she'd told him. "I'm ready."

"Of course," Paul had said. "I'm here. I'm waiting." We said good-bye to Hugo and Isabelle and came back to Colorado. Paul and Mom were married within months. He wouldn't take any chances—not that a marriage license had helped him hold on to her the first time.

"What did Mr. Tynan say?" I ask, trying to divert attention from the state of my clothes. Apparently he didn't say anything very good, because Mom looks over at Grandma, and they both frown.

"He says he thinks you need to talk to someone," Mom says, "so I've made an appointment with Dr. Reisner. You and I can go to Durango tomorrow and stay in a hotel. We can have dinner at East by Southwest. When's the last time we ate sushi?" She claps her hands as if it's all settled. I cast a glance over at Grandma and Matthew. He finally seems to be calming down. Wails have given way to occasional little blipping sounds, and his funny old-man eyelids have started to droop. Grandma doesn't dare halt her bizarre, rhythmic movement, but she returns my gaze with a measure of alarm.

"I don't see why we have to spend the night," I say. "It's only an hour and a half away. And what about Matthew?"

"Hey," my mom says, her voice strained. "You're still my baby too, you know. I have to take care of you, too, right? Paul can deal with Matthew just fine."

"But, Mom," I say. "He's three weeks old. Do you really think you should leave him overnight?"

"Let me worry about that," Mom says. I feel an old, familiar sinking. In the past I was the only one of three children she ever worried about, and I don't want to become the only one of four. Matthew, over there wailing in Grandma's arms, is supposed to be keeping me company in the mothering section of her brain.

*   *   *

When Mom tells Paul her plan—to leave Matthew with him and go on an overnight to Durango—his face drops. It goes so pale that even I feel sorry for him. Clearly the idea of her loading me into a car and taking off without him, to say nothing of his child, is flatly traumatizing. Which is why the next day finds me, my mother, and Matthew driving together to Durango with plans to return that evening after we attempt sushi. The hotel idea struck me as strange anyway, since it only takes about ninety minutes to get from Rabbitbrush to Durango. However, I start to see the appeal of Mom's original plan when Matthew spends the first sixty minutes or so screaming. If Paul thought that insisting she bring the baby along would ensure her return, he may have been shortsighted. By the time Matthew finally falls asleep, Mom looks like she's been through a war— and she kind of has been, leaning over his backward car seat to nurse him, singing, waving a little cloth face with legs and cloth flaps sprouting out all around it.

Mom crawls back over the seats to sit next to me, her agility impressive for a forty-five-year old woman who has just given birth to her fourth child. She leans her head back and closes her eyes for a minute. Then she says, "All I wanted was one day to myself. Do you think that was too much to ask?"

I keep my eyes on the road. Even though I found the crying ordeal admittedly horrifying, most people would not consider a daughter's suicidal leanings an opportunity for vacation. "Well," she says when it's clear I don't plan to answer. I hear an edge of irritation in her voice. "Do you think it's too much to ask?"

"Sorry," I say, glancing sideways. Her eyes are open now, and she sits with her long legs tucked beneath her. "I thought it was a rhetorical question."

Blowing out a long stream of air, she says, "I guess it was." She glances into the rearview mirror, which is aimed at another mirror on the backseat so that she can see Matthew even though he's pointed away from her. This communication between the glass strikes me as a metaphor for constant vigilance, and suddenly I feel sorry for my mother, who does so famously ill in captivity. It was one thing to be pregnant, playing at perfect motherhood, another to put that perfection into action.

"It's funny," she says. "He doesn't look anything like me."

"Well, Mom," I point out. "Why would he?"

"I know, I know," she says. "It's just got me thinking about babies, about all my babies. I know this is the kind of thing a person's not supposed to talk about, but my whole life everyone's told me I was so pretty. I can't remember a time when people didn't tell me that. And I heard the words, but I never saw it in myself. I used to stare into the mirror, and all I ever saw was this kind of pale, crooked face. I'd walk down the street feeling okay, and then I'd glance in a store window and think, *Yikes*.

I never felt pretty. I never liked my face even a little bit until I had the twins. *Their* faces were so beautiful, they were so perfect, and they looked just like me. When I looked in the mirror, suddenly I would see pieces of them, and finally I liked my own face."

This is enormously interesting. Before this minute I have never heard Mom speak of Jill and Katie as babies, her own children.

"It kills me that they call me Hannah," she says. "Do you know they called Francine Mom? For years they called her Mom, even after Paul left her."

"I thought she left Paul."

Mom waves her hand and says, "Whatever." I grant her the ambiguity, as we all know Paul left Francine emotionally long before she left him—if he was ever present emotionally in the first place.

"But, Mom," I say, now that she has opened this long-closed door, "how could you do it? How could you leave them?"

From the backseat Matthew gives a little hiccup, as if seconding the question. Mom looks into the rearview mirror with intense, wide-eyed dread. Clearly, nothing in the world—swerving off the road, a heart attack, a sudden forest fire—would be worse than the sleeping baby waking.

Luckily, it turns out to be a false alarm. Mom turns her gaze back to the road, staring intently. She doesn't seem to have any intention of answering, so I prod. "Seriously," I say.

"I don't know," she says. "I can't explain it. It was a kind of antsyness, like I didn't have any choice. I was so young, and they just wanted, wanted, wanted, wanted all the time, every second around the clock. I didn't sleep for nearly two years. Maybe if it had been just one baby, it would have been different. But suddenly I could see my whole life, with no movement whatsoever. Every second of it in that little town, the same people, the same experiences."

"So why did you keep coming back?" I ask. "Why did you come back and marry Paul?" She shrugs as if she doesn't know herself. Then she says, "I was forty-two. I felt seasick. I couldn't stay with Hugo anymore. I was done with that. And I thought, where do I go from here? Where's my security? Do I really want to be a forty-year-old vagabond? A fifty-year-old vagabond? How many more men can there be, after this?"

"And you knew Paul would take you back."

"He always said he would. And he did, immediately. No questions asked. He's very forgiving."

I remember how devastated Hugo was when Mom told him we were leaving. He and Isabelle both cried, and he refused to take us to the airport. I tried to hug him good-bye, but he couldn't bear it. Seasoned sailor though he was, he'd never come across a storm as unpredictable as my mother.

"Don't think I haven't asked myself the same question," Mom says, finally returning to my original prompt.

"How could I have left my own children? I think it's part of the reason I held on to you so ferociously. Mom and Dad would have taken you, and sometimes I could see how that would have been a better life. Jesus Christ, I could barely even feed you. But then what would that make me, if I did it twice? And if life in Rabbitbrush was so terrible, what was I doing leaving all my children there?"

This story veers so dramatically from the one she's always told me, about how her deep, fierce love prevented her from ever parting with me, that I almost want to pull over to the shoulder and catch my breath. Instead I press a little harder on the gas, pushing the car well over the speed limit toward eighty. I wonder if Mom will comment, worried for Matthew's safety, but she just keeps staring at the road in a steady, sleep-deprived fog.

Assia Wevill turned on the gas oven. She placed a blanket on the floor beside it and laid her sleeping daughter down. Then she lay down too. She not only left; she brought her daughter with her.

"I never looked anything like you," I say to my mom. This truth has always been part disappointment— missing out on her beauty—and part relief, a point of separation, the possibility of escape.

She turns toward me, surprised and maybe even a little wounded. "You don't think?" she says. "I do. We have the same chin. The same forehead. The same jaw.

And you have my hair—a different color, but the texture's the same. I always think of you looking like me."

"I look like my father," I say.

"Yes," she says quietly. "You look like him, too. He was lovely, Tressa. He was really beautiful."

I try to picture my father's face but can't conjure adjectives to attach any more accurately than I could to my own. What I see instead is the scenery changing, the landscape a colorful blur through the car window. Mom touches the top of my head. I can see Durango now as we come up on the city limits. In a few minutes I'll be out of this car, out of this conversation. It can't happen soon enough.

Dr. Reisner has an office in town, and this is where he wants to meet me. I feel thankful for this bit of normality, not making me return to the halls of the hospital but letting me wait in a room built for normal neurotics, with *People* magazine and *Good Housekeeping* spread out across the glass table.

"I'm worried about the baby," I say as soon as I sit down across from him. "My mom seems like she's getting ready to take off again."

He tilts his head, then drums his fingers on his knees. Dr. Reisner is a telemark skier and always looks like he'd rather be on the slopes. I like this about him. For one thing, it makes him seem less like a psychologist. He has long, gray-blond hair that he wears in a ponytail, and a permanent wind tan, pale around the eyes where his goggles block the sun. Even in early summer, when I stayed at the hospital, that tan persisted. Now, in the midst of ski season, his skin is red, freckled, and peeling— making those pale rings all the more dramatic. I'm touched that he would forfeit today's sunny blanket of fresh powder to meet with me.

From the waiting room the baby wails. Matthew woke up when we got out of the car, and now Mom must have just stopped nursing him. "That baby's kind of a handful," I tell Dr. Reisner.

"Newborns tend to be," Dr. Reisner says. "But that's something your mom can discuss with her own therapist. I'm interested in you, Tressa."

I lean forward and roll up my sleeves. I show him my scars—still red, raised and violent.

"I'm okay," I say. "Look. Same old wounds. No fresh ones."

"A teacher was alarmed?"

"A teacher overreacted. I'm not subject to thought control, right?"

"Of course not. I just want to check in on those thoughts, not control them. Make sure you're all right."

I pull my sleeves down and sit back in my chair. Dr. Reisner crosses his arms. I think about everything I can't tell him—Luke's visits, and saying good-bye to Carlo. Dr. Reisner imagines that his own power and knowledge surpass mine. And yet he will never know what I do, about loving so deeply that it brings back the dead. I like Dr. Reisner, I do. But unlike during the old days at the hospital, before Luke came back, I don't feel as if there's anything he can do for me except maybe give my English project the green light.

Dr. Reisner asks his gentle, prodding questions, some of them implying it wouldn't be a bad idea to go back on Prozac, or some other SSRI. Of course I don't say the first phrase that leaps to mind, *Over my dead body*. Outside in the waiting room the baby continues to cry. Outside the window the San Juans rise—covered in snow, the blue sky behind them, with thin wisps of clouds that might be spirits, angels.

(22)

TRESSA

Matthew gives Mom a break and sleeps through dinner.
With his car seat perched on one of the chairs, she drapes
a blanket over him like he's a parakeet she can trick into
silence. We eat spicy tuna rolls and unagi. She orders
hot sake and pours a glass for me. I leave it sitting there
beside me, untouched, until finally she reaches across
the table and drinks it herself.

"I think Dad's going to let Paul build his theater,"
she says.

"No." I dip my eel into the dish of soy sauce and
wasabi. "He said he never would."

Mom shrugs. "It's really not up to him. He gave the
land to me. Anyway, I guess they had a good talk at the
diner."

I remember Grandpa's face at the diner. It didn't look

like a particularly good talk to me, and I start to tell her so. But she interrupts me.

"Did I ever tell you about that guy in Ireland?" she says. The waiter appears, to clear away our empty plates. "The one who fell off a cliff?"

I sip my water and stare at her over the rim of my glass, wishing she'd fill me in on Paul and Grandpa, and wondering how she could possibly think I want to hear a story about a guy who fell over a cliff, when just a couple months ago she didn't consider me strong enough to hear the word "mortified."

"I had just found out I was pregnant with you," she continues, "and your father took me to see the Cliffs of Moher. There was a sign saying 'Caution,' but every-body went right to the edge. That's what we were there for, right? To see the cliffs? So Sean and I go right up to the edge. We sit with our feet practically dangling over. It was so beautiful, Tressa, so green and wild, so different from Colorado but still so clearly the same Earth. You know? Anyway, this other couple comes up beside us, goofy and laughing. An American couple in jeans and their new hand-knit Aran sweaters. The wind was kind of fierce and cold. I remember saying to Sean that I wished I could buy one of those sweaters, and he said his mom would make one for me. Anyway, the guy poses so his girlfriend can take his picture. He's young, younger than Sean and me, maybe still in college. He crosses his arms and smiles. The girlfriend snaps the picture—one of those old thirty-five millimeters, they were very fancy back then—and in that exact second his heel slides on the precipice and he disappears. Sean and I and all the other tourists saw the fall, but for the girl-friend it must have been, one second he was in the frame of her picture, and after the camera snapped he was gone. Vanished."

My water glass has gone clammy. Mom goes on. "I've thought about that moment my whole life, how you can never know what's going to happen. One minute someone's there, the next—poof. Gone. We can't count on anything; it's all fleeting. It's all just this video on fast-forward, except we never know if someone's going to press pause, or stop, or eject."

"How about rewind?" I say.

My mother reaches across the table for my hand. I put my glass down and give it to her, my fingers slightly moist.

"That would be nice," she says. "I used to think about that boy. How one second he was here and the next he was just gone. But ever since what happened to Luke, I've wondered about the girlfriend. Where did she go? How did she get home? How did she live the rest of her life, knowing anyone she loved could just disappear in a single instant?"

Mom lets go of my hand and covers her face. Back in his office Dr. Reisner had said I could do my English project as long as I promised to send him a copy of the paper, and to make an appointment if I started to feel overwhelmed. Perhaps this permission has unleashed my mother's strong propensity toward carelessness.

"I must be drunk," she says. "I shouldn't be saying this to you. But I'd like to track that girl down now. I'd like to find out how she is and how she got through it."

"Me too," I say.

Mom peers at me through her fingers. "Let's stay in a hotel," she says, her voice slightly muffled.

"Mom."

"Seriously. I'm too drunk to drive back. You're too tired. Right?" She pulls out her phone and starts texting.

"Mom," I say. "You're going to text him?"

"That way he can't argue." She punches out the text slowly, awkwardly, then turns off her phone and drops it into the diaper bag.

"Mom," I say again.

"Oh, give me a break," she says. She picks up her water glass. Before she sips, she says, "What's he going to do? Divorce me?"

She takes a long, deep drink, looking more energized and more like herself than I have seen her in a long, long while.

On the way from the restaurant to the DoubleTree hotel, Mom pulls into the Safeway for formula. "Let's just see if he'll take it," she says. "Then you can get up with him once or twice and I can get some rest." She hasn't asked if this plan is okay with me, making the old assumption that I'll go along with whatever she decides.

We stand together in the baby aisle, me swinging Matthew back and forth in his portable baby seat, Mom studying the different boxes of powder. I can't believe that she would want to give the baby something packaged in a way alarmingly similar to Crystal Light.

"Oh, who cares," she says when I mention this. I notice she has to hold the canister a little bit far away in order to read it, like Grandpa when he forgets his reading glasses. "I bottle-fed the twins, way back before the lactation Nazis took over the world."

"What about me?" I ask.

"With you I couldn't afford formula."

I take a baby bottle off the shelf and read the back of the package. "Mom," I say. "We have to sterilize everything with boiling water. How are we going to do that in a hotel room?"

"Crap." Mom puts the canister back on the shelf. "It'll be easier to just nurse."

I follow her back into the parking lot. She gets into the front seat, allowing me to buckle Matthew in backward. He opens his mouth as if he's about to wake up, but only makes a bleating noise, like a little sheep, and goes back to sleep.

"Great," Mom says immediately as I settle into my seat. "He'll probably wake up just in time to keep me awake all night."

"Hey," I say, "if he does, just nurse him when we get there, then hand him over to me. I'll stay up with him. I don't mind."

"Good," Mom says. "I was thinking we could get adjoining rooms."

I know I should be freaking out at this shift in her personality, this shift toward the old, self-serving Mom. And I do feel exasperated, but it's a familiar exasperation. I almost feel like for the past three years there has been some sort of stand-in—an alien being possessing her—and now all of a sudden I have my real mom back.

In the old days it would have been a splurge to stay at a Motel 6. We would have slept together under a polyester quilt, in a double bed whose springs made themselves all too apparent every time we rolled over. Now we have two rooms at one of the nicest hotels in the state, but for several hours I don't get a chance to contemplate the change in our fortunes. Instead I frantically pace and jiggle and coo, dealing with this little baby who doesn't understand why his mother has suddenly become unavailable. When I finally get him to sleep—lowering him back into his car seat—I tiptoe into Mom's adjacent room to see if she's getting any rest.

The lights are on, and she sits sideways in a wide easy chair, her gazed fixed out the window toward the luxurious view of the Animas River and the mountains—snowcapped and therefore shining through the darkness.

She sips a glass of wine she must have ordered from room service. Her leggings and cashmere sweater are cozy enough to sleep in, but she doesn't sleep, just swings her legs and stares out at that expensive view.

I sit down on the edge of the bed. "I thought you wanted to sleep," I say.

"I do. But this is nice too. Do you want a glass of wine?" I see she's ordered a bottle. It sits on the table beside her next to an empty glass. She reaches for it, ready to pour.

"No, thanks," I say. It annoys me that she keeps offering me alcohol when she got so mad at Luke for supposedly getting me drunk.

She takes her hand away from the bottle and says, "That's right. You have no vices. Luke was your only vice."

Something in my spine goes very cold. "He wasn't a vice." I remind myself to use the past tense and hope that my voice sounds foreboding enough to make her change the subject.

Instead she shrugs. "I guess that's a matter of opinion."

"I could just as easily say Paul is your vice."

"But that wouldn't be accurate," she says. "It's me. I'm his vice."

I turn my head and stare out the window along with her. Maybe this conversation, this transformation, means she has stopped being afraid of my committing suicide again. I wonder what has precipitated this change in her, and I only need to rack my brain for a moment to remember Hugo and Isabelle's visit.

"Mom," I say. "Did you see Hugo when he was here?"

"See him?" She lets out a short, self-pitying bark of a laugh. "How could I see anybody? I'm under house arrest, remember?"

"Mom," I say, again with the cautioning tone I haven't had to use in years.

"I did speak to him on the phone," she admits. "I liked hearing his voice. It was fun, *n'est-ce pas*, living on that boat? *Sur la mer?* All wild and free?"

"You said the opposite when we left. You said it was confining, claustrophobic."

"Isn't that odd," she says. She leans her head back, her voice going dreamy. "All that sky. All that water. Miles and miles. And still I felt hemmed in."

She stops talking abruptly, and I know she's pondering her own psychological makeup. We sit there quietly for a long time, staring into what wilderness gives itself back through the darkness. Maybe there's something she can sense that I haven't realized yet, like a part of me has shifted back, just as it has in her.

And then, as if they were on some kind of delay, my mother's words sink in: "I'm his vice." Even though I don't like Paul, have never liked him, I think of all the damage my mother has done to his life and his family (poor Francine, my poor sisters, poor Luke), and I feel sorry for him.

"You won't do it, will you?" I ask. "You won't leave him again."

I think at first when she doesn't answer that she's considering her reply. But when I look over, I see that she's asleep, her head flopped back, her hand still resting on the table by the wineglasses. Her chest rises and falls slowly, steadily, and in this forgiving and luxurious light she looks just the way she always has, only briefly at rest, a person whose future has yet to be decided.

From the other room I hear a baby wake. It takes me a minute to remember that he's ours, my responsibility, and I jump to my feet and rush in to him, hoping I can calm him without feeding, giving my mother a little more time to sleep.

(23)

LUKE

Weird. Very weird. I can walk into town during the day and see things like a new sporting goods store, and a new clerk behind the counter at the Mercantile. Little things like that, telling me this could be the after-Luke. One afternoon I stand outside the Rabbitbrush Café and watch my father drink coffee. He sits at a table by the window. He's got a sandwich and fruit in front of him, but he doesn't eat it, just nods when the waitress comes by to fill his mug. I don't know that waitress. Plus, something about Dad's face makes it seem like after. He looks different. Probably I've been remembering him wrong for a long time. I always think of him the way he looked when I was a kid. Now he looks kind of old. Gray hair, lines, all that. On top of that it looks like he's lost weight. I wonder why he's not eating. He must have wanted the food when he ordered it.

When I was a kid Dad would get home, pat me on the head, then go into his study and close the door. All the things I ever did, all the activities, I did with my mom. Never him. He never tried to see me after we moved out, he didn't want any kind of custody. It pisses me off especially now that I'll never have my own kid. Dad had something important, he had me, and he just tossed me out like I was nothing.

But the weirdest thing? I still want him to look up and see me standing here on the other side of the glass. So I knock on the window but even I can't hear the sound it should make. On the other side of the glass my dad doesn't do anything. He just looks crumpled.

What would happen if I walked into the café the normal way, through the front door? Maybe I could sit down at my dad's table and he'd be able to see me. *Why not give it a try?* The bell jingles in my head before I have a chance to even open the door. Instead of being in the café, I'm walking through the front yard at my Dad's house, the house where I grew up.

Out of nowhere, day turns into night. Snow crunches under my feet. I stare up at Tressa's window and I can't see anything. I can't sense anything either, no thoughts or feelings. She must be at the Earnshaws'. From upstairs I hear a baby cry. My brother, I think, and I know I can't stay here, not even for a minute.

* * *

So I head for the river. Tressa used to tell me about living on the ocean. What she liked best was walking along the shore. I've never lived anywhere near the beach. I like to think of the waves lapping over her bare feet.

I don't know why the river still feels like my friend. Maybe by now I've learned my lesson. I remember the way the current forced me under when I tried to swim toward shore. I never knew the water would be so much stronger than me. I held my breath as long as I could. At first I didn't breathe because I wanted to live. But then that same thing, wanting to live, forced me to breathe. That's when water flooded my lungs. I tried to hack it out but I couldn't, and by that time it was like I'd already left. I felt sort of shocked but not so much in pain. I was just leaving, whether I wanted to or not. For a while there my body was the river and me at the same time. And then my body wasn't me at all because I'd left it. No going back, no matter how much I wanted.

Now I start walking again, to the Earnshaws' house, but somehow I end up at mine. Mom's house. The place is so familiar that I breathe in. I breathe in so deep I think I taste river water.

All the lights are on. I walk inside, down the narrow hallway, over the floorboards that splinter if Mom forgets to mop sideways.

She's sitting in the living room watching TV. There's

a blanket over her knees. The local news is on, something about the Rabbitbrush drive-in movie theater, how zoning has been approved and it might open this summer. To me it's pretty incredible that I can hear this and know this. But Mom just snorts and says, "Of course it will. He always gets everything he wants."

She'd never say that if she knew I was there. I always figured she hated him, but she never would've said it to me. Maybe I can touch her, I think, and put my hand on her shoulder. Mom's body goes tight for a minute, like I startled her, but then she relaxes. I can't feel her shoulder under my hand but I tighten my grip anyway.

"Hey, Mom," I say. "Hey, Mom. It's me. Luke."

She picks up the remote and turns off the TV. For a second I think she's going to talk to me. But she just pulls the blanket up to her neck and lies down. I wish she'd go into her room. She never used to sleep on the couch.

But I guess with me gone things are different. Mom closes her eyes. Her breathing gets slower but I can tell she's not asleep yet. She used to have this habit of waking up in the middle of the night. The blanket slips a little and I pull it up and tuck it in around her. Then I stand up and go through the house, turning off lights. Mom looks like she needs rest. Maybe with the house dark she can sleep a little longer.

(24)

TRESSA

School has been back in session for nearly three weeks. Every day Evie and I sit together and eat lunch. It's nice to have company, especially company that doesn't insist on conversation. She doesn't say anything when Kelly crosses the cafeteria holding hands with her new boyfriend and sits down two tables away. After Kelly empties out her brown bag, she looks over at me. I look back. We don't wave, just like when we pass each other in the hall we don't speak. We just watch each other, carefully, knowing there's this same kind of sadness between us.

With Dr. Reisner's approval, Mr. Tynan has given me the green light on my project. I haven't said anything to Evie about it yet, but now I take the books out of my backpack and place them on the table, a confession. "So I have to admit," I say to her, "I'm copying you."

She nods, a little grave and also bemused—remnants of her brother in that expression. I watch her reach out and run her finger down the spine of each book, tapping the titles.

"Weird, isn't it," she says, "how reading this stuff doesn't make you sad. At least not in a bad way."

I think of all the possible bad ways, and how Evie has stayed immune to the worst of them. She doesn't cut, or starve herself, or take drugs, or do anything to dull the pain of everything that's happened to her. I wonder if befriending me represents, in a way, forgiving her father. Forgiveness, I think, is the business of survivors.

After my lunch of an apple and sliced cucumbers, I sit in the school library and work on my project. My stomach grumbles and complains. Mr. Tynan has excused me from class for the next few weeks. Sometimes I use the time to take notes; sometimes I just read. As I sit at the carrel, light outside dapples and shines like springtime even though it's only the end of January. I can't look at my books. I can only stare out at that bright sunshine, the trees and eaves dripping with melting ice, patches of grass and red dirt peeking through what's left of the dirty snow. I understand that this only represents a brief preview of spring, that the snow will keep returning as late as May and sometimes—crazily—June. But in spite of that and long before, spring will make itself known—bringing with it the anniversary of that day by the river.

I slam my book shut and leave school through the library door. As a senior (second-year senior, no less) I am allowed to leave campus during the day. I have two more classes this afternoon, and I have never cut a class in my entire life. Probably I will be back, in an hour or so, in time for AP French. But right now I feel restless. Hungry. The skipped meals and the late-night exploring have been working, and today I'm wearing a pair of my old jeans. So I walk down Main Street and turn in at the Rabbitbrush Café, which serves breakfast all day. I remember Mr. Tynan's meal, the one I coveted back when I first embarked on my project, and how good that one salty piece of bacon tasted.

I don't do a survey of the place, just find myself a table in the corner and settle down with my books. With its huge glass windows the room is unnaturally bright. When the waitress comes by, I order eggs over easy, whole wheat toast, hash browns, and bacon.

"I'll have the same," a deep voice says, sliding into the chair across from me. I have to shield my eyes to see H. J., clean-shaven. He wears jeans and a thick cotton sweater—it's warm enough that he hasn't bothered with a jacket—and his hair is combed, looking neat enough that he may just have come from having it cut.

I close my book. "Hi," I say. Except to occasionally wave to him when he's on his front porch or in his yard when I'm on the way to my grandparents', we haven't interacted since that night after skiing with Evie. He doesn't make any reference to the time that has passed since we last spoke; he just pulls one of my books toward him and closes it to inspect the title: *Birthday Letters* by Ted Hughes.

"Ah," he says. "You've inherited Evie's obsession."

"Obsession?"

"Well. 'Interest' would definitely be understating. Maybe 'preoccupation' would be more fair."

"Can you blame her?" I say.

"No. I really can't." He pulls the next book toward him, a biography of Sylvia Plath. He taps the cover the same way Evie did. It's a picture of Plath and her two children—a boy and a girl. Before sticking her head into the oven, Plath left them a tray with their breakfast. She also sealed off the cracks in their bedroom door so they'd be safe from the gas.

"He committed suicide, you know," H. J. says. "Sylvia Plath's son. Not too long ago."

I hate this information. I hate that her careful sealing of the door has gone to waste. "How did he do it?" I ask.

"Hanging."

"Oh," I say, remembering that boy's advice at the hospital. Then I say, "Not a naive method."

"What?"

"Nothing." I can tell by H. J.'s steady, knowing gaze, the bemused rise and fall of his brow, he has already made the connection.

The waitress slides our plates in front of us. She's a

new girl, not from around here, so we are spared the usual chitchat. H. J. picks up his fork and breaks into his eggs. The yolk runs slowly across the plate, and he grabs a piece of toast and dips it in. This is exactly what I had planned to do, but I don't want to look like I'm mimicking him. I realize the idiocy of that as I think it, but just the same I take a bite of my hash browns instead. They taste crunchy, greasy. Perfect diner food. My stomach, long-deprived, does an unaccustomed little churn of happiness.

"It runs in families, you know," H. J. says. "Suicide."

"Really?" I say. For the first time I wish that he could occasionally find his way to talking about the weather, or reality TV, instead of always going immediately to the most loaded topic possible.

"Would you like to know how I feel about suicide?" he asks.

I sigh, and break open my egg. They've cooked a little longer than H. J.'s, so it doesn't ooze quite as perfectly, but I don't have the heart to send it back. I dip my toast in and must look disappointed, because H. J. says, "Here. Take mine. I've only had one bite."

Because I think it may lead to a change in conversation, and because I really want those runny eggs, I agree. We trade plates, then sit for a long time, H. J. letting his question go, the two of us eating in silence. It feels natural and companionable, not unlike lunch with Evie. When the check comes, H. J. pays, to my protests.

"I want to," he says. "What about you? What do you want? A little walk in the high-altitude sunshine, perhaps?"

"I should get back to school."

"Come on," he says. "It's all a rerun for you anyway, right? Play hooky. I'll carry your books."

"I have a backpack," I point out.

"I'll carry your backpack."

We walk down the street together, my pack slung over H. J.'s left shoulder. Before handing it to him, I'd stuffed my jacket inside so I can feel a nice cold breeze through my long-sleeved T-shirt. We stop by the construction site where Paul is having the field torn up for his drive-in movie theater. Trees have already been cut down, and carpenters work on a snack shack. In front of it all stands a sign that reads COMING SOON! A THEATER NEAR YOU. When Mom and I got back from Durango, Grandpa told me that Paul was going to win. The property belonged to him by way of marriage, and the zoning was legitimate. Grandpa said he was tired of fighting with him, but for the past few days he's been scowling and muttering as if each lost blade of grass is a personal affront to him.

"The truth is," H. J. says, though I haven't said anything about the battle, "it'll probably be a lot of fun, having this theater." I think of warm summer nights, buttered popcorn, and first-run movies, the last of which we now have to drive to Cortez or Telluride to see.

"It might be," I admit. "But don't say that to my grandfather."

"I won't," H. J. promises. We start walking again, past town, and in a minute we find ourselves on one of the flatter, more winding nature trails. We've barely walked a hundred feet before H. J. says, "Here's what I think about suicide."

I sigh. "I was wondering when you'd get back to that."

"Don't you want to know what I think?"

I stop walking and look at him. I can hear the Sustantivo River, its slow and meandering winter pace, not far ahead. I'm surprised it doesn't bother me, walking in this direction without Luke, maybe because this spot is so far away from the accident. I decide that if H. J. insists on broaching loaded, personal topics, I will no longer respond with tentative politeness.

"Don't you worry about it?" I say. "After what happened with your dad. If it really runs in families, don't you worry about yourself, or Evie?"

He doesn't react facially. Instead he gives the back of my shoulder a little push, propelling me onward, and we continue walking toward the water. Our sneakers squish over melting snow and slush.

"Evie is a survivor," he says. "I never worry about her committing suicide. And I don't worry about it myself particularly. The way I feel about suicide is, I like knowing it's there. I like having it as an option. Because if I'm going to kill myself, then nothing really matters, so I might as well stick around for one more day. Just to see what happens. Out of curiosity. If I'm going die anyway, then nothing is of particular consequence, so why not see what happens next? That way all I have to do is live until tomorrow. I know I can always handle one more day."

"I couldn't handle one more day." We step through a small stand of pine trees, and the river comes into view. "I couldn't even handle one more hour."

"Ah, but you have. Just look at you. All those days and hours since last spring."

I pick up my pace, toward an outcropping of large gray rocks. I climb up and perch on the very top, staring out at the river, which looks and sounds gentle, companionable—as if it's trying to make peace. H. J. takes a seat next to me.

"I'm sorry about your dad," I say after a little while.

"Thanks," he says. "I'm sorry too." I wonder why I'm able to talk about these things to H. J. when I haven't succeeded with Evie.

"Do you ever wish you'd done something differently?" I ask him. "With your dad, I mean. Some key thing, something that might have changed everything?"

"Of course I do," he says. "That's what grief is, right? Wishing things were different? Wishing it so hard, you think you might break open. Or die."

I nod, I guess a little too vehemently, because H. J. says, "What could you possibly have done differently? It was an accident, what happened to Luke Kingsbury. You didn't do anything to cause it."

Actually I did a million things to cause it, from being born to getting drunk to keeping him all to myself, but for the sake of this conversation I stick to that day. "He was at the river because of me. I dropped my dog's leash, and he fell into the river. Luke was trying to save my dog. If it hadn't been for me, he would still be alive."

"If that's how life works," H. J. says, "then maybe you saved him a hundred times before that without even knowing it. Maybe one day you two were heading somewhere and you realized you forgot your keys and had to turn back, when if you'd kept going, you would have been hit by a truck. Maybe one day you twisted your ankle on the Ethel White trail, so you and Luke never ran into the mountain lion up around the bend. Maybe one day when you wanted to stop skiing early and get some hot cocoa, he would have skied into a tree. You could have saved his life over and over, right up until that day last spring. There's just no way of knowing."

I think about this awhile, staring out at the river. I have to admit, I love the idea that in some alternate universe of other decisions, other actions, without me Luke might never have survived as long as he did.

Then I say, "Luke and I saw somebody die once, after

269

hitting a tree. We were in the infirmary at Mountain Village. I had hurt my knee. This guy came in. He was completely blue, and his wife kept yelling at him for going too fast and ruining their vacation. Then he lay down on the table next to me, and within, like, five minutes he was dead."

"Think how his wife must have felt afterward," H. J. says. "Think how she must still feel."

"Maybe she doesn't know how many times she saved his life before that."

H. J. smiles without showing his teeth or looking at me, glad this possibility has sunk in. For the first time in a long time, I think about taking someone's picture. I would like to photograph H. J., the exact expression on his face in this moment. Maybe instead I'll draw a map, these woods, this rock—a picture of H. J. to mark this rock.

We sit quietly again, listening to the river. After a minute H. J. says, "You know the main thing I wish? I wish he hadn't taken Evie's dog. It seems weird to wish that most, when my father died, when he killed himself, which was bad enough—abandoning us like that. But taking Evie's dog just felt so mean. Like he didn't care at all, about anything. It makes me angry enough to hate him, and I hate hating him. He's my dad. The poor guy lost his wife, and now he's dead."

I think of Assia Wevill and that little girl. "You don't have to hate him," I say. "He couldn't help it. He was just in so much pain."

"He could help it," H. J. disagrees quickly. "And pain is no excuse. Not for suicide, and certainly not for murder."

I feel my face go red. I don't like to hear those two words in the same breath, as if they're comparable. "The thing is," I say, "it's hard to explain. But when you're in it? You don't think it's going to hurt anybody else. You think just the opposite, that everyone else will be better off once you're gone."

H. J. thumps my back with the flat of his palm, and I wonder when he got so comfortable touching me. "Hey," he says. "I don't mean to make you feel bad. But I'm guessing you've figured out that nobody would be better off with you gone. Which is why I mean to keep you alive."

This last statement feels alarmingly personal, so I say, "That's really not your responsibility."

"I know it's not. It's my want-ability. I want to do it. I want you alive."

"Just till tomorrow?"

"Just till tomorrow. Every day all you have to do is stay alive till tomorrow."

We don't say anything else, just sit there for the longest time letting the sunlight widen and narrow through the trees, listening to the rustle of squirrels and birds and marmots. Watching and hearing the river, incongruously cheerful—meaning no harm whatsoever, just making its way through the world, the day, these next few hours.

* * *

Since school's back in session, I've been staying with Mom and Paul again. H. J. drops me off after dark at the end of the driveway. He doesn't pull in front of the house, perhaps sensing that my family would get the wrong idea if they saw him. He leaves the car running and keeps his hands on the wheel. His face looks flushed and suddenly young—much more like Evie's brother than her dad—and this moment before good-bye feels awkwardly like a date. I shift sideways in my seat, away from him, my fingers on the door handle.

H. J. doesn't seem to notice my slight retreat. "It was nice running into you, Tressa Earnshaw," he says.

"Likewise, H. J. Burdick. Thank you."

I grab my backpack and open the car door in one fluid movement, then stand for a second and wave, waiting for him to pull away. He leans forward and rolls down the window.

"I'll wait till you're inside," he says.

Walking down the driveway, I remember all the nights I've walked for miles, alone or with Luke, and think how silly it is, H. J.'s careful eyes upon me. When I reach the front door, I push it open and turn and wave in a shaft of light from the front hall. H. J. answers with a little beep, then pulls away.

I had planned on making an excuse to avoid dinner, but instead of the aroma of my mother's cooking, I'm greeted by Matthew's wails. I walk into the kitchen to find Paul, pacing and jiggling and trying to calm the baby. At the sound of my footsteps, he whirls around, a hopeful expression on his face. When he sees it's only me, his expression collapses back into a frown. He immediately thrusts the baby into my arms, and I wonder where my mom is.

"Tressa," he says. "Where is your mother?"

"I don't know," I say. I have to yell over Matthew's crying. "I haven't seen her since this morning."

He sinks into a chair at the kitchen table. We both look at the wall clock: 5:45, certainly not an alarming time of day. But of course, like my grandparents and me, Paul has begun to notice the glaze in Mom's eyes, the tapping feet, the too-apparent dreaming of elsewhere.

Despite all the noise Matthew's making, we hear the sound of tires crunching on gravel. My mother must hear the wails even from the driveway, but there's no sense of hustle in her approach. She enters the house through the front door instead of the kitchen. We hear her arrange packages in the foyer. Then she saunters in to us, her face flushed and calm. She stops for a moment and stares at me holding Matthew as if she is trying to place each of us, our relationship to each other, our relationship to her. Then she sighs and reaches out her arms.

"Give him to me," she says resignedly. She carries him to the seat across the table from Paul and pulls up her shirt. The baby snorts and grunts and sets to nursing.

It's a noisy process, punctuated by sad little shudders from having cried so hard, so long.

"Where were you?" Paul says in a low voice. I see the anger, but also the fear of letting the anger show through. My mother has become restless, and he knows he shouldn't act like any kind of captor. He continues tentatively: "I came home, and your mother was here with the baby. She left more than an hour ago. I don't know when he ate last."

"I left formula," Mom says. She gestures toward the refrigerator with a jerk of her chin.

"Formula," Paul says, disgusted, and I think he is an unlikely La Leche League activist. "He wouldn't take it," he tells my mother. "He wanted nothing to do with it."

My mother shrugs. "Just keep trying," she says. "He'll drink it if he's hungry enough."

The baby looks plenty hungry to me, but I've had enough of this conversation. "Speaking of hungry," I say, "I had a late lunch, so I don't need any dinner. I'm just going to go upstairs and study."

"Fine," they both say at the same time. I carry my books up to my room and put on my iPod, not wanting to hear another word of whatever spoils there may be—from Paul's misguided devotion, and my mother's inevitable longing to escape from it.

(25)

TRESSA

During the night I wake, thinking I hear something. I get out of bed and go to my window. When I look down, *there he is*, finally, standing on the ground, staring up at me. Luke! He's here! I thunder down the stairs, not caring whether I wake up the baby, or my mother, or Paul. Just let them try to stop me. Luke has come back. He's waiting for me.

Downstairs the little alarm panel reads READY TO ARM—they've forgotten to turn it on. Victory! I still have to crawl through the dog door to avoid that announcing Australian voice. Outside, frigid air envelops me as I step into the driveway and run around to the spot beneath my window. My bare legs tingle with the freezing air that's too cold even for snow. The weather changes quickly at this altitude, and this afternoon's balmy sunlight feels worlds and worlds away. I look around wildly. But Luke's not here.

"Where are you?" I call. "Luke. Luke!" I reach out my hand to feel the air in front of me, as if maybe things have shifted and now I'll be able to feel but not see him. But I just *did* see him; I know I did. He was standing out here, and now he's gone, and for a second I want to leap out of my skin and run after him, no matter how cold it is and no matter how flimsily I'm dressed.

One more day, I say to myself. *Just one more day, to see what happens.*

That voice in my head startles me, and I wonder if I'm getting better. Is "better" the right word? What if, as I get better, healthier, the need to keep Luke here, hovering around this world, fades, and then—he fades too? I think of Carlo, walking away forever. What if Luke does the same thing? What if he's supposed to? And me, so selfish, keeping that from happening. But to never see his face again—*never*—I can't. I can't!

I won't. I stand here in the cold. It must be ten degrees or less. My body shivers and my skin stings. But I will myself not to care, not to wish for warmth. I will myself to court this danger, this pain, if only it will bring him back to me.

How can I want to get better if that means sending Luke on his way? At the same time my body rebels, urgently, against the frigid air that feels wrong, violent, in my lungs and against my skin. If I don't know how to wish Luke gone, I also don't know how to freeze to death. So finally I turn and walk into the artificial warmth of my artificial home.

LUKE

Don't ask me why, but I disappear as soon as Tressa comes outside. Then I'm back, but standing in the woods. I can see her through the trees but she can't see me. I try to walk over to her but it doesn't work. This could drive me crazy. Her face looks way too pale, like she's already got frostbite. Plus her lips are turning blue. All I want to do is head toward her but my legs don't move.

"Where are you?" she yells.

I'm here. I'm right here. But I can't hear my voice. I don't think she can either.

Tressa stands there so long that I start to remember what cold feels like. It's like her bare legs are my bare legs. Why is she wearing a nightgown in winter? It must be ten degrees out. *Go inside,* I yell.

Suddenly I feel guilty. If I went away like Carlo did, Tressa wouldn't be out here with bare legs, looking for me, the kid who wasn't strong enough to stop fighting and stay in this world. The same kid who can't fight his way toward her now, out of these woods.

Go inside, I yell again. Maybe she hears me, or maybe it's just that the cold finally gets to her. She turns back toward the house. I see her hugging herself and I can't stand how much I want to walk over to her.

Maybe I *should* leave. But I can't.

TRESSA

At the hospital, before they let me see him, before Francine arrived, I hit the EMT who told me Luke was dead. Maybe she thought I blamed her. It took so long for them to find us, the hiker who'd come upon us having shouted hysterical directions into his cell phone. But that wasn't why I hit her. In my heart I'd known Luke was gone before the hiker even dialed 911.

The sheriff had driven Carlo to my grandparents, and I rode in the ambulance with the EMTs. On the ride they worked over Luke's body too constantly for me to get near him. I hunched in a corner. When we arrived at the hospital, they handed the stretcher to medical personnel, and I slid out of the back behind them. One of them, the woman—not much older than me and not much taller— turned and placed one hand on my shoulder. She meant to be kind, to be honest.

"I'm sorry," she said. "You should know, there won't be anything else they can do."

"What do you mean?" I asked.

"He's gone," she said. "We did everything we could, and I'm so sorry. But he's already gone."

Before that moment I had never hit anybody in my life. But I hit her. Even though I already knew Luke was dead, I lifted up my hand, and I balled it into a fist, and I punched her right in the face, knocking her backward. The two other EMTs ran to help her. Part of me wanted to run from them, away from the hospital, screaming at the top of my voice: *No, no, no, no, no.* But before they could reach me, or her, I felt a pair of arms encircle me, even though nobody stood nearby. A strong, dis-embodied, invisible pair of arms—wrapped around my waist, holding me steady.

Then the arms disappeared. I stepped forward. "I'm sorry," I said to the woman. "I don't know what hap-pened."

"It's the shock," she said, rubbing her jaw. The other EMTs looked at me, dubious. "It's okay," she told them. And I left them to walk inside and find Luke, before the rest of the world descended.

LUKE

I can't get back to Tressa. I don't know why. I try and I try and I can't get there, so instead I visit my mom. Sometimes I sit at the table while she eats breakfast. Or else I sit on the couch while she gets ready for school. I like to hear her moving around the house like she's still got important stuff to do.

One time I sit next to her in the car while she's driving. I talk a lot, even though she can't hear me. "I love you, Mom," I say. Not something I told her much, the last couple years. And then out of nowhere, I tell her, "Hey. Mom. Watch out for Tressa. Okay?"

I know it's not fair to ask. Probably she's had enough of looking out for people, especially Hannah's kids. But I can't help it, and anyway, she can't hear me.

I get out of Mom's car and walk a long way, hours or days or weeks. I'm losing track. On what looks like a very cold night I turn up at my dad's and find a kitten in the well of a basement window. It's wedged up into a little ball, barely breathing. What's a little kitten doing out in this weather? It'll die out here. I reach in and touch its spindly back. There's some warmth from the house, which I guess kept it alive so far. But that won't last long. I know nights like this. If I leave it where it is there'll be nothing but a kitten Popsicle come morning.

So I scoop it up. Just like I could feel Carlo when he was alive, I can feel the kitten. I hold it to my face. Its nose is freezing. How can I hold a kitten, feel a kitten, but not Tressa? It makes no sense. I close my eyes and try to will myself to Tressa's room. When I open them I'm still standing outside. I stare up at the stars a moment. I'll try again.

This time I head for the front door. It pushes open. The alarm panel blinks away, but for some reason it doesn't go off. I guess I don't register in the after-Luke, even when I open doors. So I go through the kitchen, up the stairs, past my old room.

When I get to Tressa's room, she's sleeping. I wish I could crawl into bed with her and just sleep. The kitten moves a little, like maybe it notices things have warmed up. I put it down next to Tressa.

I get onto the bed too. I lie down and put my arms around Tressa. She doesn't wake up, but that's okay. I'm here. I'm here. I close my hand around her wrist, feeling her skin. I know that if I close my eyes this'll be over. When I open them I'll be someplace far away. But I can't help it. I close my eyes, so that just for this minute we can sleep, wrapped up. Together.

TRESSA

The strangest thing: I wake up, and here's this tiny black kitten—a kitten!—no more than eight weeks old, curled up right on my chest, purring the creakiest little purr I have ever heard. I close my eyes, wipe sleep away, then open them. She's still here. I'm not dreaming.

I lift her to my face. She opens her eyes, a thousand layers of emerald, a thousand more flecks of jade. "Where did you come from?" I ask, though I know right away. She is a gift to me. I am a gift to her. *Luke was here*.

I can smell it on my pillow, that sandalwood scent. I can feel it in the pulse of the kitten's heartbeat beneath my thumb, pressed against her fragile rib cage. Luke was here. Luke brought me this kitten, and he wants me to take care of it. And I know, I know, exactly what he's telling me: He wants me to stay alive.

I think about what H. J. said, about the chain of events we unknowingly halt or set into motion. I have thought about my life in terms of monumental moments that can't be undone. My mother's letter to Paul, all those years ago. That first day meeting Luke. Our last walk by the river. The X-acto blade across my wrists.

I have neglected the seemingly less monumental moments. The decisions we never think of again, the actions that change the course of time without our ever knowing. In another world and time I am a high school graduate. Luke and I live miles away, we walk hand in hand beside Boulder Creek. We have left Rabbitbrush and its inhabitants, our families, behind.

In still another world my mother stayed put. She never sat down at that table, never wrote that letter to Paul. Instead she endured, took care of the twins, stayed with her husband. She never traveled, never met my father. Francine married someone different. Luke and I never existed at all.

But where I sit, in my room. It's *this* life, here and now. My mother went away and came back, over and over again. Somewhere in the midst she went to Ireland, so I was born. She left room for Francine, so Luke was born. Luke and I fell in love as easily and naturally and unavoidably as lightning or rain. I may have saved his life a hundred times until the time I didn't.

One day Luke walked by a field of larkspur and picked a purple flower. Toward the edge of the trail he dropped it. Its seeds blew in a Chinook wind, and now another field waits beneath the snow to erupt in spring.

Beside my ear the kitten lives, it purrs. Every single step of my life led up to this moment. And so I will do as Luke wishes. I will stay alive, at least for one more day. Though the winter continues in pale, white loneliness, and he does not return for two long, cold, and endless months.

part four

staying or going

(26)

TRESSA

The world stays mostly frigid—fewer signs of spring and thaw than I have ever known in Colorado. I see Genevieve Cummings wearing a snowsuit at the Mercantile. She's with her new babysitter, so I go over to say hello. "Genevieve," I say, kneeling in front of her. She looks at me, her puffy down hood circling a red-cheeked face that shows zero recognition.

Soon word from colleges will arrive. This season is a strange mirror of last year, when Luke and I waited for letters from Boulder. We had a happy celebration the day we both received fat manila envelopes, suddenly tasting it, the time when we would be together, unimpeded, uninterrupted. This time waiting to hear, all I feel is vague curiosity. Katie has already found a house in Boulder with enough room for both of us. I figure I can wait till the last possible moment to break the news that I want to stay in Rabbitbrush. Maybe I can go to one of those online colleges. It's hard to imagine my mother objecting, since we've never been apart for very long. Even though I'm living with my grandparents now, I see her nearly every day because she always drops Matthew off with Grandma for a couple of hours.

It was the kitten that made me finally move out of Paul's house for good. The morning she appeared, the first thing I did was carry her downstairs to the kitchen and open a can of tuna fish. I knelt beside her, stroking her tiny spine as she attacked the food. The softness of her fur made my heart expand, already falling in love.

"What's this?"

Paul stood in the doorway, buttoning the cuffs of his shirt sleeves. He looked scowlish, angry, full of dislike— the look he would always have, regarding me, if there were no one else to see us together.

"It's a kitten," I said.

"I can see it's a kitten. Where did it come from?"

I wondered what he would say if I told him the truth: *Luke gave her to me.* If ever there were a prototypical nonbeliever, it would be Paul. Then I remembered his faith in my mother, his belief that she might stay in this new life.

"She was crying outside last night, so I let her in. She would have frozen to death."

Paul stepped over us and headed to the coffee

machine. "You can take your mother's car to school," he said, "and drop the kitten off at the shelter on the way."

I didn't look up, just kept petting the cat. "I was thinking of keeping her," I told him.

"That's not possible," he said brusquely. "Not with everything we have going on here, with the baby. The cat will destroy the furniture." I wasn't sure how these two things were connected and almost said so, when Paul added, "Anyway, I'm allergic."

This probably wasn't true; he just wanted to present as many inarguable points as possible. The bowl of tuna empty, I scooped up the kitten and held her to my chest. Upstairs the baby woke, his cries filling the house. Paul and I both looked at the ceiling, waiting for my mother's footsteps. The coffee machine hissed and dripped with dramatic, explosive exhalations. Matthew cried. No footsteps.

"Shit," Paul said, and left the kitchen. I heard him take the stairs two at a time, impressively fit, impressively youthful. Still holding the kitten to my chest, I crossed the room and picked up the phone. My grandfather answered after two rings.

"I found a stray kitten," I said. "Paul won't let me keep her."

"I'll be right over," Grandpa said, joy in his aged voice at a new pet for me and the opportunity to thwart Paul for him. Conceding the movie theater still rankled.

I named the kitten Emily and moved in with my

grandparents. A couple weeks later Grandpa bought himself a new truck and gave me his old one so I wouldn't have to ride the school bus. But within a few days he decided he missed his old truck, shot muffler and all, so now I have a brand-new Toyota flatbed. It's cherry red, and the color makes me think Grandpa meant to give it to me all along. He always drives blue trucks.

One Friday afternoon I drive home from school in bright sunlight that does nothing to penetrate the thick, crusted mounds of snow that line the side of the road. I slow down when I pass a young woman—lithe and graceful with a long, fair ponytail. As I pull up alongside her, I see that it is not a young woman at all but my mother, the tips of her ears bright red from the cold air.

I stop the truck and push down the passenger window with a sleek electric buzz. "Hey," I call to her. "You should have worn a hat."

She sticks her head through the window and reaches out her hand. "Hi," she says. "Can I have yours?"

I hesitate for the barest fraction of a second. This particular hat was a gift from Francine. She gave it to me my first winter back in Rabbitbrush, before the nature of Luke and me made itself apparent. If I give the hat to my mother, there is a good chance I will never see it again. Still, my pause doesn't last long before my natural obedience kicks in. I take it off my head and hand it over.

Mom pulls it over her ears, still looking unsettlingly

girlish. "Soft," she says, approving, and then adds, "I can't get used to seeing you in this truck."

"It's nice," I agree.

"Dad bought me one, very similar, when I was your age."

It's easy to picture her driving off to college in her red truck, leaving town, hoping it was for good. These days every time I see her, I expect her to ask me to come home. But she hasn't, not once. She's barely even referenced my absence. If she's mad at Paul for driving me away by not wanting the cat, I haven't heard anything about it.

"Where's Matthew?" I ask.

She narrows her eyes, weary of everybody asking this question. "I sold him to the Indians," she says. Instantly realizing her mistake, she turns bright red.

"The gypsies," I say. "It's the gypsies, in that expression."

"I realize that." She looks away, down the road, toward the direction she'd been walking. She can't wait for me to leave. I imagine Matthew, a squalling little bundle in a basket on Francine's front stoop. A single flash of confusion would cross Francine's face before she gathered up the basket and took the baby with an electric air of renewed purpose.

"Bye, Mom," I say. I wait for her to ask me to come to dinner, or go for a walk. "Bye, Tressa," she says instead.

I drive away. In the rearview mirror I can see my

mother, wearing my hat, her hands in her pockets, standing still, watching me go.

Heading home, as I pass the Burdick house, I see H. J. shoveling the walk to his front door. I wave, but he doesn't see me. For a second I think about stopping but decide against it. Inside my grandparents' house it smells like banana bread just out of the oven. There it is, cooling on the stove.

"Tressa," Grandma says. "Sit down." She slices the banana bread and butters a piece from the block of good, Irish cream butter she always keeps on her counter (covered these days, to protect it from Emily) and slides the plate in front of me. Emily jumps into my lap, her creaky little purr setting immediately to work. Grandma pours me a cold glass of milk—whole, of course—and puts it on the table with the food. These past weeks with her have destroyed all my dieting efforts, but how can I say no? The little girl who still lives inside me, who always wanted to come to Grandma's and be fed, demands that I accept these offerings.

I close my eyes and bite into the warm, buttered bread. Heaven. Grandma sits down across from me. She takes an envelope out of her back pocket, unfolds it, and shows the front to me. It has an impressive collection of colorful stamps, a bust of the queen in their left-hand corner. I recognize my father's slanted handwriting, always faint—as if he doesn't believe his words deserve the full pressure of his pen.

"It came yesterday," Grandma admits. "I don't know why I didn't give it to you. I almost read it myself."

"Why?" I ask, surprised. My father has never been considered a loaded topic. He's barely ever been considered at all.

"I'm not sure myself," Grandma says. She frowns, more thoughtful than displeased. "I suppose things have just been humming along so peacefully these last few weeks, with you here. I didn't want anything unsettling to happen."

Without thinking, I close my right hand around my left wrist. I hate the worry that I continue to cause my grandmother, who's never been anything but kind to me.

"I won't even read it, if you don't want me to," I say.

"Oh," she tells me. "No. I don't want to keep your father from you. He's a harmless fellow, generally, isn't he?" She looks relieved that I haven't expressed any particular emotion, and hands over the letter. I scan it quickly, then fill her in.

"He wants me to come to Wales next year. He says I can stay with him, and maybe apply to the university in Swansea."

"Swansea," Grandma says, horrified. "So far away? That won't do. We just got you back!"

I think of all the various places from where she's got

me back. "Don't worry, Grandma. I'm not going any-where." *Not even to Boulder,* I don't say.

At that moment we hear a car rumble up the drive-way—not Grandpa's truck, which announces itself all too clearly with its broken muffler. Grandma rolls her eyes. "It's your mother, coming to hand over the baby." She doesn't fool me with her reluctance. I know that Grandma is happiest when she has a crying baby to soothe or a small child to feed. She once told me her greatest sadness was having had only one child instead of a whole houseful. Who could have predicted that one wayward daughter would provide her with a lifelong stream of little children?

"It's not Mom," I say. "I ran into her earlier. She was taking a walk."

Grandma gets up and looks through the storm door. I hear a car door slam. "It's Paul," Grandma says. "Now what could *he* want?" I hear another door slam. "He has the baby," she says. She glances back at me worriedly. Every one of us, I realize, has been standing poised, waiting for the day Mom takes off.

"I just saw her," I say again, referencing but not directly stating the unspoken, shared fear. "She was on foot, just taking a walk."

"In this cold," Grandma says. As if summoning the temperatures to prove her point, she opens the door, let-ting in a chilling gust. Paul strides past her, the baby over one shoulder.

"Is she here?" he asks.

We tell him no, and I say again that I just saw her, she was going for a walk. The repetition sounds like too much protesting, but Paul's hearing it for the first time, so he heaves a sigh of almost-relief and sinks down into a chair. Grandma steps forward to collect the baby, but Paul doesn't want to relinquish him. He holds him close to his chest, absentmindedly patting him every few seconds.

"I came home," he says, "and she had left the baby with some stranger, a girl from the café."

Grandma and I look at each other. Any other mother in the world could hire a babysitter without making anyone bat an eyelash. But with *my* mother, it sets off abandonment bells in everyone's head. I feel a stab of sympathy. Mom would have to be perfect to the nth degree to stop everyone from worrying. I guess Grandma has the same reaction, because she says, "Maybe it's good for her to feel like she can get out of the house now and then."

Paul looks over at me. "Tressa," he says. "I was thinking maybe you should come home. You could help her take care of the baby. You could give her another reason, you know. To be there." He won't come out and say that he knows she's in the crouching position, ready to run. Grandma's face darkens.

"Tressa will stay here," she says. "This is what works best. It's not her job to keep your wife happy."

Paul looks over at me, his face pleading. I consider

what his face means to me, what it should mean and what it doesn't. It's not like he never abandoned anybody.

"I'm sorry," I tell him. "I think I'm better over here."

"You can bring the cat," he says, his voice desperate.

I feel badly for Paul, I do. But there's nothing I can do about my mother. There never has been. So I say, "I'm sorry. But I need to stay here right now."

A dark cloud passes over his face, changing it from pleading to angry. The thing is, and we both know it, having me at the house wouldn't make her more likely to do anything but take me with her when she leaves. Paul stands up, thumps the baby again. As a father he has a mixed track record—devoted and frazzled with the twins, distant and angry with Luke. Who will he be to this baby, this boy, Luke's brother? And will he be that person on his own, or with my mom, or with someone else?

Paul leaves, ducking through the cold to his car. Grandma and I stand together and watch him through the door. He buckles Matthew into the backward car seat and hustles around, rubbing his hands together before he starts the engine. Even Paul's fancy new SUV sputters in protest at the freezing air.

"If she has to leave," Grandma says, "I wish she'd just come here."

"When has she ever done that?" I say. My voice sounds harder then I meant it to.

"Maybe we're just jumpy," Grandma says. "Maybe this time will be different."

Her voice cracks on that last word, and I feel a rush of anger, not only toward Mom for always doing this but at all of us, too, for always believing things will be different. Maybe the only ones who have it right are the twins, who completely gave up on her years ago.

Grandma puts her arm around me. "If she deserts that baby . . . ," she says, her voice uncharacteristically hard. I wait for her to finish the threat, but she can't. Because both of us know that as much pain as my mother's exoduses cause, her parents will never be able to stop taking her back.

We stand there for a while, arms around each other, watching the space Paul has left empty, until finally we hear Grandpa's truck on Arapahoe Road, heading toward home. It seems impossible that my mother sprang from two people who've lived in the same place for so long. I can't remember my grandparents ever even going on a vacation. Maybe that's what gave Mom the freedom to roam in the first place, this unwavering, unchanging home base.

"There's a storm coming," Grandpa says as he walks into the kitchen with a gust of freezing air. The cold emanates from his skin. Grandma and I let go of each other to let him pass, and at that exact moment the phone rings. I feel a little tingle in my palm—the mystic cross, perhaps, and I know it will be Evie, inviting me over. Before I pick up the phone, I tell my grandmother not to expect me for dinner.

(27)

TRESSA

H. J. pours a huge bottle of burgundy into a stainless steel pot, the bottom of which carries the charred scars of a long-ago spaghetti dinner. "Finally," he says. "You've come for the mulled wine."

A couple weeks ago I gave Evie the map I drew of their kitchen, and one of them has already had it framed. It hangs right above the stove, the glass fogging up from the steam off the hot wine. Evie and I sit at the kitchen block, sticking cloves into oranges. The wine glugs and glugs into the pot with an increasingly cheerful rhythm. He is making enough for a whole roomful of people, and I imagine most of it poured down the sink tomorrow morning.

"You know," I say, "I don't really drink wine."

H. J. picks up a bag of sugar, bypassing the Pyrex

measuring cup next to it. "I'll make it extra sweet for you," he says, letting the sugar sift into the pot almost as generously as the wine. He throws in some cinnamon sticks and slices of lemon. We hand over the oranges and start in on some new ones. The room smells wonderful, an infusion of wine and citrus and cloves. Outside the wind kicks up, stormy and cold, and I find I'm eager to taste H. J.'s warm brew.

He makes popcorn in the microwave while the wine simmers, and for a few minutes the fake butter smell wins out over the wine. The three of us sit on the battered couch in the kitchen for a good while, watching the storm work its way over the mountains. The snow falls sideways in violent gusts.

"You'll probably have to stay here tonight," Evie says through a mouthful of popcorn. "It looks like a big storm." I wonder if my mother made it out of the woods, home safe. I picture her and Paul, a shaky truce formed in the bad weather, Paul overjoyed that at least for tonight there's no chance of her escaping.

"We'll see," H. J. says, maybe worrying that the thought of being stranded here will scare me off.

I shrug, feeling surprisingly complacent, then excuse myself to call my grandparents. "The storm looks like it might be bad," I tell Grandma. "So I'll probably stay here tonight if that's okay." When I come back into the kitchen, Evie asks if I've heard from any colleges yet.

"No," I say. "Nothing yet."

"Evie got into CU," H. J. says.

"Really?" I say. "That's great, Evie." I don't say anything about my possibly going there too.

"Yeah," Evie says. And then, "H. J.'s selling the house."

I turn abruptly to look at him. I don't know why this news should alarm me. But everything about the place, the family photos and the worn but cozy furniture, the kitchen smells from hundreds of meals—successful and unsuccessful—spell permanence. I can't imagine another family inhabiting these walls.

"But where will you go?" I ask H. J. He's sitting on the other side of Evie, so I have to lean forward.

He shrugs and tosses a piece of popcorn into the air, opens his mouth, misses. For no particular reason I think that Luke would have caught it.

"Hither and yon," H. J. says. "Out and about." He grabs a handful of popcorn and eats it the normal way. I sit back on the sofa.

"My father sent me a letter," I say. "He wants me to come to Wales and stay with him next year."

"Oh, yeah?" H. J. says. "I didn't know your father was Welsh."

"He's actually Irish," I say. "But he lives in Wales right now."

"Cool," H. J. says, not investigating further. "You should go."

"But what about college?" I say, instead of *What about Rabbitbrush?*

"Big brick buildings. Very heavy. Difficult to move or destroy. Likely to be here when you get back." He stands up, moves to the stove, ladles out mugs. Snow pelts the window, and I bring the warm wine to my lips. It enters my nose first, a wonderful, head-clearing blast. When H. J. sits down, this time it's right next to me.

"Let's go into the living room," Evie says, "and sit by the fire."

LUKE

Today I go for a walk with Hannah. This in itself is weird. I'm pretty sure the last time I walked anywhere with her, she was taller than me. But what's even weirder is, I think she knows I'm here. She keeps stopping and looking over at me. Once or twice she reaches out like she wants to touch me. It makes a certain kind of sense, her being Tressa's mother.

Hannah heads through the woods toward the river. She's wearing the hat my mom gave Tressa. When we get to the riverbank Hannah starts pacing up and down. I can tell she's trying to figure out the exact spot where I went in. She goes too far and stops at the beaver dam. I see her take a deep breath and then squat down on the ground. She puts her elbows on her knees and stares out at the water.

Don't ask me why but I feel like telling her I'm sorry. Maybe it's because I haven't been looking out for Tressa the way I should. I'm still taking her places nobody thinks she should go. So I tell Hannah, "I'll do better from now on." But I can tell she doesn't hear me.

She stands and walks upriver. I follow her. After a while she starts running, so I run too. I can hear her counting under her breath. Maybe she's counting out how long it would have taken me to drown. She stops in the wrong spot again.

Hannah pulls off her left glove. She's got two wedding rings, one just plain and one with a giant diamond, and she screws both of them off her finger. She shoves the diamond ring into her pocket. I can already see it in the case of some pawnshop in Denver or Grand Junction, and I laugh. Hannah turns and looks straight at me. I freeze. Then she laughs too. She throws her other wedding ring into the river. She doesn't put her glove back on, just shoves both hands into her pockets and stands there awhile.

I walk away and leave her there. I'm losing track of time. I'm not sure when I last saw Tressa. Maybe it was just a couple days ago, or maybe it was a lot longer. I can't figure it out. All I can do is move in the only direction I know, toward Tressa.

* * *

TRESSA

The wine tastes so different from any alcohol I've tried before. It feels good, happy and warm. I become different. I move more; I laugh. I sit in the Burdicks' living room beside the crackling fire and listen to H. J. and Evie exchange their barbed brother-sister banter. It strikes me as the funniest thing in the world. I love the intensity of their connection, and I say so: "Watching you two makes me wish I had a brother or a sister."

"Um," Evie says. "Hello? Don't you have two sisters?"

I laugh. I'd forgotten Jill and Katie, not to mention Matthew. "Yeah," I say. "But it's nothing like what you two have."

"Well," Evie says, ever forgiving. "Your family is unusual."

"To say the least." I take another sip of mulled wine, as if I've been drinking for forever, as if intoxication is the most natural thing in the world.

H. J. regards me, noting I'm buzzed, which clearly amuses him. "Tell me, Tressa Earnshaw," he says. "What's your passion?"

I laugh, a short burst, taken by surprise. "My what?"

"Your passion," he says. "What makes you tick? What makes life worth living?"

I have one immediate, obvious answer to this question, but I know it's not what he's looking for. He doesn't mean a person or a romance. He means something else, an avocation, something that drives me outside of human relationships.

My answer is the lamest one possible. "I don't know," I say. "What's your passion?"

He sits back and considers. "It keeps changing," he says. "When I was younger, it was physical—skiing and skating, being outside. Then in high school there was acting, being in plays. Like your sister. Then I thought it was teaching, but that didn't work out. Now I'm thinking, maybe travel. Travel might be my passion."

"Oh, no," I say. "Not travel."

He and Evie both laugh. "Why not?" H. J. says. "Wasn't it kind of great, moving around the world like that? Seeing new places and meeting new people?"

I remember uncertainty, the feeling of rootlessness, the longing for home. But I also remember something else, the waking up in the morning, my eyes fluttering open, not sure where I'd find myself. And I confess to something airy and wonderful in that moment. I remember an evening in Key West, sitting on a pier with my mother. To get there we'd driven through Georgia, where we had seen a little market whose sign had read BEER, WINE, GROCERIES, HUMAN HAIR PRODUCTS. We couldn't stop laughing about that sign. "It couldn't be wigs," my mom said, "because then the sign would just say 'wigs.'" We made guesses about the alternatives—brooms, pillows, voodoo dolls—while eating fried

shrimp and drinking fresh-squeezed lemonade. A home-
less sailor who called himself Peg Leg tried to flirt with
Mom, and she laughed him off in her brave, inclusive,
irresistible way.

"Sure, I liked the adventure," I admit. "It was fun
sometimes."

H. J. smiles and takes a deep sip from his mug. "There
you go," he says, and I smile back at him.

LUKE

I end up at the Burdicks' house. I've walked by this
place a thousand times but I've never gone inside. The
other night Tressa asked me about them. Evie and H. J.
But I can't think why she would be here.

The wind picks up and snow begins to fall sideways.
It's kind of cool how I can just stand out here with no
coat. I walk over to the window and wipe away the
snow so I can look inside.

Someone's built a fire. I can't hear the noise it makes
over the wind, but it looks warm. Cozy. The room is
pretty messy, with skis and boots piled in one corner
and the furniture all crowded together. I can see the
back of some guy's head, he's sitting on the couch. It
must be H. J. Evie's sitting in an old wicker chair on one
side of the fire. And Tressa's there too.

I press my face closer to the window. It's a big,

comfortable-looking chair Tressa's sitting in, facing the window. She's got on a black turtleneck sweater. It's too big for her. I think that used to be my sweater. I remember the itchy wool. She's got her hair pulled off her forehead with a little brown clip, but the rest falls over her shoulders. I used to like it when she had her hair that way. I still do.

Tressa doesn't see me yet. She's holding a steamy mug and I think it must be some kind of alcohol. Don't ask me how I can tell this, maybe because of the way she looks so relaxed. The whole scene looks very wrong to me. Nothing is the way it used to be. I'm surprised I don't just disappear.

I can't see H. J.'s face but his hands move so he must be talking. Evie looks more grown-up than I remember. Her eyes droop like it's hard work to stay awake. But Tressa looks *wide* awake. She leans toward H. J. and laughs.

All I want to do is walk inside. I want to pour myself one of those warm drinks. That chair Tressa's sitting in looks big enough for both of us. I don't like how I'm *watching* this. I want to be there inside joining this party. So I bang on the window.

The other two don't hear it. But I do and so does Tressa. I see her face go still and I feel a little bad about interrupting. Then she looks out the window. For a second I'm scared she won't be able to see me, like Hannah or my mother. But she can see me, and she smiles. She smiles way wider than when she was talking to H. J.

He turns and looks toward the window. But I don't look at him. I look at Tressa. I wave to her. *Tressa Gentle.* She sees me mouth the words and I can tell she wants to wave back at me.

She puts her mug down and gets up. H. J. gets up too. They talk for a couple minutes. The conversation is easy enough to guess. Tressa's saying she's got to go home, and H. J.'s telling her no, no, it's crazy to go out on a night like this.

Finally Tressa gives up. At least she pretends to. But I know how it goes when someone tells her to stay away from me. Before she heads out of the room she glances toward me, toward the window. *Don't fade away*, is what that glance says.

Outside the storm gets stronger. All I have to do is wait.

TRESSA

I don't sense him at first. I don't feel him coming at all, maybe because so many weeks have passed, or maybe because of the wine. I'm so unused to the wine, it settles at the bottom of my brain, it cushions itself around my heart, and honestly for the first time since last spring— maybe for the first time in my entire life—I'm not think- ing about Luke at all, just talking to H. J. and Evie— mostly H. J., because Evie might be falling asleep. Her head nods a little. She's like a little girl determined to stay up with the grown-ups.

And then I hear a knock, sharp like an alarm clock, snapping me awake. For a moment I freeze. I know exactly what that knock is, and I feel as though I've been caught. Caught drinking wine. Caught being relaxed, and happy, and worst of all caught forgetting, *forgetting*, even for a moment.

But then I see his face. Luke, standing outside the window, white snow gathering in his black, black hair. His beautiful sharp cheekbones, his beautiful dark eyes, his beautiful red lips. His beautiful gathering of my own face in his gaze, and I feel pure joy explode in my chest.

That joy disrupts the room. H. J. turns, staring out the window, trying to figure out what I'm looking at. Evie stops nodding off and sits up. I put down my mug and get to my feet.

"You know," I say, "it's so late. I think I'd better head home."

"Head home?" Evie says, groggy, and not sure she's heard right. "We're in the middle of a blizzard."

H. J. stands up too. "You can't drive in this weather," he says. He sounds confused, a little hurt. In a single second everything has changed.

"It's so close," I say. "I'll just walk."

"Walk?" H. J. says. "Are you insane? It's, like, two degrees out there. Maybe even colder. Look at the snow. You won't be able to see three inches past your face."

A sort of panic rises in my chest. Luke outside the window, so close, and me not able to get to him. "Okay," I say, wanting to set the night in motion as fast as possible. "Do you have a spare room, then? I'm feeling pretty tired."

"Tired," H. J. says. His face falls, he looks perplexed and a little crestfallen. I realize two things in that moment. I realize that his face has become handsome to me, and also that he has been picturing the two of us alone, together on the couch after Evie finally gives up and goes to bed. Thank goodness Luke showed up.

Evie gets up from her chair. "Come on, Tressa," she says. "I'll get you some blankets." We head upstairs, leaving H. J. alone in the middle of the living room, staring after us.

The Burdick guest room must have been H. J.'s once. It has a pair of twin beds with matching blue quilts, and bare walls with scars from thumbtacks and Scotch tape. I lie underneath the covers, fully clothed and fully awake, staring at the ceiling. I know I could blow it by trying to leave too soon, but my whole body twitches. I can't wait another second. I have listened to H. J. move around the house, rattling pots and putting out the fire. I listened to him bang around the bathroom and finally close his bedroom door.

I know it hasn't been long enough, but I can't help it. I push the covers aside and creep downstairs. The steps are quiet beneath my feet. I take my parka from the bench in the hallway and pull on my gloves. I curse my mother for stealing my hat, and I take a striped navy scarf that probably belongs to H. J. and wrap it around my head. Catching a glimpse of myself in the hall mirror, I change my mind and unwind the scarf with sharp, sudden movements. I don't want to be wearing H. J.'s clothes when I see Luke.

If anything will wake H. J. and Evie, it's opening the front door—the wind blasts inside with a loud cartoon howl. But all I have to do is get outside; as long as nobody stops me, I'll be okay. I step into the wind and snow and pull the door shut behind me.

The snow stings my face. H. J. was right—I can barely see past my own nose. I reach out my hand and touch the side of the house, feeling my way around it. Occasionally my fingers glide from splintery wood to ice-crusted window. Finally I guess I have reached the living room window, and I turn toward what I think is the stretch of forest that leads to my grandparents'. I think of Sturm and Drang, safe and warm in their barn. Then I push away from the house and head into the night, the snow, the storm.

Already my ears feel frozen. I want to call out Luke's name but don't dare. The wind could carry the word back to Evie or H. J. And then I hear my own name:

Tressa. Tressa Gentle.

I step forward, and Luke's arms are around me. I see

him, of course, my face pressed against his shoulder. He's wearing his red and black flannel shirt, and I try to decide whether that shirt also still exists, hanging in the hall closet back at Francine's. I wish Francine and I still had a relationship, some kind of friendship, so that I could go to her house and ransack the closets, solve the mystery of whether his clothes exist in two places, on his body and where he left them.

I block out these thoughts and concentrate on Luke. In a way I do feel him. The memory of Luke holding me is so precise and so huge. It coincides with this moment so exactly that I almost feel him, his hair against my freezing cheek, his arms around me keeping me warm, cracking the small of my back.

"Luke," I say. "Why did you stay away so long? I wanted to see you so much."

"I know," he says. "But I haven't been away, I've been here. All around town. I saw my mom. I saw your mom too. I saw *now*. Tressa, I think you can tell me about now."

I pull away a little and look at his face. He smiles. I have wanted, every day, to tell him about my world. I sift through everything that's happened in the past months, the things I've longed to tell him—my mother's restlessness, his father's worry, my father's invitation.

"The kitten," I say. "I named her Emily."

He nods, vehemently. "Cool," he says. "Is she all right?"

"She's perfect," I tell him. "I love her." A huge gust of

wind kicks down from the San Juans, and I find myself kneeling underneath its pressure. The skin on my face and ears screams in stinging protest. I know in a moment they will go numb. I don't care. The only thing I want to do in the whole world is stay here with Luke, and tell him everything.

He kneels down in front of me so that we're face-to-face. "You have a brother," I yell over the gusting wind. "His name is Matthew."

"Matthew," Luke yells back, testing the word, this piece of the world that has continued without him. He pushes the sleeves of my coat up and closes his bare hands around my scars. His palms feel wonderfully warm.

"He doesn't look like you," I say, and Luke laughs.

I am about to tell him the rest, I am about to tell him everything, when from somewhere in the distance I hear my name. The voice in this moment sounds so foreign that I can barely place it. My hands through my gloves ache like needle pricks, so do the scars on my wrist. A strange look passes over Luke's face, not sorrow exactly, just a kind of wordless *Oh*.

•

LUKE

It feels so good to be with her, I do everything wrong. I make her come out in the blizzard. I watch her skin go from pink to red to white. I spent my whole life in this part of the country. In middle school we took courses in mountaineering. I know what it means when a person's skin goes white. Part of me wants to send her back indoors but another part wants to keep her with me.

A living voice snaps me out of it. I know I can't do or have what I want. I fade backward before I have a chance to remember and tell her the most important thing, the reason I can reach her.

Tressa.

I feel myself fall away, backward, to someplace deeper. Damn. Damn! For the first time I'm scared I won't be able to find my way back.

TRESSA

"No," I yell. "Luke! Please don't go. Please stay here with me!"

There's still so much I need to tell you.

But it's too late. His face has changed, become vague and helpless. We try to hold on to each other, we cling and grasp, we get to our feet and struggle with all our might to hang on.

The wind blows. The snow assaults from every direction—east, north, west, south. The sky and the ground. I can't see a thing. My eyes force themselves shut, I press my fists against them, and when I open them, Luke is gone, just as I knew he would be.

"Luke," I scream. "Come back."

A hand I can actually feel comes down on my shoulder. I turn to see H. J., bundled in a down coat and fleece hat, and the scarf I rejected wrapped around his neck.

(28)

TRESSA

I don't want to go back to the house. I want to stay here with Luke. I have to find him again. So I try to kick H. J. away, but my stupid legs won't move, my arms won't move. H. J. is pulling me, and finally one leg kicks out— Luke! I wriggle away from H. J., and we both fall into the snow.

"Tressa!" H. J. yells. "Stop it! I'm going to lose my sense of direction. I won't be able to find the house!"

His voice scares me. It sounds frightened, urgent. A flash of us freezing to death, lost in a blizzard just a few yards from his warm house, enters my head. If it were only me, disappearing to wherever Luke goes, I wouldn't care. At all. But I think of Evie, waking up to find the last member of her family gone. I think of Assia Wevill, laying her little girl down on the blanket.

Turning on the oven. I get to my feet. H. J. hangs on to my waist, as much to support himself as me. It doesn't seem possible for the wind to blow harder, but it does. We duck our heads and follow H. J.'s homing device for what seems like hours, toward the back door, and enter through the kitchen.

I don't take off my coat, though it drips wet snow onto the floorboards. The kitchen feels like a hothouse, drenched with the aroma of mulled wine. I sink down onto the ancient sofa and try to pull off my boots, but my hands won't work. H. J.'s not wearing his glasses. They would have only frozen over outside. He ladles a luke-warm mug for me and presses it into my hands, pulls off my boots, and quickly starts building a new fire. He still wears his hat and scarf. I can see him shaking as he rips up newspaper and tries to light it, squinting.

I gulp down the wine. Warmth enters my body with violent pain. It's the pain of coming back to life. It sears down to the center of my bones, razor sharp, so that I almost want to scream. Instead I whisper. "H. J.," I say. "H. J."

He turns and looks at me. He's had no luck with the fire; his hands are shaking too hard. My body shakes too, violently. My teeth do what they couldn't do in the blizzard, they chatter. It sounds like wood knocking against wood. H. J. goes pale. I see him glance toward the living room, probably considering the phone. Does he want to call 911? My mother? My grandfather? Whoever it is, I see him decide against it. There's no hope for help without endangering our rescuers. We're snowbound.

He walks across the floor on his knees, toward me. He takes off his hat, his scarf. He kneels in front of me, his hands gripping the belt loops of my jeans.

"Tressa," he says. "Why did you do that? Why *would* you do that?"

I stare into his face. It blurs in front of my eyes, I shake so violently. He is the forest ranger, saving me against my will, and at the same time he's someone else. I let him help me to my feet. If he hadn't come out to get me, I would have frozen to death out in the storm. I know this now. Maybe I could have stepped right out of my body, a ghost, and walked away with Luke. But H. J. *did* come out to get me, and I lean against him as he pours more wine, then helps me up the stairs.

We go into his room, what must have once been his parents' room. A wide bed, with iron head- and footboards, down comforter, and quilts piled high. H. J. lifts the mug to my lips. I drink. He puts the mug on the nightstand. It's surprisingly neat in this room, the floors swept, the surfaces clear, the bureau drawers closed. Only the bed—where H. J. tried to sleep before my newest disaster woke him—has been disturbed.

He takes off my coat. He unzips it so carefully. He slides it off my shoulders. The same with my gloves. He pulls them off one finger at a time. Then he pulls a down comforter off the bed and wraps it around me. "Can you take off your clothes?" he asks.

My hands fumble toward my jeans, but they're shaking so hard, my fingers won't uncurl. H. J. steps closer. He pulls the comforter closer around my shoulders, shielding my body. He keeps his eyes on my face as he kneels to unzip my jeans and pull them down around my ankles. I step out of them like an obedient child.

I know what H. J.'s doing. He wants to stave off my hypothermia. He will undress me, and then himself, and we will crawl under the blankets together and huddle, sharing our body warmth, returning us to 98.6, the temperature of the living.

H. J. takes off one of my soaking wool socks, then the other. He gets to his feet. I'm shivering so hard. He should get me into that bed, under all those blankets, but first he places one hand on either side of my face. I have to tilt my head all the way back to look at him. I can feel how cold my skin is against his palms. It's like a layer of ice has formed underneath the top layer of my skin. Vague lines cross H. J.'s forehead above his hazel eyes. I see the stubble across his cheek, the tremor in his lips. He looks . . . I don't know how else to say it. He looks like a man, a grown-up man. He looks, in this dim moment, against my freezing limbs, the storm raging outside, the heat inside pulsing noisily from a too-old furnace—he looks like the other choice. Like possibility. He looks like a person who wants to save me.

H. J. guides me over to the bed. I drop the comforter and climb under the covers. My body still trembles, my teeth still chatter, but I manage to get out of my sweater and T-shirt. H. J. puts the comforter back onto the bed, on top of me. Then he starts taking off his clothes. I close my eyes, my teeth still chattering. The mountain of blankets does nothing to warm me up. I can't stop shaking. Every edge of my skin burns.

It's survival, I tell myself as H. J. joins me in bed. His chest feels broad and strong, pressed against mine. His lips press against my forehead. He doesn't kiss me, exactly. He just pushes his lips there, another part of his body warming up mine. And it's working. His hands press against my back, holding me even tighter. Gradually I can feel the blood returning to my body. The shivering subsides. I can breathe in.

H. J. holds me. He feels warm. He feels naked. And I hate to admit it, but he feels good. He feels close. Every few minutes he asks, "Why would you do this? Why?" The question seems clearly rhetorical, his lips moving against my forehead. And if I start to cry, lying with him the way I only have with one other person, it's not just the difficulty of coming back to life. Which H. J. must understand.

"I will keep you alive," he says anyway, with certainty and determination. I surprise myself by feeling grateful for that promise.

For a long, long time neither of us sleeps. We just

press close together, bringing our temperature back to normal, H. J.'s lips against my forehead. Outside, the wind keeps roaring. After a while he starts to nod off. I pull away ever so slightly and watch him fall asleep. He looks like Evie as his lids droop, struggle, and then finally close.

My eyes stay open. I sit up, leaning back against the pillows, H. J.'s arm draped heavily across my waist, his sleeping breath against my rib cage. His long johns shirt landed on the nightstand. I reach across him carefully and pull it over my head. I watch the snow slow down, fall straight, still a storm but no longer a blizzard. Light arrives, despite the still falling snow. At some point I hear Evie wake up and head to the bathroom. I hear her stop beside the guest room, the door wide open and the bed empty of me. I hear disquiet and maybe a little woundedness in her pause. Then she goes into the bathroom, clicking the door shut with palpable irritation. I can't stand to know what she must be thinking.

My emotions come flooding back, hours behind my body temperature. What am I doing, lying in bed with a man who's not Luke? A *naked* man. I sit up abruptly and lean off the bed, reaching for my jeans, which are still crumpled on the floor. They're wet and clammy. I give up for a moment and lean back, my heart thumping guiltily inside my chest. Beside me H. J. breathes. I hear the slight hint of rales, the kind of deep but vaguely troubled rest that follows trauma, intensity. Part of me wants to shake him awake and ask him why he couldn't have just left me where I was. Another part of me wants to kiss *his* forehead and whisper my thanks. I wish he were wearing clothes.

The light widens through the room, a white mingling of snow and sunlight. I can't be sorry to be alive. The aged slant of the floorboards is lovely, and so are the soft down blanket, the heavy handmade quilt. This room reminds me of my grandparents' house.

I remember last night, Luke peering through the living room window. What would he think if he looked through this window now? I pull the covers over my head as if I could hide from him. Last night I left to be with Luke. Not H. J. Surely if Luke knows anything, he must know that. Right?

I didn't mean to, I promise him. *It's not what it looks like.*

Out in the hall the bathroom door clicks open. I hear Evie walk downstairs and open the front door. She must be staring out at an impressive accumulation of snow. Then I hear the door close, and Evie comes back inside. No one's going anywhere today.

H. J.'s lashes flutter against my skin. He stirs a little, then reaches up to stroke my forehead. It's unbearably intimate, and I flinch, moving away from his touch. He ignores my ungrateful recoiling and says, "Hey. Did you sleep at all?"

I think about lying, which immediately strikes me as ridiculous. "No," I say.

"Did the snow stop?"

"I don't think so." I don't know why I haven't bolted for the door. Then I remember my jeans. "My clothes are still wet," I say.

"I'll put them in the dryer." He starts petting the top of my head, and suddenly I'm too tired to stop him. It was a very long trip, out toward death and now back to life. His hand feels nice.

H. J. sits up on his elbow. Gently he pulls me from the waist, sliding my head down on the pillows, bringing me face-to-face with him. He moves his hand from my head to my cheek, still stroking. Then he says, "Tressa. Go to sleep."

My mind starts to fog, and I remind myself that all H. J. did was keep me alive. All I did was let him. Never mind how flatly affectionate it feels, this insistent stroking. I know that his attentions, and the way he cares, have to do with so much more than just me.

What I wanted to do was go to Luke. Having failed, maybe I at least deserve a rest. Outside, snow might still be falling. But sunlight manages to filter in, brightening, and with it comes the deepest, most dreamless sleep.

(29)

TRESSA

Everything in Rabbitbrush stops. Power lines are down, phones don't connect, roads need to be plowed. The day after the storm, late in the day—following a long sleep—I pull on my boots and coat and borrow H. J.'s scarf to hike back to my grandparents'. H. J. insists on coming with me. We trudge together up the unplowed road. He stands at the bottom of the porch steps until I have closed the door behind me. Through the window I watch him turn, hands in his pockets, and head down Arapahoe Road toward home.

I spend the two days of canceled school in my room sifting through my biographies of Sylvia Plath and Assia Wevill. I try to start writing the paper in a spiral notebook. Every time I think I have fueled my brain enough to come up with a thesis, an opening paragraph, something to say, I prove myself wrong. I can't extract these stories from my own, and at the same time I don't want to compare them.

Out in the world the sun shines strongly, courting spring, but the snow piles high in thick, beautiful drifts. It doesn't seem possible that May lurks around the corner. I can't consider how these very drifts will feed the river. And after that I will turn nineteen, alone.

When school reopens, I drive my new red truck down icy roads, carefully, past the Burdick house. It occurs to me that I should stop and offer Evie a ride, but I don't. I'm not ready to face any questions about H. J. and me. The place looks dark and quiet, as if no one has stirred. Maybe she's staying home today.

I pull into the parking lot at school a little early. Mostly teachers bundle from their cars into school; the buses haven't shown up yet. At the far edge of the parking lot, between two empty spaces, I see my mother, sitting on the hood of her Lexus. I close my eyes, hoping I'm imagining things, but when I open them, there she still is, cross-legged and wearing the gray cashmere hat Francine gave me. An absurd thought goes through my head, that at least she has backed in, a nod to my grandfather, who always says it's safest to leave a parking space facing forward.

From beneath the hat her hair falls in bright, beautiful waves, and I wonder if she will be able to maintain those skillful highlights away from Paul and his fat bank accounts. Because I know. This is it. She's leaving. I wait for my stomach to knot, the way it always used to on the morning of my mother's flights. But now, seeing her, what I mostly feel is numb.

I walk across the parking lot and stand in front of her car. She wears jeans, sneakers, and a light blue down vest. I peer around her into the backseat, looking for Matthew. But there's no room for a baby; the seat is down, and the car's piled high with suitcases and boxes.

"Hi," she says.

"Hi." I put my hands into my pockets. "Do you know where you're going?"

"I'm going to start out in San Francisco," she says, her voice light, easy, guilt free. "Isabelle got into Stanford. Did you hear? Hugo's going to dock his boat in Sausalito for a while, while she gets settled. Not too close, not too far. He's thinking of opening a bar there. I'm going to help him look for a space."

"So you're getting back together with Hugo," I say.

She shrugs. "Not necessarily. I just need to go somewhere else for a bit. Hugo understands that impulse."

That impulse. Somehow that phrase breaks through my numbness. It infuriates me, the way she says it, like she's talking about something normal or healthy or unavoidable. *That impulse*—the impulse to abandon children, and parents, and people who love her. People who trusted her to stay.

"Jesus Christ, Mom," I say, almost like I didn't know this was coming.

She slides off the hood and stands in front of me. I look at her face, still beautiful but more changed than she would probably like to admit from the face she owned more than twenty years ago, her original exit.

"I thought I could make everything all right," she says. "But it's too much to atone for. The twins will never want a relationship with me. I have to accept that. It only insults them, my pretending to be their mother."

"You *are* their mother. It's not *pretending* to be something you actually *are*. And what about Matthew? Were you just pretending to be his mother too?"

Mom exhales and rolls her eyes, like I'm the one being difficult. It's what she's always counted on—other people, especially me, behaving reasonably in the face of her desertions.

"It's not like I don't feel bad," she says. "But what am I supposed to do."

This last has not been intoned like a question, because if it were, I have plenty of answers. *You're supposed to love him,* I could say. *You're supposed to finish what you started. You're supposed to be a mother to this baby you brought into the world. You're supposed to keep your promises and stay put for once in your life.*

"Tressa," Mom says, as if what she's about to say will stop my being angry at her. "Do you want to come with me?"

The question explodes in my head like a firecracker. There it is. The invitation that has shaped my entire life. The way she implicates me. Apparently she hasn't noticed the expression on my face, because she adds, "We could swing by Mom and Dad's, and you can pack a bag or two. You can even bring Emily. I left room in the passenger seat." I can't help looking into the car to see if this is true.

"Mom," I say. "I'm just a couple months away from graduating." My hand flutters backward, indicating Rabbitbrush High. "The second time."

She puts her hands into her pockets. "That's just a formality," she says. "The only reason they didn't let you graduate the first time . . . Well. You know."

I nod again. Mom says, "I'm not asking because I'm worried, or because I think I need to watch you. And I'm not asking because I expect you to say no. This is no hollow gesture. I'd really like you to come. It feels wrong, leaving without you. You're my traveling buddy."

My traveling buddy. Maybe a better word would be "accomplice." And I don't want to be her accomplice anymore. "I was never your buddy," I say, willing myself to ignore the way her face falls. "I was a little kid, and you dragged me all around the world. You wouldn't give me a home. And now you're deserting this little baby. He didn't ask to come into this world. You *made* him come into it. And now you're just leaving him, like you left Katie and Jill."

Finally I've accomplished it—making her angry. Mom's eyebrows go into a *V* formation, and she takes a few steps back from me. "Make up your mind, Tressa," she says. "Which is the bad thing? Leaving kids behind or taking them with me?"

She crosses her arms, and I stare at her. Nothing I say will make her stay, or even admit to the damage she's caused. But I can make my voice hard too. "Thanks for the invite, Mom. But I think I'd like to finish school, and find out about college. I think I'd like a normal life."

Mom nods. She's mad at me still, I can tell that, but I can also tell she likes the sound of that last thing I said. *I'd like a normal life.* It makes her feel relieved to hear me saying I'd like any kind of life at all.

"Bye, Mom," I say, trying to sound like I couldn't care less, and I wish I didn't. I turn to walk away, but when she calls my name, I can't help it. I stop and look at her.

"I want to tell you something," she says. Her face looks flushed, like she's letting me in on a secret. "That day before the snowstorm I went for a walk by the river. And for the longest time I could have sworn Luke was with me. I could feel him right next to me. I could almost swear I heard him laugh."

Every inch of my body turns to airless, weightless pixels. I don't dare say a word, and I can't help the tears that pop into my eyes. Mom holds out her arms so I can hug her. And I can't help myself. I step forward. "Good-bye, Mom," I say into her shoulder. "Safe travels."

She moves back, away from me. She takes off the gray hat and places it on top of my head. She keeps her hands there for a moment, staring into my face. Then she looks down and takes my hands in hers. She stares at them for a moment, then closes her hands around my wrists. "Never again," she says without looking up. "Okay, Tressa? Never again."

I stand there with her, feeling the pressure through my sleeves, not quite knowing whether my skin itself responds to her touch. I think of my mother's promises, to Paul, to the baby, and I won't make it. No more promises.

"I'll do my best," I say. "Every day I will do my best."

"I need better than that," she says, not looking up.

"Don't we all."

She looks at me then, a little frightened, not wanting to deal with any more of my anger.

"Did you at least tell him?" I ask.

"He knows," she says, which doesn't answer my question. She looks away from the expression on my face, then says, "I left my cell phone. I'll let you know when I get a new number."

"Okay."

She hugs me again, then gets into her car. I stand in the parking lot and watch her drive away. I'm tired of being the one who forgives her, who makes her feel like she's not so bad.

Students have started arriving, and almost immediately someone takes the spot she vacated. My mother's car glides down the snowy street, then disappears. Suddenly school does not seem like the best idea. So I dig into my backpack for my phone and press the only number on speed dial, the one he himself programmed a few days ago, before we walked back to my grandparents'.

"Hey," I say. "It's me. Do you feel like skiing?"

"Sure," H. J. says immediately. From the tone of his voice I can tell he has already risen to his feet, he is already on his way. Within half an hour the two of us are driving to Telluride. When we make the turn his father intentionally missed, coming from the opposite direction, H. J. doesn't look toward the wall. He doesn't register any kind of recognition or emotion, though I know for him this longitude and latitude holds every bit as much weight as a certain curve in the Sustantivo River does for me.

It turns into the perfect day for playing hooky, the post-storm snow powdery and deep, the sun bright and warm on the backs of our necks. H. J. talks me into trying out the black diamond runs and stays with me around every mogul, guiding me, instructing me, impressing me with his vigilance. We don't bother stopping for lunch; we ride the chairlift over and over again, our legs weighted down and swinging. For the first time ever I think that maybe one day, years from now, skiing is something I'll be halfway decent at. That phrase—*years from now*—trails me, foreign and inviting.

For the last run of the day we decide to take it easy. I find myself back at the top of See Forever, looking out across the San Juans, and farther south toward the Sangre de Cristos. Above it all, the sky does not hold a single cloud. Everything looks so clear and blue that I appreciate the trail's corny name. But of course I can't really see forever, no one can, because nothing really *is* forever. Not even these snowy peaks, towering everywhere around me and everywhere off in the distance. The seemingly endless range of the Rocky Mountains will not stand permanent, but one day will crumble and fall, or be subsumed by the rising ocean. Somewhere out there, at the four corners of these states or the four corners of the world, my mother journeys away—the one pattern on which I can rely, her inconstancy strangely constant.

"All my life," I say to H. J., picking up a conversation we must have started at some point, "I felt like I could never be sure of anything. When the truth is, that's how everybody lives. Nothing can be certain, ever, not for a single second. You could set out on a nice vacation and end up skiing into a tree. Or pose for a picture on a high cliff and fall before the shutter even snaps."

"Or," H. J. says, "you could go for a walk by the river and your dog could fall in. Your boyfriend could drown trying to save him."

I stare out at the layers of sky and mountain. Then I say, "Your mother could get cancer and die. Your father could get so sad that he drives into a wall and kills himself. He might even take your sister's dog with him."

"Bad things happen," H. J. says.

"Terrible things. There's no way to be sure about anything, ever."

"No way at all," H. J. agrees. He walks sideways, stepping his skis closer and leans toward me, pressing his shoulder against mine.

Nowhere on the planet can the sun be as bright as it is over our heads, the world continuing below us, barreling downward for nearly twelve thousand feet. At the top of See Forever the whole world stretches its wide, wide wings below us, and the future refuses to make a single promise. The only thing we have is the sunlit height of the present tense—immediate and fine and ever so fleetingly sure.

(30)

TRESSA

I don't see Paul at all over the next few weeks, but Grandma goes over every day to help take care of Matthew. Grandpa stops grumbling about the drive-in movie theater. Suddenly that victory seems like the least thing he can give to Paul, after everything his daughter has taken from him.

That night Mom left, after I got home from skiing with H. J., Grandma and Grandpa sat me down in the living room. "Do you know where she is, Tressa?" Grandpa asked. His rugged, sunburned face looked stern.

"No," I admitted. "But I know where she's going." Not wanting to aid or abet in any way, I told them everything I knew about her plans to go to California, but the information didn't help much. And even if we knew where she was, what could Paul do? Go out to

Sausalito with a net and wrestle her back here? Mom had left, again. Paul's only hope was to wait until the wish for her return subsided.

Finally Paul calls. The phone's ringing as I walk in the door, home from school, and I pick it up blindly. My grandparents have no use for such modern inventions as caller ID.

"Tressa," he says. I realize that I expected him to sound angry the first time I spoke with him, but he doesn't, just sad, maybe defeated.

"Hi, Paul," I say. "Just a second. I'll get Grandma."

"I'm calling for you, actually," he says. I can hear Matthew crying in the background. "I hoped you could come over and help me out with something."

The last thing I want to do is go back to Paul's house and be alone with him. I know his primary goal is not help with the baby but information about my mother. Still, I hear Matthew wailing. Probably Paul wants to wail right along with him. I remember those brutal, terrible first days—the ones that followed losing the person I loved best in the world.

"Okay," I say. "I'll be there in ten minutes."

The scene I find is more organized than I expected. There's a girl taking care of Matthew. I recognize her as the new waitress from the Rabbitbrush Café, which surprises me, because I assumed Paul wanted me to babysit. But when I walk into the kitchen, the girl picks up Matthew and gets ready to leave the room. Paul takes a bottle that has been warming in a pot of hot water on the stove and hands it to her. She carries the baby away.

"He's taking formula now?" I say.

Paul looks at me without answering, then opens the freezer. I see it's stuffed with bags of frozen breast milk, what looks like tens of them, all neatly dated with black ink.

"These were in here when she left," he said. "I guess she'd been stockpiling them, maybe in the freezer in the garage. Then yesterday I got a package from FedEx, addressed to Matthew. More little packets of breast milk, packed on dry ice."

"Wow," I say.

"I guess she plans to keep sending them, who knows for how long."

Paul must have stayed home from work today. He's wearing jeans and a gray hoodie. He actually looks a little more relaxed than he did in the weeks leading up to Mom's departure. As if reading my mind, he says, "It's really almost a relief to have her gone. I thought I would go crazy that last month waiting to see what she'd do."

"I'm sorry," I say.

"It's not your fault." He says this quickly, and his voice sounds hard, not quite convinced.

"I wasn't apologizing," I say. "I was sympathizing."

Paul frowns. He has not softened toward me. In fact, I see that he has hardened in general, the one point of softness he retained—his weakness for my mother—finally freezing over, the middle of the lake. Mr. Zack could park a Mack truck on what used to be Paul's devotion to my mother, now covered by a thick layer of ice, buried too deep for any spring thaw to ever reach it again.

"I wanted to talk to you," Paul says, "about several things." He walks into the living room, and I follow him, noticing as I pass the hall table that all photographs of my mother are gone, though he has left a couple of me, and of Carlo. In the spot where he kept a photograph from their original wedding, he now has a picture of Luke at around eight years old, sitting on somebody's horse and smiling at the camera. I stop for a minute and touch the frame, then go and sit down on the red velvet love seat. Paul sits on the couch across from me.

"Do you want coffee, anything?" he asks.

"No, thanks."

I place my hands in my lap and wait for him to speak. After a moment of awkward silence, Paul says, "I'm wondering if you've heard from any colleges yet."

"No," I say. I know I could check online but want to wait for the letters. "Any day now, I guess."

Paul nods. "Well," he says. "I just want you to know, I had a college account for Luke that I switched into your name after he died. I want you to use that for Boulder of

course, but also if you get into Stanford or CC or wherever. There's enough money to cover whatever you
decide to do." He sounds slightly embarrassed at this
generosity, but to his credit he doesn't look at his hands,
or the coffee table, but squarely at me. I find it harder to
return this gaze, not sure at all how I feel, no longer a
threat to him now that she has already gone.

"You had an account for Luke," I say.

"Of course I did." He sounds more emphatic than
defensive.

"But why would you give it to me?" I ask. "You could
switch the account again, couldn't you, into Matthew's
name?"

"It's in your name," he says, suddenly gentle. "I want
to pay for your college. I want to make sure you're all
right. Not for your mother, but for my son." I frown in a
moment of confusion, thinking he means Matthew, and
then Paul clarifies. "I want to do it for Luke," he says.

A small sob has collected itself in my throat, and I
battle not to let it out. Paul presses on. "It's not your
fault your mother took off again," he says. "And it's certainly not your fault that I trusted her."

I wait, but he doesn't exonerate me for the most
important crime. He can see that I'm waiting for that,
but he can't grant it. Instead he says, "I'm not going
to pretend you and I have been close. We both know
we've had issues, you and I. But whatever your mother
does, wherever she goes, you and I are family. You're

my daughters' sister. And I've got plenty of guilt of my own, Tressa. You must know that."

I lean forward and cover my face with my hands. For a minute I wait for tears to come, but they don't. When I speak, still hiding behind my hands, my voice sounds laced with the same anger I directed at my mother. "Paul," I say. "It almost sounds like you're saying you're sorry." He blows out a thick stream of breath, and I take my hands away so I can look at him.

"Yes," he agrees. "I was wrong. We should have let you two be. We should have respected your feelings. I'm sorry."

Hearing the apology, after all this time, the tears make their way into my throat. I know I should say thank you, but I don't want to cry. Not just now. Paul rubs his hands over his denim-covered knees, not nervous exactly, just emotional. "Since Hannah left," he says, "I've been thinking that maybe what I couldn't stand about seeing him, and about seeing the two of you together, was that it gave me a mirror of my own feelings, my own relationship, and what it would look like if it were actually reciprocal."

"That can't be easy to admit," I say, finding my voice again.

"No," he says. "It's not. But I need to do it, because I feel terrible for what I stole from him."

I lean toward Paul, hoping the weight of my words— the simple truth—will help him the way he's trying to help me. "But you didn't steal anything," I tell him. "You couldn't."

He stops the OCD movement of his hands and nods. "I'm not going to file for divorce," he says, which somehow doesn't seem like a non sequitur. "What's the point? If she wants a divorce, she can file. This all serves me right for walking straight back into it."

"Don't be so hard on yourself," I say. "You couldn't help it. You loved her."

"Loved her?" Paul says. "You know the crazy thing? The infuriating thing?"

"You still do."

It's his turn to cover his face with his hands. I do the only thing I can think of, which is reach across the coffee table and pat the top of his handsome, graying head. I wait for something to break the silence—the baby, a magpie, a car rumbling down the road. But the room stays preternaturally still and quiet, the weight of this unlikely truce hanging in the air around us.

Never one to leave well enough alone, when Paul walks me out to my truck, he says, "I hear you've been spending time with H. J. Burdick." I don't ask who he's heard this from, or point out that it began before I left his house, when he had more pressing concerns to attend to. I don't say anything, just wait for him to tell me that H. J.'s too old for me. But instead he says, "I'm glad. I hope you're moving on with your life. That's what I'm going to do. Move on. Your mother has left so many times, I can hardly keep them straight."

Something in his voice acknowledges the cycle, and the fact that she may end up back on his doorstep. But love her though he may, Paul has finished taking her back. I expect his resolve not to divorce her will last a good month or two.

"Listen, Tressa," Paul says. He makes a gesture with his hand, waving it outward, away from his house, toward the world. "The thing to do is to move on. Alive or dead, you have to let it go. This thing we feel, however huge it seems. It's madness. We have to leave it behind, once and for all, to save ourselves."

I know Paul means well, and I recognize the truth in his words, the danger of keening toward the unattainable, the just-out-of-reach. But I would feel too much like a traitor agreeing with him. So I just say "Thank you" and do one of the most unlikely things of all. I hug him.

The wheels of my truck slosh through new snowmelt; the sun's bright, cheerful glare has continued since that day H. J. and I spent on the slopes, and all around me spring finds ways to make itself apparent, in buds on trees and the increasingly green shimmer of aspen leaves as I drive down the road, this old familiar route. Part of me wants to turn around and head out of town. What would happen if I truly became my mother's daughter and hit the gas, heading down the highway, not leaving word, just disappearing?

You can't really fault people for leaving. They do it, whether they want to or not. I may be angry at my mother right now, and she may have left, but I still love her and I always will.

Luke left, but his love stayed behind. It stayed behind so big and huge and permanent that after a while it brought him back. I know that no matter what, that love will never go anywhere, will never diminish, will never stop defining me.

Then why not let yourself get better? a voice from somewhere says.

I nod as I drive and take the turn onto Arapahoe Road. My sleeves are pushed up to my elbows. I have stopped trying to cover up the scars. What's the point, when everyone knows they're there? They look less dramatic than they did in the fall, less red and raised.

Respectfully, we summoned a spirit, Ted Hughes wrote. *It was easy as fishing for eels / In the warm summer darkness.*

My chest is full of tears, my eyes blur so that I can barely see, and I remember my good luck, my good fortune, in knowing a place so well I can navigate my way without the benefit of sight.

* * *

LUKE

I'm fading. Stepping back. Before. Now. The after-Luke. Everything blurs together. I can't feel my feet on the ground. I know Tressa's next to me but I can't see her face. Sometimes I hear her voice but I don't think she hears me when I answer. I know she's there, exactly next to me, but I can't make contact.

From someplace far away I hear a dog barking. It may be time. I know I'm on my way. But I haven't left just yet.

(31)

TRESSA

The next day I skip homeroom; I can always go to the office later and let them know I'm here. Not that it matters at this point, if I cut class. Nobody worries about me failing, or taking drugs, or loitering my life away. A glimpse of me walking the halls, safe and sound, has become all that anyone—including myself—requires.

The sign on the faculty lounge door says NO STUDENTS ALLOWED UNDER ANY CIRCUMSTANCES. THIS MEANS YOU. I ignore it and push the door open. The teachers just look up from their coffee and smile. Mr. Tynan sits at a round table, going over quizzes with red ink. "Tressa," he says. "I've been meaning to schedule a meeting with you. How's the paper going?"

I sit down across from him. "That's what I want to talk to you about," I say. "I've read all the biographies, and the poems. I've got all the pertinent information."

"Has that been okay for you?"

"It's been hard," I admit. "They're sad stories."

Mr. Tynan nods. "They certainly are."

"At first I thought I would hate Assia, because of the little girl. But somehow I can't hate her. I just feel sad for her. I just want to run back in time, into that room. I want to turn off the oven and open up the windows."

Mr. Tynan nods gravely. "Do you think she'd thank you for that?"

"She might not," I admit. "She might never appreciate it, and there'd be all that shame from trying. But still I'd know I'd done the right thing, saving them both." I lean down and open my backpack. I take out my copy of *Birthday Letters* and slide it across the table to Mr. Tynan. "It's a good book," I say. "I can't say whether he was a good man, because I didn't know him. But he's a good poet."

Mr. Tynan tilts his head to one side. He furrows his brow, more fond than consternated. "What's wrong, Tressa?" he asks.

"Nothing," I tell him. "Nothing's wrong. But I can't write this paper. I can't think about all this anymore. So instead of handing in the paper, I'd like to give you this book. As a present."

He leaves the book sitting in the middle of the table. Then he opens his grade book. He leafs through it till he comes to my class. Of course he hasn't entered any final grades yet. Those spaces are blank. But he runs his finger down the column, and it doesn't take him long to get to my name. In permanent red ink he writes a large, capital *A*. Then he pushes the Ted Hughes book back to me.

"I hate to return a present," he says, "but I think maybe you should keep this. It was written by the survivor, after all."

I hesitate, then nod. "Thanks," I say. "For everything. For that especially."

"You're welcome," he says.

I leave the lounge with a light step, testing that new word—"survivor"—in my head, and realizing, among other things, that I don't have to go to high school English ever again. I'm not sure why this makes me happy, since it was always the class I enjoyed most. But it does.

I am moving forward. I am leaving things behind. When I pass Kelly Boynton in the hallway, we both stop. We stand there a moment, examining each other's faces, until finally Kelly says, "Hey, Tressa."

"Hey, Kelly," I say. When she walks away, I turn and head in the other direction. Her footsteps click behind me, calm and even. The sight of me will never make her cry again.

May looms, bright and shimmering, just around the corner.

* * *

Evie has avoided me since the storm, and since this has turned into a day for putting things in order, I go searching for her. I find her in the library, sitting on a couch by a western-facing window. She has an American Civil War textbook open on her lap, but she's staring out at the mountains and doesn't notice me until I perch on the table right in front of her.

"Tressa," she says, not startled, just a little dreamy.

I decide to channel H. J. and get straight to the point. "I miss you," I say.

She sighs, and then nods. "Sure," she says. "I miss you, too. H. J. says your mother took off."

"Yes," I say. "She moved to California."

Evie nods. "Did H. J. tell you he decided not to sell the house?"

"No." For no good reason this information makes me light-headed. Something that won't change—the Burdicks staying in their family home. "Does that make you happy?" I ask.

"It really does," she says. "I feel relieved. I feel like I need that house for a couple more years, you know? A place to come home to." We both nod. Evie says, "You should call H. J." Something in her voice makes me feel guilty. At the same time I recognize her granting me permission.

"Did you hear about college yet?" Evie asks.

"Not yet," I say. I can tell she's about to tell me to check online, then changes her mind. She understands I have my reasons for waiting. She doesn't need me to be any different than I am.

"I bet you will today," Evie says. She smiles, her eyes lit from within, reflecting sadness but also an unflinching optimism—the tenacity of her commitment, to forgiveness and continuing, despite the curveballs life has thrown her. I decide to put her permission to use.

H. J. answers on the first ring. "Tressa," he says, not one of those people who pretends the cell phone hasn't already told him. "Let me come get you," he says. "I want to talk."

"Okay," I agree. "But I'll get you. I want to check the mail anyway."

When I pick up H. J., there are two letters on the passenger seat—a rejection from Stanford and an acceptance from Colorado College. H. J. picks them up before sitting down, then pretends to weigh them with his hands.

"This one's hefty," he says. "Congratulations."

"Thanks."

"Do you know what you're going to do? CC or Boulder?"

"No," I say. We drive about five minutes to Silver Lake, then walk silently over the damp ground—the snow in patches, dirty and gray. Although that sun has been increasing over the past several days, I am not prepared for the sight of the lake itself—completely thawed, reflecting the blue sky, not a single chunk of ice floating on its placid water.

"Wow," I say. "I wasn't expecting this."

H. J. kneels beside the lake and dips in his hand. "Still too chilly for swimming," he says, then flicks the water at me. I duck away, but not before a few freezing droplets connect with my cheek and dribble down my neck, inside my shirt.

I resist the urge to retaliate, and walk over to the log. H. J. sits next to me. "Evie tells me you decided not to sell the house," I say.

"Not for a couple years, anyway. I figure we can swing in-state tuition that long."

"So you'll stay here?"

He shrugs. "I don't know what I'll do. Maybe some traveling. I was thinking about buying an open-ended ticket to London. I could fly over there, spend a year going through Europe. A backpack, hostels, the whole thing. And just make my way back here whenever. Maybe in a year. Maybe two. Maybe I'll come back to Rabbitbrush, maybe I'll go to New York City. Maybe I'll enroll in culinary school. Mostly I won't make any plans for a while."

"That sounds nice," I say.

"Yeah?" he says. "You want to come with me?"

I close my eyes, wondering why the invitation doesn't surprise me. Then I breathe in deeply. Like any place a person calls home, Rabbitbrush has a very particular smell. Sage and pine, of course. Wildflowers in summer, and the chilly, elusive, persistent scent of snow in winter, also infused by pine. The damp moon fragrance of red dirt. And something more, something far less identifiable lying beneath it all, so personal it might come from someplace inside, my own reaction, my own senses.

The truth is, in addition to Rabbitbrush I have another home, and it's called the world. Before I ever set foot in Colorado, the first place I lived was nowhere in particular—wheels traveling over asphalt, the sky in motion above my head. For the first time in ages, maybe ever, returning to that known uncertainty, to travels, feels very appealing.

But I can't answer, not just yet. So I say, "Maybe. I don't know. Let me think awhile. Okay?"

"Okay," H. J. says. He reaches out his hand and closes it over mine. Inadvertently, I am sure, his thumb brushes over my wrist. And I can feel it, the slightly calloused skin, its warmth, its good intentions. We don't turn toward each other, or say anything else. We just sit there, holding hands. We stare out together, across the lake. Beneath that small and local body of water, a thousand frozen creatures stir their way back to life.

(32)

TRESSA

May offers no guarantees. Sometimes in Rabbitbrush it snows as late as June. But for now we enjoy a stretch of extremely warm weather. In the early nineteenth century tuberculosis patients traveled to Colorado hoping that the dry, high air would open their lungs. Rabbitbrush never boasted a sanatorium, which was another tourist boat missed, because it would have been perfect—the air here carries oxygen so clean and painless, the sun beats down so insistently, so lovingly. It could cure any illness at all.

I decide to let Grandpa teach me a few chords on the ukulele. What harm could it do? After dinner we sit in the living room and play old Doc Watson songs. Then Grandpa puts his guitar aside and stands up. He walks over and places his large hand on my head.

"Tressa," he says. "I have something to show you."

It's early, not quite six thirty, and through the open windows light evokes summer evenings. I follow Grandpa out of the house and across the wide eastern field, Sturm and Drang following us with huge, lazy footsteps. Grandpa walks a few paces ahead of me. He has only become a shade wider or thinner, or grayer, a little at a time, in all the years of my life. He wears the same Carhartts and flannel shirts. He turns to me with the same expression of kindness and love, intent on concealing the worry that always accompanies those first two emotions in this uncertain world.

"Close your eyes," he says, and then—not quite trusting me—he places his wide, rough hand over my eyes. Once when I trip over a root he catches me by the elbow. When he takes away his hand, we stand on top of the hill overlooking town. Since Paul has cleared trees for his theater, we now have an unobstructed view of Main Street, and the high school, and the Rabbitbrush Café. The movie screen hasn't been installed yet, but I can see the marquee, the snack shack, the flat grass where everyone will park, and the rows of speakers.

Grandpa and I stand beside an alien apparatus that I don't quite recognize, a tall metal pole with a funny black box on top. I stare at it, confused, long enough to realize that it's another speaker.

"You see?" Grandpa says. "This was part of the deal. On summer nights you can pop a bowl of popcorn and walk out to this hill and watch the movie. You can invite your friends if you want to. "

Friends. I know he means H. J. and Evie. If Grandma and Grandpa suspect that H. J. is anything more than a friend, they haven't said a word. Maybe this is their way of apologizing for ever going along with the anti-Luke campaign. I haven't told them yet that I wrote to Colorado College deferring for a year, which doesn't necessarily mean I'll be traveling with H. J. I also wrote to my father, telling him that I might visit Wales. For all I know I will apply to Swansea, too. Maybe I'll stay in Rabbitbrush. Maybe I'll go to Boulder and live with Katie. All I know for certain is, I'm not ready to decide.

But before all that, no matter what, I'll have the summer here. On hot nights it will be kind of magical, walking up to this hill with a bowlful of popcorn and staring through the wilderness at a big, flickering screen. I can't wait to tell H. J. and Evie, and then I feel surprised—that my first thought wasn't sadness that Luke would miss it.

"How great, Grandpa," I tell him, and he puts his arm around me and squeezes me close.

Finally it arrives. The anniversary, one year exactly since that day by the river. I never thought I'd do it— wake up on this day, to the first slow rays of dawn. Outside my window a magpie's complaints are at war with the gentler mourning dove. The sleeping kitten has grown heavier on my chest—a well-fed adolescent—and I push her off gently before dressing in layers, jeans and T-shirt and fleece vest and heavy Windbreaker. I lace up my hiking boots and put on a baseball cap. Downstairs I stuff a backpack with Nutri-Grain bars, water, a book, my iPod, and sunscreen. The wait may be long, the day will move in cycles, and I mustn't risk missing this most necessary ambush.

It's not what you're thinking. I don't go down to the river.

I park my truck on Aspen Street and head to the trailhead, wishing I could open the passenger door of my car to let Carlo out with a jingle. Words will never do it justice, how acutely I miss my dog while hiking. Heading up through the conifers, he should be beside me. He should be running ahead to chase squirrels. He should stop to wallow in Butcher Creek, spraying me when he shakes off the freezing mountain water.

It's not even three miles to the top. It doesn't take me long to find myself alone at ten thousand feet, staring out at town, at the ski area, at Bridal Veil Falls. I sit down in a grassy spot, the sun heating up to midmorning. Despite the warmth I put on the hat she gave me. Instead of pulling out my book or iPod, I just sit quietly. Francine is an early riser. She'll be here before too long.

I sit there in the gathering sunlight—the gathering day—through two or three false alarms, hikers who stop awhile to share the view. One couple has a black Lab. He jingles over to me and licks my face in greeting, still showering runoff from Butcher Creek. But when Francine finally arrives, nobody else is here. She wears shorts, her legs as brown and strong as a teenager's. She wears her hair in a long braid, and I see she looks more like herself, less puffy, less red-eyed. This purpose—one last thing to do for him—has energized her.

She carries a backpack over her shoulders. I know its contents, and my heart constricts. For her part Francine does not look surprised or dismayed to see me. She looks resigned, like she knew all along I would be here waiting. She walks over to where I sit and takes off her pack. Noticing the hat, she touches the top of my head briefly, then lowers herself onto the ground beside me. In biology I learned that mothers keep their children's living cells inside them even after they're born. So I don't think about that urn filled with half of Luke's remains. What's more important is that I'm sitting next to the only living piece of Luke left on earth, his own cells floating around inside his mother.

"Hi," I finally say. She doesn't answer.

We sit there for a while, not saying anything. Another group of hikers appears, taking a few minutes to look out over town, and then disappears down the other side of the trail.

"You'd think they'd want to look out there longer," Francine says. I nod in agreement. Now that she has found her voice, Francine goes on. "So your mother left town," she says.

I nod but don't say anything. The reason we're both here has nothing to do with my mother. After a while Francine says, "I thought that he would be here. Paul. All the way up this trail, I knew someone would be waiting for me, wanting to be here. But I felt sure it would be Paul. Now I feel like I should have known, of course it would be you."

"We're the ones who miss him most," I say.

"Yes," she agrees. "Katie and Jill miss him. His friends do. I know Paul misses him too. But nobody misses him the way you and I do."

She closes her fist around a tuft of grass and rips it up out of the earth. I see the pain in her face, in her dark eyes that look so much like Luke's, and I think how she has just carried the ashes of her only child to this point on top of the mountain. After performing such an immense task, so early in the day, she shouldn't have to deal with me, too.

Francine doesn't look at me as I try to assemble the right words in my head. She just continues staring out at the world, spread far and wide and glittering beneath us. Then she blows out a thin stream of air, her lips pursed, and I remember her telling me once that it's impossible to feel stress while you're exhaling.

"I want you to know," Francine says when her breath is finished, "I'm not going to say I forgive you, because there's nothing to forgive. I understand it's not your fault, what happened to Luke."

"Francine," I say. "That's not why I'm here."

She takes in another deep breath, meant to stop me from speaking, and then says it again: "It's not your fault, Tressa. None of it. It was a freak accident, and it had nothing to do with anything any of us did. I want you to know that and go forward, into the world, and live a full life. Love. Work. Have children. Be safe and well. It's what Luke would want."

She reaches behind her neck to unclasp a necklace, and as she holds it out, I see it's Luke's—the peace sign with the pearl stone, dangling from its leather string. The one he still wears when he comes to visit me.

"Here," Francine says. "I was going to give it to Paul, but you're the one who's here. You should have this. Luke would want that, too."

I take it from her and clasp the leather thread around my neck. Cold silver that rested against Luke's skin for so many years, now resting against mine. I will wear it until the leather crackles and splits, and then I will find a new thread. I will wear this pendant the rest of my life. "Thank you" seems like too pale a phrase.

Sunlight shifts a little, settling in for the day. The light around us mutes. I can feel it dappling on my bare arms as I sit here, staring down the trail, half expecting the next hiker who appears to be Luke himself.

"All the same," Francine says, her face going hard again. "I don't want you here now. I need to do this by myself, just Luke and me. You weren't here when he came into this world. You don't need to be here when he goes out."

I nod. Francine is his mother. If she needs to do this alone, then so be it. I'm not the only one Luke left behind, so I get shakily to my feet. Before I duck down into the trees, Francine calls out.

"Tressa," she says. "I want you to do something for me."

My hurt at being excused evaporates. Finally—something I can do for Francine. The last thing I expected to feel today, joy, grips me as I turn and stand still, waiting.

"I've put it in my will," Francine says. "But people don't always follow those instructions. You know? So I want you to make sure that when I die, they scatter my ashes here. Okay?"

I understand her intention, to extract two promises—because making the one presumes my outliving her. I nod, then turn to head down the trail, not looking back to see Francine—sitting there, cross-legged, staring out at the view. A mile or so down the path I think I feel a tactile mist brushing against my cheek.

Luke's mother has thrown his body to the wind, and—more than I can say—I hope this brings her peace. But as for me I know he hasn't left. Not yet.

* * *

And still I don't make any decisions, and I don't go to

the river. May turns away, the waters rise without me, and I find myself wanting to milk this knowing—the approach of one last time—for at least a few more days. Nobody complains when I stop going to school. This town has wished me well despite everything, and for whatever reason it seems to consider the mission complete.

Paul opens the Drive-in on June second, a Friday, the night before our birthday. For almost my whole life that's how I've thought of it, *our birthday*, and I know that will continue year after year. I haven't asked Paul if he registered the significance of the date, even though I spoke to him a week ago, when I called to let him know I wouldn't be starting college in the fall. He voiced the expected concerns about whether I'd ever get back to school. "You're a smart girl," he said. "You need an education."

"There's plenty of time for that," I told him. "Big brick buildings. Difficult to move or destroy." The words out of my mouth sounded instantly familiar, and I realized I had stolen them from H. J.

"Well," Paul said. "If you want to go away, if you need money to travel . . ." I held the receiver to my ear, thinking of the weight those words must carry for him, and I said thank you.

And then the next day, walking down Main Street, I saw something that took me by surprise. Francine and my sister Katie, walking together. Katie had an ice cream cone, and for a moment they stopped, and Katie held out the cone to Francine so she could have a taste.

I ran across the street and ducked into the pharmacy. Paul hadn't said a word about Katie visiting. She must be staying at Francine's, I thought.

Through the store's plate-glass window I watched them. They looked like a mother and daughter. Where Katie went, Jill would be soon to follow, and I felt great relief at the thought, of my sisters reclaiming the only mother they'd ever known. And of Francine welcoming back her living children.

The night before our birthday, Grandma fills brown paper bags with popcorn—popped on the stove, of course, dripping with butter and salty brewer's yeast. H. J., Evie, Grandma, Grandpa, and I carry lawn chairs out to the east hill. Sturm and Drang follow. We settle in, waiting for the sun to set. For opening night Paul has invited the whole town free of charge, and we watch a steady stream of cars make their way to the grassy stretch of land. The smells of popcorn and hot dogs waft up the hill from the snack bar, and we know that, free admission or not, Paul will make a mint tonight.

The five of us watch cartoons in companionable silence, the huge horses grazing beside us. Above the screen the moon rises in the distance. When the movie starts, it announces itself as a harbinger of summer with its action-packed inanity. After an hour or so Grandma falls asleep, her light snoring inspiring Grandpa to wake her and head back home.

"I'll bring the chairs," I whisper, as if there's a theater full of people to disturb. I turn away from the movie, watching them walk back down the hill, their companionable shadows leaning into each other.

H. J. and I stay for the second feature, a crackly black-and-white movie starring Clark Gable and a small woman with great, dark eyes. Evie excuses herself, collecting the empty, greasy brown bags and heading back down the hill.

"You can take the car," H. J. calls after his sister. "I'll find my way back home."

With Evie gone, H. J. and I get off our chairs and sit together on the grass. For an hour or so we watch the movie, our knees resting against each other. He does not put his arm around me or attempt to kiss me. In fact, if I don't count that night he breathed me back to life, he has never kissed me. Though H. J. and I have never said a word about what's between us, I imagine that if I take him up on his offer, of traveling, eventually there will be kissing. One more thing I can't think about yet.

At some point, the two of us staring ahead at that screen, H. J. says, "Have you thought any more about what you're going to do?"

"I've thought," I say. "But I haven't decided."

On the movie screen credits have begun to roll. Cars file out onto Main Street, an orderly stream of headlights, probably the entire town of Rabbitbrush making its way home. I turn to look at H. J. His face in profile, clean-shaven tonight, looks young and very vulnerable.

He doesn't look back at me, just reaches over blindly and closes his hands around my wrist, which he brings to his lips. My fingers bump the rim of his glasses. He kisses my scars, deeply and intently, and I can feel it—his hands and his lips, my own wronged flesh, this crime I committed against myself and everyone who loves me. And I realize that although H. J. might not love me yet, he could one day, especially if I decide to go away with him. Stranger than that, I could love him, if only I gave myself time, and permission.

I can't make any promises, or plans. But there is something I can give him, for now, something I owe him, and I tap his temple, lightly, to make him turn and look at me.

"You make me want to live," I say, making sure the words sound clear, not faltering, a definitive statement.

Looking at me now, H. J. doesn't look distracted at all, but focused, and even happy. Then he stands up and offers me his hand. I take it, getting to my feet beside him. We gather up the lawn chairs and fold them under our arms—two for me and three for him. Then we clatter down the hill, lit by the moon and headlights, accompanied by Sturm and Drang, making our way, in the increasing darkness, toward home.

(33)

TRESSA

I have waited out the spring, letting the river rise with-out me. But I have not kept Luke waiting. He has been right here all along. Today, June third, the day we turn nineteen—I know I'll see him when I reach the river.

This morning I sleep late enough that when I go downstairs, Grandma and Grandpa are gone. There's a brightly wrapped box waiting for me on the kitchen table, along with a card, and I decide not to open it until they can be with me. Getting ready to go, I want to assure myself that scene will occur, but I can't, not just yet.

Yesterday I got a package from my mother, a gray cotton cardigan and a black postal bag from a shop in San Francisco. I use the bag now, opening its unnatural stiffness to pack bread and apples, a bottle of water, and the cardigan, even though the day is warm already, flirting with hot. Slung across my torso, the bag's light weight presses against the small of my back as I walk to the banks of the Sustantivo River, a particular spot, the imprint of his lost foothold still impossibly visible to me. I take off the bag and sit down, cross-legged, on the red dirt. Luke won't keep me waiting long.

LUKE

I see her across the river. She looks calm. I know she's waiting for me.

TRESSA

In another week the weather will become more reliable and the river will be—if not exactly crowded, busy with human life, kayakers and white-water rafters and fly fishermen and kids in fat inner tubes screaming their way down the rapids. But for now I have this stretch to myself. The sun works its way through treetops, but the river runs too fast to catch or reflect its rays. My face feels drops of water from that top layer, a chilly mist that makes the hair on my arms stand on end.

I know Luke is close, and I know I'm safe. Whatever happens, I will be all right. At first I don't feel it, the hand on my shoulder, but after a while I see it, his fingers there. I look up and see Luke, standing beside me, looking down, smiling. And the old reaction in my chest, erupting, eclipsing everything. Shouting, *Finally. Finally, finally, there you are.* Now I am truly and fully among the living.

I get to my feet and throw my arms around him. I can't feel his arms, but I can feel my feet, lifting off the ground as he picks me up and swings me around. I can't feel his lips as he kisses me. I close my eyes and block out that frustration, trying to summon the memory of all those thousands of kisses, and fuse them into this one moment.

"Happy birthday," he says when we pull apart.

"Happy birthday," I tell him.

LUKE

We sit down, and I close my hand around her wrist. I can still feel the scars. I know they're fading, but I also know they'll never totally go away. Meanwhile, I can't do this much longer. Time's running out. I've got to tell her the whole reason I came back in the first place.

TRESSA

I can't feel it anymore, his hand around my wrist. The realization hits me with a giant lump of sadness, forming in my chest, under my ribs.

"I can't stay long," he says. "But I've got to tell you three things." He tilts his head and looks at me, not quite a smile, just a settled and contented expression, the two of us—twins, in synch.

Nineteen years ago today the two of us were born, the same day of the same month of the same year. Maybe even the same hour, the same minute, the same second. Luke—with his reliable and organized mother—knows the exact time: 9:32 a.m. at the Mercy Regional Medical Center in Durango. My own birth certificate has long since been lost. There is a seven-hour time difference between Durango, Colorado, and Galway, Ireland. My mother remembers I was born in the afternoon but can be forgiven for not remembering the exact time. She was almost all alone, an unwed mother in a Catholic country, no one but an ex-lover's mother to attend her. One day, if I really need to know, maybe I can write to the hospital in Galway and request a copy of my birth certificate. I wonder if she recorded my father's name, or if, determined to keep me absolutely for herself, she had them write "unknown."

"It's a word we have to live with," Luke says, still holding my wrist. If he has lost the ability to feel me, too, he doesn't say so, but clearly he has retained the ability to read my mind.

I nod and wait for him to speak, to tell me what he needs. But he stays quiet.

* * *

LUKE

I shouldn't have said anything. I've stayed too long. I used up all my hours. All my words. I can steal these last minutes with Tressa because I have to. But I don't think I can talk again.

TRESSA

I see the voice leave him, the ability to speak. But it's okay. I think I know what he needs to tell me, and I can do this for him. "I know the first thing," I say. "You want to tell me that I need to stay alive. That I can't hurt myself again."

He looks down at my wrist, and opens his fingers, releasing his grasp. His movements have wound down; I can't exactly see through him, but part of me feels as though I can. To me he looks translucent, painfully temporary. He nods, his face very somber and also relieved, his head bobbing in a graceful kind of slow motion.

"The second," I say, "is about you and me. How we'll always be you and me, no matter what happens, even if one of us is gone. I can mourn the loss of you, but I don't have to mourn the loss of *us*, because that continues."

He nods again, less slowly, and also—I think—less certain. This is a mission, a duty. He knows what he has

to do but feels no more certain than I about these messages.

"The last one," I say, "is that it's okay for me to move
on, and love someone else."

Luke stops nodding; his eyes become unfocused. He
stares off over my shoulder. An expression that I can
only call *pained* transforms his entire lovely face, and
I'm afraid I've got that one wrong.

I touch my fingers to my lips, then press them against
his. No feeling, just the sight of it. And I can't ask forgiveness for what comes after, because I don't have any choice.
I can't even call it a decision. It's only what I do next.

I step forward. I don't slide like he did, I don't stumble.
I spring from the balls of my feet and jump into the river.
The water rises around me, and my head bobs above the
current. I can't believe the river's strength, or its temperature, stronger and more frigid than I ever expected
or knew.

From the banks I can hear his voice. Summoned one
last time, for me. "Tressa," he shouts. And then, the same
running, springing step and splash.

The water is freezing. It pushes me under, then pulls
me back up. I know what I have to do. I learned the
lesson from watching Carlo and Luke. I saw the one who
fought go under, and the one who gave in come out the
other side. So I don't move my arms or my legs, I don't
listen to what every last nerve or instinct screams to
do, which is swim, fight, battle against the current. If

I fight to stay alive, I will die; wanting one will cause the other, and I don't know what to do, because I don't know what I want.

I feel rocks scrape my legs and arms. Every time I go under, at the very moment I think I will have to give in and breathe—filling my lungs with water—the current delivers me back to the top, the air, just long enough to take in a gulp of dry oxygen.

And then, very suddenly, I stop going under at all. Instead I float on top, like a kayak, facing upward, my head pointed downriver, my arms flung out at my sides. Not even feeling cold anymore, I watch the blue, blue sky moving over my head, along with the clouds and sun. The flickering pine needles and aspen leaves, the world up there and more, beyond it, everything I will never understand if I live to be a thousand years old.

And I *feel* them, his hands on my back, his body beneath me, holding me above the current, refusing to let me sink.

LUKE

I don't need to breathe. Water surrounds me for the last time. When we get to the calm it'll finally be over. *Goodbye,* I say, but the words turn to bubbles in the current. Tressa gives in. She stops fighting. She's going to live.

I am gone.

TRESSA

Once and for all, as I make this trip; I know that it wasn't my fault, or my mother's, or Paul's or Carlo's or Luke's or anyone's at all. The blame belongs to the wanting, and the longing, and the trying with all your might. And how can that possibly be avoided? By anyone?

I remember one version of death, the light and the tunnel and every departed loved one waiting there to greet you. I can't know if that's true. But I do know that when I survive this trip, there will be a line of beloved faces waiting for me somewhere on the other end—my mother, my grandparents, my sisters. H. J. and Evie.

A few minutes, a hundred years, a thousand. I float where the current stops, by the beaver dam, faceup, alone. If I feel sorry, it's only for a moment. The sky above me so blue and harmless. The whole world, welcoming me back.

Good-bye, I say, for the second time this year. *I will miss you my whole life.*

I climb out of the river. The light widens—my skin frigid and scraped, my bones aching, the familiar pain of resuscitation.

I walk up the river shivering, back to my postal bag, and trade my soaked T-shirt for the gray sweater. I take off my shoes and socks and perch them on a rock to dry.

Then I lie down on the bank for a long, long time, drying off in the increasingly hot sun. Finally the color of the light changes. The sun dries my skin, my shorts. It's June after all, so night's still a long way off. I stuff my socks into my bag and pull on my sneakers. They still squish, but I get to my feet and walk through the forest.

At home I stand under a hot, hot shower, then change into long sleeves and pants so my scrapes and bruises will not be visible. My grandparents give me their gift—a new camera. I take a picture of them, arms around each other, smiling at me. They're still standing there when I put the camera down.

Birthday calls came while I was gone—from H. J. and Evie, my sisters, and Isabelle. Grandma asks me if I want to invite the Burdicks over to share the chocolate cake she baked. I say I'd rather be with just her and Grandpa. He plays my ukulele and they sing "Happy Birthday." I blow out twenty candles, that lovely, traditional, optimistic wish. *To grow on.*

The next day I walk through near-dawn, my sneakers still damp, a squeak in their soles that may never go away. When I get to the Burdick house, I'm surprised to see H. J. already awake, sitting on the front stoop, a steaming mug in his hand. He wears gray sweatpants and a faded life-guard T-shirt. No glasses, but as I walk up, it looks like he recognizes me—my form, my outline—without squinting.

Birds make a racket all around us. We can hear the

frogs from Silver Lake, half a mile away. Morning light has yet to make itself apparent. I stand in mist left over from last night.

"Hi," I say when I reach him. "You're up early."

"I had this feeling you were coming."

"Oh, yeah?"

"Yeah." He hands me his mug of coffee. I don't take a sip but let my hands close around it, warmth pulsing into my palms.

"It's not light yet," he says. "Predators are still stirring. When are you going to learn not to wander around after dark?"

"Probably never," I say.

He shrugs, giving up, and says, "Happy birthday, Tressa Earnshaw."

"Thanks, H. J. Burdick." I take a sip of coffee. It tastes thick, chalky, and good. It warms my bones, my body. H. J. watches me. I hand the mug back and sit down on the step beside him.

"Have you been thinking?" he asks me.

"I have."

"It would be fun to travel together."

"It would," I agree.

"But you're not ready to decide just yet."

I stare out across his front yard. The sun has picked up steam. Before long it will shine brightly enough that puddles of sunlight will look like puddles of water. Yesterday I said good-bye. Honestly that feels like a big enough decision to last a long while. I have started to feel certain that autumn won't find me here in Rabbitbrush. But just now I can't say which direction I'll decide to take.

"I'm only nineteen," I hear myself saying. My voice sounds lighter than it has in a very long time.

H. J. puts his arm around my shoulder. He moves slowly, not in any kind of a hurry. "That's true," he says. "You've got all the time in the world."

"Oh, yeah? You said I only had to get through one more day."

"Well," says H. J. "They have a way of mounting up. If all goes well."

I nod, feeling the weight of his arm. It's a good weight. H. J. and I watch as a small pack of mule deer clatter out of the woods across the street. Arapahoe Road at this hour—at most hours, really—is quiet enough for them to graze without being disturbed. It occurs to me that it's been years since I drew a map of this road, and that I'm due for a new one. By now the houses represent such different things to me.

But that's a project for another day. I take a sip of coffee. H. J. gets up and goes inside, probably to pour another cup for himself. I know he'll be back in a minute, to sit here on the stoop with me. Later on plans will be made, and maps will be drawn. But right now I just want to watch those deer while the last bits of night fade away. Life can work itself out later.

I have all the time in the world.

part five

one last after

(34)

TRESSA

I want to end there. I swear I do. But a part of me too will always be waiting.

That day by the river was Luke's last. I know that. But if there's one thing I've learned this past year, it's that not everything we know turns out to be true.

I knew my mother would always keep moving. Then I knew for certain she had settled down. I knew Luke and I would always be together, and then I knew he was dead and never coming back. I knew I wanted to die. Now I know I want to live.

So I will travel this world with the best intentions. I will explore its countries and its continents. The sun will beat down on my head, and the ocean will wash over my feet.

Meanwhile hope will never entirely leave me. One

day I'll be walking. Maybe there will be a premonition, or maybe he'll take me by surprise. I might be hiking up the Jud Wiebe Trail, or by the Sustantivo River. I might be on a beach off the coast of Georgia, or a city street in Jerusalem. I will turn a corner. Luke will be there.

Tressa Gentle, he'll say.

The old joy will explode around us—firecrackers, a native dance. Saluting the universe and all its secret, pulsing possibility. And I won't be able to help it.

I will run to him.

acknowledgments

My agent Peter Steinberg not only championed this novel from its first draft, he came up with the title. I can never thank him enough for his tireless work, faith, and friendship.

I still have a hard time believing how much love and sweat Caitlyn Dlouhy poured into this story. I couldn't have written it without her determination and vision. She is every writer's dream editor.

Dr. Lori Birdsong helped me understand Tressa's mental state and her treatment. Early readers—Danae Woodward, Daisy Barringer, and Kristina Serrano—gave me insight and encouragement. Bill Roorbach helped me with Luke's voice. My mother, Carol de Gramont, proofread the galleys.

Cassie Wright was walking by a river on a November day in 1998 when her dog was swept away by the current. Cassie is always loved and dearly missed.

As always, all my love and many thanks to David and Hadley.